THE LORDS OF NIGHT

A SHADOW BRUJA NOVEL

THE LORDS OF NIGHT

A SHADOW BRUJA NOVEL

J. C. CERVANTES

RICK RIORDAN PRESENTS

Disney • **HYPERION**   LOS ANGELES   NEW YORK

First Edition, October 2022
1 3 5 7 9 10 8 6 4 2
FAC-004510-22231
Printed in the United States of America

This book is set in Aldus Nova Pro/Linotype
Designed by Phil Buchanan

Library of Congress Cataloging-in-Publication Data
Names: Cervantes, Jennifer, author.
Title: The lords of night : a shadow bruja novel / by J. C. Cervantes.
Description: First edition. • Los Angeles ; New York : Disney-Hyperion, 2022. •
"Rick Riordan presents." • Audience: Ages 8–12. • Audience: Grades 4–6. • Summary:
When fourteen-year-old godborn and shadow bruja Renata embarks on a quest to stop
five rogue demigods from awakening the nine Aztec Lords of Night and overpowering
the Maya gods, she confronts questions about her family, her magic, and her destiny.
Identifiers: LCCN 2021055620 • ISBN 9781368066563 (hardcover) •
ISBN 9781368066617 (ebook)
Subjects: CYAC: Witches—Fiction. • Magic—Fiction. • Mythology—
Fiction. • Gods—Fiction. • LCGFT: Mythological fiction. • Novels.
Classification: LCC PZ7.C3198 Lo 2022 • DDC [Fic]—dc23
LC record available at https://lccn.loc.gov/2021055620

Reinforced binding
Follow @ReadRiordan
Visit www.DisneyBooks.com

For all the girls who are told no

1

In the beginning (sort of)
Seven months before

Once upon a night, there was a girl who didn't know who she really was. She didn't know how her shadow magic worked, or even where it came from. Only that it was there, deep in her blood and bones, and maybe even deeper than that.

But to understand everything, it's important to go all the way back to the *sort of* beginning.

It started like this:

There she was, all cuddled up on her bed with her weighted blanket, reading a book about Maya gods and magic and curses and some overly dramatic kid named Zane Obispo. She didn't want the story to end, but it was inevitable. The end always comes.

Ren was just about to close the book when the last words on the last page started to glow a greenish gold. She blinked over and over, thinking—hoping—she could pretend the iridescent glow wasn't really there. No such luck.

Someday when you least expect it, the magic will call to you.

Then, like the need for breath, Ren had a sudden urge to say the words out loud. "The magic will call to me...."

At first nothing happened. But then, four minutes and

fifteen sighs later, a familiar tune being played on a viola rushed from the kitchen, down the hall, and under Ren's closed bedroom door.

Ren's heart ballooned so big and so fast she thought it was entirely possible it might explode. This wasn't just any song—it was her dad's favorite, and he had written it especially for her. But that was impossible! He had died six years earlier and been buried with his beloved instrument.

Jagged stripes of lightning flashed outside. Anyone paying half attention would have thought an electrical storm was approaching. They weren't unusual in Galveston, Texas.

Something indeed was approaching.

The music grew faster, louder, more urgent. Ren was sure now. The melody was definitely coming from her father's viola, the one that creaked when he played it.

In that first moment of panic, Ren wondered if she could take the words back, unsay them. *Maybe if I repeat them backward . . .* she thought just as another blinding-white light flashed across the night sky.

Then came the scratching on the pitched roof. Her mind immediately conjured the image of a corpse trying to claw its way out of a wood coffin. Not that she would know firsthand what that looked like, but she had, regrettably, watched too many zombie movies in her thirteen years.

Ren knew the drill. She had practiced for this exact moment. She threw off her blanket, swung her legs over the side of the bed, and tugged on her red cowboy boots.

Just as she opened her bedroom door, her abuelo appeared

in the hall. His gray hair was sticking up all over like a storm cloud. "It's happening." His low voice carried a strange tone that sent a shudder down Ren's spine.

There will come a day when your shadow magic is discovered, her abuelo had told her. *On that day you will have to leave. To run. To hide.*

Ren felt sick. Had she done this? Just by saying those words? *But it's just a book.* A book still in her grasp.

Ren was breathing heavily now. "Do you hear Papá's music, too? It's my song!"

Abuelo shook his head, his eyes roving the ceiling. "Mira," he whispered, "we are going to get in the car very quietly just like we've practiced. ¿Me escuchas? And we are going to follow the music. Your music."

There was no time for arguing or explaining, no time to grab her laptop with her blog articles about aliens or even change out of her spaceship-patterned pajamas before her grandpa nudged her into the garage and into the car.

The music got even louder.

Instead of using the remote control, Abuelo manually opened the garage door, slowly, carefully—each inch a lifetime.

Lightning flashed again. A terrible growl clung to the night air.

Rain began to plummet from the sky as her grandfather slipped inside the car. He pulled the little Honda out of the garage gradually, checking the side mirrors every two seconds.

"Abuelo..."

"Shh..."

It was the dead of night. There was no traffic, no people, no life.

The rain came harder. The lightning flashed so bright it could've blinded the sun.

"Tell me which way the music wants you to go." Abuelo wiped his forehead with the back of his hand.

Ren hesitated, not trusting herself with something so big. What if she picked wrong? But no way would her dad let her down when she was running for her life. She took a deep breath, tuning her ears to the instrument playing so clearly. "Turn right."

Abuelo hooked a hard right, not bothering to slow down at the stop sign. "I know you can't control the shadows yet." He pulled in a long, ragged breath. "But that will change. Your power will grow."

"But where am I supposed to hide? And for how long?" Ren thought these were excellent questions since her drills with Abuelo had never covered this part.

Thlunk! Dark glossy wings spread across the length of the windshield.

Ren screamed.

Abuelo slammed the brakes. The Honda skidded and spun one hundred and eighty degrees, flinging the winged creature into the air.

What was that? Ren wondered. *A huge bird? A massive bat?* She white-knuckled the dashboard.

"You must stay calm," Abuelo said.

Calm?! He wanted her to stay calm? How could she? Except

that they both knew what could happen if she didn't. Stress usually sent her into one of her absence seizures, and the last thing she needed right now was to pass out.

"Turn left," she commanded.

Abuelo pressed his foot to the pedal.

A terrible snarl reverberated across the night.

Don't look. Don't look. Don't look, she told herself.

The moonlit bay came into view. Ren realized what was happening. "The music—Papá's leading us to the water." This was definitely not going to turn out okay.

"Of course," Abuelo whispered. "Can you try to bring the shadows now? To slow down those . . . creatures?"

¿En serio? I can barely breathe! But Ren clenched her hands into fists anyway, because what choice did she have? She closed her eyes and focused, nearly popping a blood vessel in her forehead. It was no use.

Less than a minute later, Ren and her grandfather had bolted from the car and were rushing down a dock. The rain had slowed to a sprinkle, but the black wings . . . Ren could sense them drawing closer. The music was rising, growing louder with every step she took.

Suddenly, the melody stopped, forcing Ren to a grinding halt, too. She looked down at a dinghy knocking against the pier. She knew the answer before she asked the question: *This is a dreadful escape vessel. Couldn't I have a yacht instead?*

"¿Eso es todo?" Abuelo wrinkled his nose.

Ren nodded as tears pricked her eyes. "There aren't even any oars." Or a blanket, or food. Or water. She tried not to think of everything that could go wrong—things worse than no food. Things like massive sharks with massive teeth and massive appetites. *Why did I have to go and watch* Shark Week?

"The magic will guide you." Abuelo's voice shook. "And wherever this boat takes you, you must always remember—"

"That I come from an ancient line of the most powerful shadow brujxs that have ever lived," Ren finished, wishing she believed that was enough to keep her safe.

"You must go, Renata."

She stepped into the boat awkwardly. She could do this. She *had* to do this.

There was another growl, deep and hungry. Then out of nowhere came a dark hideous fury of claws and wings and shiny black eyes.

Ren instinctively threw her arms over her head.

There was an explosion of shadow. A thick web covered the moaning beasts, trapping them in midair. Ren could feel power pulsing in her fingertips like electricity.

The creatures thrashed inside the net of shadow, wailing with rage.

"Very impressive," Abuelo said, managing a proud smile.

"I don't want to leave you, Abuelo!" Ren cried.

There was a rushed good-bye, a last embrace, a wet cheek. A promise to reunite.

The boat was swept out of the bay and into the sea as if magic hands were guiding it. A new sheet of shadow hovered protectively over the dinghy, making Ren invisible. She tugged her pajama hood over her head and pulled her knees into her chest, hugging herself and the book. *Don't think about the sharks.* Her heart beat faster. *Or those terrible monsters.* Her pulse started racing. *Or where I'm going.* Her pulse was definitely off the charts.

No. Not now. No stress. Not now.

I need to stay awake. I need to—

The world went black.

The boat slipped across the water, in the direction of Renata Santiago's destiny. And although her body was in it, her mind wasn't. It escaped to a place of splendor, with pink and purple and silver skies. A jade crown on a silken pillow. This wasn't a dream—it was a memory hiding in her heart.

A memory she didn't know and wouldn't recall until more than a year later.

2

Seven months later
Xiuhtecuhtli

The wind roared with the ferocity of ten thousand gods. The trees bowed and writhed. Even the sky shook in fear of the great blast from the north. Fires combusted from nothing, scorching the Kansas earth. The final explosion was only a whisper, "It is time."

And then the first Lord of Night, the Fire Lord, rose inside the flames, fueled by his rage, and opened his eyes.

It had been a very long sleep.

3

YOU'RE A LOSER!

The pizza crust was still dangling out of Ren's mouth when she opened the email connected to her alien-sighting blog, *Eyes in the Sky*, and read that first subject line.

She froze, blinked. Re-scanned the three words as if she'd misread them the first time. Nope. The message was even clearer on the second read. And then Ren's eyes floated to the next message. She gasped. The half-eaten crust plummeted onto her desk.

YOU'RE A FAKE!

Sure, she'd been gone all summer and hadn't blogged or communicated with her readers in all that time, but hello! She and her friends had been saving the world! Her cheeks throbbed with a burning white heat when her gaze fell to another email.

GET A LIFE!

Her throat closed completely when she read COUGH UP THE PROOF, CHICA from someone calling themselves Chewbaccabro.

Ren's heart felt like it was imploding—not once, not twice, but over and over.

And as terrible as the messages were, she couldn't stop staring at the hateful words. Or trembling. Something hot and unfamiliar expanded inside her as she composed a response in her head. *Proof? You want proof? How about a field trip to the Maya underworld, Mr. Chewbaccabro? And by the way, Chewbacca is too cool for you!*

Before she realized it, a shadow rose from the floor, taking the shape of a lion's paw. It crept onto her desk and with a single claw pressed the only key that mattered.

Delete.

Delete.

Delete.

Tears pricked Ren's eyes as she mentally directed the shadow to destroy each and every vile email. She knew enough about bullies, especially the ones who hide behind their computer screens, to know they weren't worth her half-eaten pizza crust. She knew they wanted to engage her. They wanted a fight. Well, she for sure wasn't going to give them one. Even though it might have felt really good to write back *Who taught you to be such a mean jerk?*

Wiping away the tears, she vanished the shadow, took a deep breath, and closed her eyes. She would do a meditation, a visualization; she would melt into a Zen world of calm like she always did when she was upset or stressed or worried. When she was ten seconds into a deep-breathing meditation, her laptop pinged. She almost ignored the FaceTime call until she squinted one eye open and saw who it was.

Pulling herself together, she answered, "Hey, Marco."

But instead of seeing her friend's face, all she saw was his bedroom floor, covered with piles of wrinkled clothes, wadded paper, and three different sets of muddied cleats.

"Hey." His voice carried across the mess. "You answered too fast. Hang on."

"Why can't I see you?"

He plopped down at his desk and adjusted the screen so she could see his face and the black shoe-polish-like streaks under his eyes. He had a towel draped over his head like a boxer resting in the corner of the ring. "I was changing out of my uniform," he said. "And cleaning up."

"You don't look clean."

"It's not like you can smell me through the screen." He ripped open what looked like a protein bar wrapper with his teeth and took a bite. Marco, son of the Maya god of war, usually threw punches first and asked questions later. "I left tons of messages on your cell," he said. "What's up with freezing me out?"

"Oh, my screen broke. I had to get a new phone, and I haven't set it up yet."

The towel slipped off his head to reveal what looked like freshly bleached-blond hair with blue stripes.

Ren gasped. "What's with the stripes?"

Crumbs spilled from his mouth as he spoke. "Whole team did it. You know . . ." He swallowed and took a swig from a metal bottle. "To bond and stuff."

"Guys bond over coloring their hair?"

He glared at her.

"Okay . . . I mean, I'm not into football," Ren said, "but, like, you look tough? Like a tough clown . . ." Then in a lower voice, "You're not using your godborn powers to cheat on the field, are you?"

Marco was out-of-this-world strong and could take on the voice and mannerisms of anyone anywhere, anytime. He'd gotten even better at it during their godborn training at SHIHOM, the Shaman Institute of Higher-Order Magic, this past summer. He could have turned himself into an NFL MVP or something.

"I don't need powers to be the best QB there is," he said. "Anyway, did you take a look at that dumb essay assignment I sent you?"

"You mean the one you want me to rewrite?"

"Ren," Marco said, clenching his jaw, "I'm serious."

"Not yet. I've been busy with...my blog." *And hateful bullies.*

"You know I have to keep up my grades to play on the team, and I don't have time to write about some dead presidents," he said. "And besides, I was the anchor who saved the world a few months ago. Doesn't that count for something?"

How long was he going to lean on that one heroic feat? Sure, he had held the golden time rope that kept Ren and the other time travelers linked to the present when they went back to 1987 to rescue all the Maya gods. But it was her friend Zane's uncle Hondo who had held on to the other end even though he was spinning in horrific darkness and pain.

"What gives, Ren?" Marco asked. "You look kinda...Are you okay?"

If Ren told Marco about the cyberbullies, he'd hunt them down one by one, bury them in trash dumpsters, and seal the lids with cement. Or worse. There was always a worse when it came to what Marco could dream up for his enemies. Ren was mortified to admit it, but she felt a spark of temptation . . . until the better part of her whispered, *Bad karma.*

She said, "Do you . . . ? I mean, has it been kind of hard . . . you know, going back to life at home, without other godborns around, to regular school, to—"

"You mean pretending to be normal when I'm not?" Marco rubbed the scar on his chin while his frown grew deeper. "You mean not being able to talk about my killer powers? About who I really am?"

Yeah. All that.

Not that Ren would change anything. She had never regretted following her destiny all the way to the island of Holbox that fateful night seven months ago and befriending fellow godborn Zane Obispo, aka the son of Hurakan, the Maya god of storms. If she'd never stepped onto that boat, she never would have found out that her mom was Pacific, the Maya goddess of time. And she never would have become besties with Ah-Puch, the god of death, darkness, and destruction.

It might sound super fun and adventurous to leave behind a normal life of school and homework and rules to go to Xib'alb'a, the Maya underworld, or to make a deal with a ruthless ancient calendar, or even to defeat the wicked bat god and faceless goddess, but it had been super scary, too.

And sometimes, when Ren was alone, she suffered the leftover effects of it all. She felt the heavy burden of being labeled the most powerful godborn ever just because she was also a shadow witch and now in possession of her mother's golden time rope.

But most of the time, she ignored the feeling, stuffed it all down. Pretended she was like everyone else. Even though she could sense the future tugging at her, pulling her in a direction she wasn't sure she was ready to go.

Her fingers went to the time rope in its chain-necklace form around her throat.

Just then, an email window popped up on Ren's computer from someone calling themselves Sir Switchblade with the subject line: DANGER. ALIEN SIGHTING. HELP!!!!

Her eyes scanned the words. Seemed some kid in Kansas had seen strange activity in a cornfield: jagged bolts of lightning that looked more like a "monster light show" than an act of nature. And there'd been six figures out there—one with blue skin and glowing eyes and fangs that dripped yellow.

It sounded more like a demon sighting than an alien invasion. Maybe Ixtab, goddess of the underworld, was doing some kind of training drills outside of Xib'alb'a?

And then Ren got to the last words:

The blue thing was with five kids, and one of them turned into a snake right before my eyes. A big red snake longer than the cereal aisle in Walmart!

Marco hollered, "REN!"

She jerked her attention back to him on the main screen. "Didn't anyone ever tell you not to yell at people?"

"WHO'S YELLING?"

He was definitely still yelling.

"We've got bigger problems than football and your terrible manners," she said.

Quickly, she read the message to Marco.

"So?" Marco said with a smug expression.

"Sooo, this has to be the work of the godborns who defected in Montana."

"That's a pretty big leap of logic," Marco said.

"Who other than Serena can create a serpiente grande?" Ren asked, hitting the Send button. "And five? That's the number that bolted, including her."

Ren would never forget that awful night when Zane stood on that table in the meadow and asked the rest of the godborns to join him in rescuing the Maya gods. It was all good until Serena (daughter of the moon goddess, Ixchel) and her little band of renegades demanded that this was the time to rise up. Serena had wanted to take advantage of the fact that the Maya gods were trapped in 1987 so she and her gang of misfits could come to power.

Marco was nodding. "Yeah, I was there. I don't need another rundown."

"It was like a banana rotting before my eyes."

"That's a bad metaphor."

"It's a simile."

Marco blew out a frustrated breath. "Why would the loser patrol be in Kansas?"

It was the same question Ren had, one without an answer . . . until a small voice rose inside her.

They want to finish what they started.

4

"Maybe there's a portal there," Ren guessed as she hurriedly pressed all the right buttons to set up her new cell phone.

"To where?" Marco barked. "The Chiefs' Loserhead Stadium?"

"Chiefs?"

With a grunt he said, "They're a football team?" Then, "Besides, it's like"—he tapped on his keyboard—"fifteen hundred miles from Montana to Kansas. How'd they even get there?"

"It *has* been a few months . . ." said Ren. "Maybe the cinco somehow got their hands on a gateway map. Maybe they were trying to do something terrible. Maybe—"

"Quit saying *maybe*. It's annoying." Marco's dark eyes narrowed, and he leaned so close to his screen Ren could see up his nose. "The cowards are probs in hiding."

"We need to go to Xib'alb'a," she said. "To tell Ixtab."

"*We?*" Marco grunted, and pulled back so Ren could see his whole face, including the deep scar on his chin. "I've got a huge game tomorrow night."

"Marco," Ren said. "You'll be back in time. The rogue godborns are up to something—I can feel it." Seeing her friend's unchanged expression, she added, "They're with a demon. That's not normal." Of course, nothing in the Maya world ever was. But at least in that world she felt like she belonged.

"Yeah, Ren. That's gonna be a big N-O from me. I am *not* going back to the body-part factory. I really don't need to revisit another demon freak show or Pus River. Besides, five puny godborns aren't going to do any damage, or at least not to the gods."

"So football is more important than finding the defectors and figuring out what they're up to?"

Marco raked a hand through his dumb blue-streaked hair, and just when Ren thought he had come around to her way of thinking, he rolled his chair back and said, "Dude, yes. Here in Waco, football is everything."

"Marco!"

"This is my future, man. If I want to play in college, I have to get scouted out of high school."

"But you're only in eighth grade."

"Exactly. And I have to make the JV team next year, which means I have to kick butt this year."

"Fine," Ren said, pushing her overgrown bangs out of her eyes. "I'll call Zane."

"Didn't you hear? He's off the grid."

"What do you mean?"

"He and Hurakan went underground to try and figure out why so many of the gods are still kids after the whole timetravel fiasco."

No way would Zane leave without saying good-bye. "Are you sure?" Ren said, doubting that Marco was in the know.

Marco rubbed one eye, smearing the black gunk all over his cheek. "Ren, everyone knows. He probably left a message on your busted phone."

Ren watched the phone's screen as it took its time to load.

Marco said, "Maybe you should quit spending so much time on that *Eye on the Stars* blog or whatever."

"It's *Eyes in the Sky*," Ren corrected. "Fine, I'll call Brooks."

"She's undercover."

"Adrik and Alana, then."

"On a world cruise."

"Louie." Surely the shy son of rain would help.

"Working on some big science project."

"What are you, everyone's social director?"

"Funny." Marco shrugged. "It's not my fault people choose to send me play-by-plays on their lives. And I bet you didn't even know that Hondo and Quinn are climbing Kilimanjaro. Well, maybe she's flying and he's climbing, but you know what I mean."

Ren felt loneliness wash over her. Everyone had moved on except her.

Marco's mom hollered for him to come to dinner. "Coming!" he shouted back. Then to Ren he said, "I bet the whole Kansas thing is a coincidence."

"I don't believe in coincidences."

"Still, you don't have to get involved. Forward the email to Ixtab and call it a day."

Ren was already shaking her head. "Pretty sure the goddess of the underworld doesn't have email, Marco."

"It's your cabeza . . ." Marco said, starting to get up from his chair.

"Fine," she said with a huff. "I'll go alone."

"Okay, but can you rewrite my essay before you cruise down under?"

A new email from Sir Switchblade popped up on Ren's screen.

Oh yeah, one more thing. There's a big fat symbol burned into the earth.

A symbol? Ren's sixth sense started rapid-firing one word: *proof.* If she could get a pic of the symbol and it was cool or authentic enough, she could post it on her blog and stick it to the meanies. She could reassert her stature as a true alien seeker.

"Wait," she said to Marco. He didn't seem especially impressed when she told him about the symbol. "How about we make a deal?"

"I hate deals."

"Forget Xib'alb'a. Come with me to Kansas and I'll write *all* your essays this entire school year."

Marco jutted his head back like he was avoiding a right hook. "All?" He sat down again.

Ren nodded, hoping he'd take the bait. She knew doing his homework for him wasn't ethical, but maybe she could end up tutoring him instead. No need to go into the specifics now, though.

He held up both hands like he was weighing fruit in each. "Let's see. Chiefs' Loserland or write dumb essays." He moved his hands alternately up and down. Then, "Two years of writing my essays and we go tonight and come right back so I don't miss my big game."

Ren squealed and reached toward the screen as if they could shake on it. "Deal."

"But you have to pick me up."

"Why?"

"Because I sort of broke my gateway map."

Each of the godborns who had helped save the gods received one. It was a pretty awesome gift because it allowed them to travel through magical portals to almost anywhere.

Ren narrowed her eyes. "How did you break a map?"

"What does it matter?" Marco's voice raised. "It's busted, okay?"

"Marco, you really need to chill on the temper stuff."

"I'm the son of war, Rena-a-a-ta," he said stretching out her name like he always did when he wanted to make a dumb point.

"Marco!" Ren heard his mom call. "Your food's getting cold!"

"Just a sec, Ma!" Marco looked at the gold watch on Ren's wrist and said, "Too bad that thing doesn't stop time anymore."

Ren glanced down at the gift from her mom. All the godborns received a different object from their godly parent at their claiming ceremonies. Each was infused with a unique kind of power. But Marco's dad, Nakon, hadn't given anything to him. Ren thought the god of war was a jerk, but Marco never even complained about it.

Ren's watch had stopped being able to freeze time after she'd used up all its magical time threads. "But it's still accurate to the second," she said with a small grin. "And it's now a gateway map."

"Huh? How?"

Ren lifted the watch to her mouth. "Show me the nearest gateway to Waco, Texas." A second later, the watch's face displayed where she could find the portal closest to her current location, when it would open, and where in Waco she would end up.

She looked back to Marco and said, "There's a Dr Pepper Museum in Waco?"

"There's a lot of things in Waco. But what the heck? I got a cruddy paper map thing and you got that?"

"I made it at SHIHOM in my technogics class—the one you refused to take, remember?"

"Because who cares about a combo of technology and magic? Boring. I'd rather learn how to win battles and be the best fighter in history."

"Well, maybe there are other ways to fight that don't include your fists."

Marco frowned. "Like what?"

"Like maybe we should get to Kansas."

"Right. The museum's all the way downtown. How long do I have to get there to meet you?"

"Thirty minutes."

"Fine, I'll take dinner to go. But remember, I'm only going to talk to this Sir Switchblade or whatever. That's all, Ren. And no matter what we learn, I'm coming back home. No quests or hunts or other junk. Got it?"

"Fine."

What Ren didn't say was *This became a quest the second I got that email.*

5

As soon as Ren's new cell phone was powered
up, she started to dial Sir Switchblade's number. But she got
distracted by a *buzz, buzz, buzz.* She had three unheard voice
mails.

"Ren!" Zane shouted. "I hope you're sitting down, because..."
There was a pause filled with rushing wind. He was probably
flying with Brooks, Ren thought. But why would he call me
from the sky? She'd barely finished the thought when Zane
yelled, "You are not going to believe what I found!"

As dramatic as always, Ren thought.

The next voice message went like this:

"Ren! Where are you? Ugh! I really need to talk to you. I
found something on Isla Pájaros. Something you're going to
love and freak over. Aliens, Ren! Maybe you're not so loca after
all. Call me!"

Ren's heart started to thump louder and harder as she listened to Zane's last message:

"Okay, fine. You aren't going to call me. Whatever. I found
a box. I should have taken a pic but some demons showed up
and I had to split, but there was a painting on the lid. Like an
ancient one. Two demons, and they were holding hands in front
of a fire, and one wore a flower wreath."

Just then, Brooks's voice piped up. "Tell her about the Cave of Doom."

Cave of Doom? Ren wondered.

"That isn't the most important part," Zane groaned.

"There was a monster that looked like Zane," Brooks said. "Or made himself look like Zane. Only creepier."

"And we asked Ixtab," Zane began, then must have decided not to finish his thought, or maybe Brooks jabbed him in the ribs, because he sucked in a sharp breath and changed the subject to "But the painting—there were flowers everywhere, like it was a party or something."

"And there was a creature, Ren!" Brooks shouted. "It wasn't a demon."

"I can tell the story," Zane argued.

Then hurry it up.

Zane sighed loudly. "And it had these eyes and—"

A blast of static cut off Zane, and Ren didn't catch what he said next. When his voice came back, all she heard was, ". . . scales. Muy gross. Anyhow, I'll text pics of the weird shell I found in the box. Check 'em out and call me. If I don't answer, it's because there's no service where I'm going. See you on the other side, amiga."

With wobbly, impatient hands, Ren fumbled the phone, nearly dropping it as she opened her text app, where she found Zane's text messages.

Here are the pics. What is it? I figured you'd know, being Dr. Alien and all.

Dr. Alien? Ren scoffed. But then she found herself smiling because she kind of liked the sound of it. Too bad the photos weren't downloading. Why was Zane so excited to show her a shell?

While she waited for the images, her mind echoed Zane's and Brooks's words about the box and the ancient painting of a demon party.

And there was a creature. It wasn't a demon.

Ren reached for the words that had gotten lost in the static as she examined the only ones she'd heard: *eyes* and *scales*.

Had Brooks and Zane found an ancient painting of an alien? It wasn't exactly a phenomenon or anything. Inexplicable "alien" images had been found all over the world, from Iran to Africa.

Quickly, Ren dialed Zane, but it went right to his voice mail. After leaving a message for him to call her, she tried Brooks with the same result.

Before Ren took off, she sent a quick text to her abuelo, who was out for his Thursday-night mah-jongg game.

Went to check out a sighting. I'll be home in a few hours.

Then she added a few smile emojis.

By the time Ren stepped out of the gateway and onto Fifth Street in Waco, the sky had turned to dusk. The air was thick and muggy as she hurried down the street. A minute later, she found the Dr Pepper Museum. Marco was pacing, and scowling.

"What took you so long?"

"I'm not even late."

"That wasn't the question."

"Well, if you hadn't broken your map—"

His gaze fell to her sweatshirt. "What is that?"

"Oh, it's cool, right? I had them made for my blog. You know, to advertise and stuff." But maybe she had been foolish to think that anyone wanted to read what she had to say about space and aliens. Maybe she needed to shut the whole thing down.

"Alien eyes. Really?"

Ren loved the tees and sweatshirts she had designed herself for *Eyes in the Sky*. She had gotten the idea when she first saw her SHIHOM uniform.

"The eyes glow in the dark," she said. "Do you want me to send you one?"

"Uh, I'm good," Marco said.

Ren looked at his shirt. "You're wearing a jersey."

"Ren, I'm a quarterback. How many times do I have to—"

"I've just never seen you in anything other than your leather jacket or SHIHOM clothes."

"Well, get used to it. This is me now. So, where are we headed?"

"Oh, I forgot to call them."

"You don't have an address?"

"I will in a sec, okay?"

Ren dialed the number. Sir Switchblade turned out to be a twelve-year-old boy who spoke like he was turning up the volume with each word.

"Do you think it's going to come get me?" he asked Ren.

Ren wasn't sure whether he meant the snake or the demon, but really, did it matter? Neither was a particularly good choice.

"No, they aren't going to get you," Ren reassured him. "And you only saw them that one time?"

"You mean you think they're still out there?" Sir Switchblade's voice quivered.

"Why don't you give me your address and I can come and check things out?" Ren suggested.

"I'm not supposed to do that," the boy said. "You're a stranger. Maybe you're not even a kid."

"I promise I am," Ren said while Marco rolled his eyes and started to pace again. "I'm only fourteen, but I can help. I'm really good at this stuff." *I've traveled to the underworld, visited a death magician, and bathed in bone dust. I threw a faceless goddess into a time loop!* "I'm the best person for the job, and you don't even have to talk to me. I just need to see where they were exactly. See the symbol."

There was a stretch of silence. "No one believes me," the boy said sadly.

Ren's heart sank. *I know how you feel.* "I believe you. Let me help."

Sir Switchblade hesitated. His breathing filled the airwaves. "Did I tell you lightning struck the ground? That's where the weird spiral-symbol thing is."

Ren felt a nervous ball of energy unspool inside her. "I'm already in Kansas and can be there—"

"You live in Kansas, too?"

"No... I, um... I'm checking out another sighting." She hated lying, but how could she ever explain that she was about to appear in Sir Switchblade's cornfield faster than humanly possible?

"I'll text you my address, but if you're a baddie or a fake, I've got a dog that will tear you to pieces." And then he hung up.

"Sounds like a drama mama," Marco said.

Ren waited for the text, and as soon as it came, she tapped her watch face and spoke the address out loud. Her screen displayed: WACO SUSPENSION BRIDGE 16 MINUTES. "Oh, we're lucky. Only one gateway. Do you know where this is?"

Marco raised a dark brow. "Follow me."

After half a block of silence, Ren said, "Why are you so quiet?"

"Running plays in my head."

"Good thinking. We should definitely be prepared for—"

"I meant for my game, Ren. The big one tomorrow night?"

They cut right onto a lively street filled with shops and restaurants. People were coming and going from them in groups of laughter and chatter.

As they made their way down the busy boulevard lined with trees, parked cars, and streetlamps, Ren told Marco about Zane's messages. "Don't you think that's weird?"

"Yeah, but Zane's always kind of dramatic."

"Have you ever heard of a cave of doom? I wish his pictures would download. What if he found something really cool? Do you think—"

"Whoa! Whoa! Whoa!" Marco held his hands up in protest. "That's way too many questions. Jeez, Ren. Not every experience is a mystery to be solved."

Ren had been so busy keeping up with Marco's pace, she hadn't even noticed that they were right in front of a massive bridge suspended over a dark river. The lighted entrance was flanked with life-size bronze sculptures of a herd of longhorn cattle and some cowboys on horses.

"What now?" Marco said, looking around suspiciously.

Ren thought he could use some chill meditation, or maybe an hour in a sensory-deprivation tank. Glancing at her watch, she said, "Ten more seconds."

Right on time, the air above one of the cows began to shimmer pink and gold and green. The few other people nearby would never see the magic playing out right in front of them. Ren was sure, though, that if they just opened their eyes, minds, and hearts, they might catch a glimpse. Maybe.

Marco's eyes lifted to the gateway. "Uh, Ren, that's, like, ten feet in the air. How we supposed to get up there?"

With a sigh, Ren opened both palms. Shadows drifted out of her fingertips and formed the shape of a small ramp.

Marco was already backing up, shaking his head. "You want me to walk on a shadow?"

"It will hold you, I promise. Well, at least for a minute, so you should hurry."

"*Psh*—promises are for chumps."

With an impatient sigh, Ren directed the shadow to go beneath Marco's feet. And before he could protest, he was lifted up. His arms windmilled, and his legs wobbled. But no matter how close he came to nose-diving off, the shadow expanded, catching him each time.

"See?" Ren said, trying hard not to look as amused as she felt. "I told you."

"Not funny, RenatAAAA! Get me off this!"

"Will you just relax?" Ren said, climbing the shadow behind

him. "Struggling only makes it worse." She tried to take hold of
Marco's arm, but he broke free, which threw him off-balance.
He shouted, "Worse?!"

Ren grimaced as she watched him fall into the portal headfirst. His words echoed back to her. "I'll show *you* worse!"

Just as she was about to jump through the portal after him,
she caught a glimpse of something near the tree line below.

No.

Some*one*.

A translucent girl, fading in and out like she was trying
to become solid. Ren didn't recognize her. A straight hank of
golden hair hugged her chin. Her mouth was moving like she
was trying to tell Ren something. Ren hesitated and then inched
back, wanting to get a better look, when the gateway pulsed
once, twice.

And sucked her in.

6

Ren stepped through a loose plank in a barn wall, knocking a wooden sign onto the floor. Its painted words stared up at her: LIGHTNING NEVER STRIKES TWICE.

Looking up, she spotted Marco about twenty feet away. He had his back to her and was staring at the opposite wall. He was probably looking for a pitchfork to skewer her after she had shoved him into the gateway. But here was the weird thing: he hadn't even turned when she'd made a racket coming through the portal. Which could mean he was either still plotting or way heated.

"Hey," Ren said, approaching him slowly. Her sneakers crunched some straw that was scattered across the floor. "Are you okay? Are you mad? Because if you are, I'd rather you just tell me. I mean, I'm sorry, but—"

"Ren, can you be quiet for all of two seconds?"

Planting herself near Marco but keeping a safe eight-foot distance just in case, Ren finally saw what had his absolute attention. The wall was filled with framed action shots of some football player. In one he was launching a ball, in another he had his hands up in the air in the end zone, in yet another he was smiling while being carried by his teammates. There were at least a dozen photos.

"You know who that is?" Marco finally said, jutting his chin forward.

"Uh...he looks like a quarterback," Ren guessed because he had the same number sixteen Marco wore on his jersey.

"That's Len Dawson, one of the greatest—a Hall of Famer, three Super Bowls. A legend, man. A total legend."

"You said the Chiefs were losers."

Marco tore his gaze from the football altar. "Don't disrespect the man."

Ren didn't see what the big deal was. "So, someone's a fan."

Marco shook his head and pointed to a sign above the barn doors: DAWSON.

Oh. OH. "You think this is his house?"

"Put your hands in the air and turn around slowly," came a voice from behind them.

As they spun, Ren stared down the barrel of a...rifle? She was hoping it was a BB gun. But didn't those have orange tips? The boy had red hair, light freckles across his nose, and a fierce glare.

Marco spoke first. "Is that thing real?"

The boy lifted his chin, keeping his aim steady. "I ask the questions."

"Are you Sir Switchblade?" Ren said. "I'm Ren, from *Eyes in the Sky.*"

"What are you doing out here?"

This is where the magical portal took us. "Uh—we thought maybe you didn't want us to run into anyone else in your family."

The boy frowned, throwing his untrusting gaze on Marco. "And who are you?"

"He's my assistant," Ren said. She didn't even have to look to know how fast Marco snapped his neck in her direction. He for sure was wearing his deep signature *I'll get you later* scowl.

The boy said, "I didn't see a car anywhere."

"Uber dropped us at the road," Marco put in. "And that rifle is just a paintball gun." Then, to Ren, "So the good news is that he can't kill us."

Glaring, the boy lowered the weapon. "The paint balls are frozen, so they would hurt pretty bad. Want to find out?"

"No!" Ren nearly shouted. "Really, it's okay. We believe you. So, can you show us—"

"Hang on," Marco said, gesturing to the wall behind them. "Is that your grandpa?"

Ren wanted to shout *Why is that relevant when we're here to investigate an alien AND godborn sighting?* But whatever, Marco. Keep fanboying.

Sir Switchblade shrugged. "What does it matter to you?"

"Matter?" Marco let out a whoop. "That's, like . . . Do you know how amazing he is? And . . ." He paused. "Why are all his photos out here?"

"He's my great-uncle, and my gramps keeps them in every single room, including out here. He says it reminds him to kick fear in the teeth and be great every single day no matter what. That's why I called you. I was kicking fear in the teeth." He turned on his heel and said over his shoulder, "Are you coming or what?"

"Hang on," Ren said. "What's your name?"

But the boy ignored her and marched out of the barn into the black night.

A minute later, they stood at the edge of the cornfield, the stalks taller than all of them and so thick Ren wondered how they would ever maneuver through it.

"It's in there," the boy said, pulling out his phone and putting it in flashlight mode. "It's a tight squeeze, so stay close."

Then he disappeared into the stalks.

Ren followed with Marco right behind. She could hear him muttering, "Why did I ever agree to this?" and something about "stupid essays." Ren pushed through the field, bending leaves to make a path, trying to keep up with Sir Switchblade, who was unusually fast for someone with such small legs.

"Are we almost there?" Marco groaned.

And then they came to an opening to a long rectangle the size of a basketball court. The boy shone the light on the burned earth. Ren inched closer, standing above the symbol, which was about three feet in diameter.

A tight spiral made up of dozens of little circles. And at the center, a seven-pointed star. She had never seen anything like it.

"We came all this way for *that*?" Marco said, now standing next to Ren, arms crossed over his chest.

"Do you know what it is?" the boy asked from somewhere behind her.

Ren shook her head and snapped a few pictures.

"Well, peace out," Sir Switchblade said. "I don't want to get near that thing."

"Wait," Ren said, turning to face the boy. "Where did you see the snake and—"

"Monster?" He pointed to the far edge of the symbol. "Over there. Sniffing around like they were looking for something. It was creepy, and I really don't want to be here, so bye."

"Hang on." Marco narrowed his eyes. "Did you see them before or after the lightning strike?"

The boy was already vanishing back into the field when he said over his shoulder, "Before."

Marco threw his hands on top of his head and took a gulp of air. "Ren, if Serena and la ganga were here before the symbol, then maybe—"

He didn't get a chance to finish his sentence because Ren was thinking the same thing. "They either knew lightning was going to strike or they caused it," she said. "But why? How?"

A mass of clouds drifted across the full moon, momentarily casting Ren and Marco into darkness.

"Perfect," he muttered.

Ren was about to use the flashlight function on her phone when the moon reemerged, casting a brilliant beam like a spotlight on the symbol.

Ren stooped and lightly pressed her hands into the earth. Involuntarily, her fingers dug deeper into the soil. A current of heat raced into her fingers and up her arm just as a tall, hissing spiral of dirt and shadow rose up, slowly, carefully.

"What the heck is that?" Marco said.

"It's hot." No sooner had Ren said the words than the swirling mass twisted toward her. Marco swiped at it, his hands passing directly through it as it drew closer and closer to Ren.

Floating right in front of her eyes.

She gasped.

And the darkness flew right into her mouth.

7

This was wrong.

All wrong.

Ren found herself floating in a dark tunnel.

She heard the sounds of a raging wind, the clicking of teeth, and a deep hungry laugh.

With trembling, freezing hands, Ren tried to cast a shadow blanket around herself, but there was no feeling in her fingertips, no power. NO magic. How? Was this place blocking her powers somehow? She stood in the freezing nothingness with the random, not-at-all-helpful thought: *Is this what a black hole is like?*

A thick, gravelly voice echoed through the abyss. *A black hole would rip you to shreds.*

Perfect! The teeth-clicker could read minds.

Glancing back over her shoulder, she noticed a faint and dying light at the other end of the tunnel. It was as if she were looking through a prism. Everything was so distorted, except for Marco. He was there but super tiny and so, so, so far away. His arm was outstretched. She thought, *The distance is too great. He'll never reach me.*

Something was trying to hold her here. She could feel its presence, its wicked and terrifyingly powerful energy. Pulsing. Growing. Expanding.

Stay, the voice said, amused. *Stay, Queen.*

Ren looked back into the dark. *Queen?*

Yes.

A terrible fear took root in Ren at that moment, a fear that felt like it came from a faraway memory she couldn't quite remember. Almost like déjà vu.

Then came the sudden sleepiness, an exhaustion down to her bones. Her eyelids were like stones, and if she could just close them for...

Yes, came the dark voice again. *Sleep.*

"Ren!" Marco's voice was muffled, as if his face were buried under a pillow. His hand gripped hers. Then it started to slip. "They're coming, Ren!" he shouted. "Hold on—I'll pull you out!"

Coming? Who's coming?

Ren wanted to open her eyes, but each time she did, her eyeballs burned with agony as if she were staring directly into the sun. But some better part of her understood that if she gave in, if she let herself fall asleep, she would never get out of this prison of darkness.

No sooner had she thought the words than the teeth-clicker corrected her. *It's a shadow prison.*

With excruciating determination, she forced herself awake and grabbed Marco's hand tighter.

That's when she saw what was coming. The earth Marco was standing on in the cornfield erupted, heaving up a dozen short ashen figures with thick hairy bodies. They looked like fat rats with long bendy arms, and all those appendages reached for Marco.

"Run!" Ren screamed, but Marco just stood there, holding

his ground, unwilling to let her go. Dumb, stupid, brave Marco. Gods, he was so annoying.

Those things would be on him in three...

You can never escape, the voice said.

Two...

Marco jerked her forward. There was a sucking sound, a sharp blast of air, and a horrific scream from Ren's lungs, a sound she didn't know her body could make. Then she was back in the field.

Marco was now facing the beasts. They had short humanoid bodies covered with thin gray skin that showed a tangled web of purple veins. The mouths in their rodent-like heads opened and closed as they clicked their small sharp teeth in a maddening rhythm.

Click. Click. Click.

Dazedly, Marco lifted his arms in the air as if in surrender. "Marco!"

Click. Click. Click.

Ren threw her gaze back at the beasts, whose bulging hypnotic eyes were glowing white. Immediately, she froze. Her ears popped. Her heart shrank. A blazing light burned across the night sky. And then she heard the voice again. *I told you that you cannot escape.*

Ren was melting inside, shrinking into herself, and all she could do was watch and listen.

And hope.

Because she knew something that this disembodied voice didn't. Her shadows were like guardians—they had always protected her, or at least until moments ago, when she was locked in that tunnel. Even when she was in one of her absence seizures and couldn't conjure them herself. It was a magic she had never understood.

And then, as if she had instructed her sombras to devour these beasts, a wave of shadow magic rose from the earth and hurled the beasts into the mass of cornstalks.

The rat-like monsters screeched and hissed and wailed as the shadows engulfed them.

"Run!" Ren shouted to Marco again.

"What the...?" He hesitated for just a moment and then they fled the scene in the opposite direction.

The two godborns hurried into the cover of the stalks. The dry leaves scratched and whipped them as they flailed and kicked their way through. The earth rumbled behind them. Ren heard more wailing and screeching back there.

Finally, the two of them burst through the corn and into a meadow, Ren slowed enough to speak breathlessly into her watch, "Nearest...gateway...with...directions."

A millisecond later, her watch flashed, and she told Marco, "A quarter mile this way." She didn't even bother to look at the destination. Who cared? As long as they were a million light-years away from that shadow prison and those beasts.

For once, Marco followed obediently without a word.

A few minutes later, across a yawning field under the half-moon and a million stars, a gateway materialized—blue and purple and silver.

Just when Ren thought they were safe, the voice came to

her again, smooth and unaffected, and so close she could feel the warmth of its breath. *Tonight is a new moon. And a new lord shall awaken. You can run, my queen, but you cannot hide.*

Ignoring the warning, Ren took Marco's hand in hers and leaped into the unknown.

8

TINY MARVELS

That's what the pink neon sign on the wall said. Ren and Marco found themselves on a black mat surrounded by all sorts of gymnastics equipment, from balance beams and uneven bars to vaults and a few pommel horses. Fortunately, the place was otherwise empty, as it was after hours.

"What the hell happened back there?"

Marco was angry. Okay, more than angry. He always got this way when he was scared. Ren understood. Anger is preferable to fear—it doesn't make you feel as powerless.

"You were there and then not there," he said. "It was like you were frozen in some creeptastic, dark, faraway place."

"It was so, so dark..." Ren agreed, trying to rub the panic out of her arms. She flicked on the overhead lights to obliterate the memory. "And I heard this voice.... How did I get there?"

With a grunt, Marco launched himself onto the gymnastic rings and swung back and forth, higher and higher, spending whatever feelings were burning through him.

"That black smoky junk went in your mouth." He did a few pull-ups and then dropped to the ground. "And then you were getting smaller but still there, and I ran after you, and I don't know, man. Even with my godborn speed and power, I almost didn't catch up." He wiped his hands together.

Ren didn't know where to begin, what to say. It was as if that abyss had stolen her voice. "Thank you," she finally got out. "You saved my life."

"Which I'm thinking means you'll be writing all my essays until I graduate high school." He attempted a laugh, but it came out as a pathetic little oomph of air.

"Did you hear the voice, too?"

"Nah." Marco glanced around for something else to conquer. "What did it say?"

"Something about a black hole, and then it called me... queen." Ren could see doubt cross Marco's face as he launched himself onto a pommel horse. "Dumb, right?" she said, trying to make light of something too big to swallow in this moment.

"Maybe it thought you were someone else," he said as he held a perfect handstand. "Like mistaken identity. Why don't they have a punching bag in here?"

Ren thought about the last words of the teeth-clicker. *Tonight is a new moon. And a new lord shall awaken.* She glanced at her watch. "It's already eleven."

Marco launched himself into a forward flip, then dusted off his hands. "And way past my bedtime. Sounds like it's time to go home."

"Marco..."

A band of silence stretched between them. "I really hate it when you look at me like that," he said.

Ren told him about the shadow prison and lord-awakening stuff.

"Sounds like someone else's problem."

"Marco, we have to find out what the voice meant, and what

that symbol in the cornfield was, and why or how the cinco found it. Think about it—Sir Switchblade said that the kids were snooping around *before* the lightning struck, which means they know something about this symbol or lord. Maybe that was a lord's voice I heard. If one lord is that creepy, I don't want to think about *two* cruising around."

"Look, I told you no quests or hunts or anything. I should be getting rest before my big game. There's no way I'm messing that up, which means I'm for sure not going to wherever you're thinking," Marco said, carefully enunciating each word like he was making a threat.

"I didn't ask you to, but don't you think we should find out what the cinco are up to so we can give a full report to Ixtab?" As Ren said the words, a part of her believed them, but the honest part of her heart spoke to her in whispers. *You knew you were going to follow the cinco's lead. You always knew. Even before that voice (lord?) called you queen.*

Ren shook off her frustration with deep breaths. Maybe it wasn't fair to drag Marco into all of this. "Okay, you're right."

"I am?"

"I'll figure it out alone."

Marco groaned. "Do not guilt-trip me, Ren. That's low. Fine! I'll hang out with you until pregame time, but that's it." He patted his stomach. "But can we fuel up first? I'm starving!"

"Deal!" Ren rushed over to a desk in the corner to see if she could find a clue about where they were and if anyplace would be open at this time of night. She picked up a brochure and spun to Marco with a smile on her face. "You're in luck."

"Oh yeah?"

"We're in Vegas."

"Sin City?"

"Ha! Home of the all-you-can-eat buffet. Come on."

"It is?"

"Yeah, I was here once with my abuelo. We saw a few magic shows and pretty much ate our way through the strip." Ren gasped when she realized how late it was. She quickly texted her abuelo to tell him she was on a quest and that she'd explain after.

Ten seconds later, her phone rang.

"Hi, Abuelo," she answered with a cringe. "Don't be mad, but it just sort of happened and it wasn't a sighting like I thought, I mean it was, but I think it has to do with the rogue godborns and now I . . . I have to find them."

"Ay, mija. How long will you be gone?"

One of the things Ren loved most about her abuelo was that he understood her magic and the responsibilities that came with it.

"I don't know." Ren chewed her bottom lip. "But Marco is helping me."

At this, Marco began to shake his head and waggle a long finger at her.

With a sigh, Abuelo said, "Cuidado, okay? And text me tomorrow."

"Te prometo."

Thirty minutes later, she and Marco sat in an all-night diner packed with people. At the far end was an area reserved for slot machines. The electronic dance music, annoying *ping, ping, ping* of the slots, and the needless chatter was enough to send her nervous system into overdrive.

Even though her stomach was still jumpy, Ren knew she had to eat something, and thankfully she had remembered to bring her debit card with her. She ordered a grilled cheese. Marco ordered two burgers, fries, onion rings, and nachos.

"That's a lot of food."

"Those were a lot of rat monsters."

Ren's phone buzzed just as the food arrived. She tugged her cell from her pocket. Zane's photos had finally downloaded.

She sucked in a gulp of air.

"What now?" Marco shoved five fries into his mouth.

"No WAY!"

Marco grabbed for her phone, but she jerked it back, showing him Zane's photo.

It was the same symbol from Kansas. The tight spiral made up of dozens of little circles with a seven-pointed star at the center.

"Whoa! Whoa! Whoa!" Marco's hands were up in the air again. "How in the heck did Zane find the same symbol in Mexico?"

Ren quickly dialed Zane's cell again, only to get his voice mail. She clenched her fist in frustration.

"I told you," Marco said. "He's off the grid with his dad, trying to get intel on why the gods are kids." He snorted. "Seems pointless, and I bet the unaffected gods don't even care. More power for the ones still standing."

"That's a terrible way to look at it."

"I'm just looking at it the way the gods would. And let's be real, Ren—the gods are all about power. That little lovefest when they banded together a few months ago? That was only to defeat a common enemy."

Ren's chest felt suddenly tight, like something was going to snap. "You know, life would be easier if you were a little more positive."

"Me? Right. I'm a QB, Ren. It doesn't get much more positive than that."

Ren picked at her sandwich, thinking, trying to connect the whys to the hows all at once. What did the cinco know about the symbol and the lord (or lords)? How was it possible Zane had found the exact same symbol? And why had that teeth-clicker called her queen?

"You look way stressed." Marco pushed his plate toward Ren. "Have an onion ring."

"You're the son of war," Ren said. "That means you're really good at strategy and seeing past the obvious."

"So?"

"So, help me with some theories, because it's almost midnight, and if that voice was a lord, a second one is going to wake up soon if he hasn't already."

Marco wore a deep frown, the one that said *I'm thinking of all possibilities.* "I've got nothin', Ren."

"Marco, you're—"

"The GOAT. I know."

Marco wasn't exactly the greatest of all time, but he was great at puzzling out anything villainy or battle related. "I can see your brain spinning."

Bells rang across the diner at a high volume matched only by the shriek of the lady who won at slots and the sound of all those coins tumbling out of the machine.

Marco said, "Fine. I'll spill, but that doesn't mean I'm in or going to do anything about it." He shoved a wad of burger into his mouth, wiped a dribble of ketchup off his chin, and chewed slowly. Annoyingly so. "I mean, okay, clearly the cinco have something to do with the symbol. Maybe they created it or they knew it was going to appear. And if that's true, then they must know whoever this teeth-gnasher is—"

"Teeth-*clicker*."

"So, my best guess is that Serena and crew are maybe in cahoots with these bad dudes, the lords. I mean, who knows how many lords there are, but..." He rubbed the back of his neck.

"But what?"

With a grunt, Marco leaned closer, resting his arms on the table. "You're at the center of a game, Ren. Think about it. *You* got the call. *You* got locked in the shadow prison. *You* are the one he called queen. So, the better question is... how are *you* involved? And why?"

Ren's pulse beat wildly. Her head throbbed, her stomach ached, and her limbs tightened. There was a truth in Marco's words that resonated throughout her whole body, as if there was a memory was buried in her very cells that she hadn't discovered yet.

"But why me? I told you, I've never heard of any lords, and I'd never seen that spiral symbol before Kansas and then Zane's pics."

Marco was thinking again. "Maybe it has something to do with you being a shadow bruja."

Ren's bruja blood came from her Mexica ancestry, something she knew so little about because her dad had never wanted to discuss it. Then he died, leaving her with only the broken pieces of a half-told story.

Marco gulped down some water. "I think it's time to call in the big guns, Ren. So, shoot Ixtab an email and call it a day."

"You just said I'm the one at the center of a game."

"Doesn't mean you have to play."

Ren crossed her arms over her chest and set her jaw. "Let me ask you a question. If it were you who'd been trapped in the shadow prison, if it were you he called queen or king or whatever, would you let it go?"

Marco looked like he might grimace, but instead his expression turned blank. Unreadable. Silent. He wasn't going to answer the question. And why should he? She wasn't really asking as much as making a point.

"You could cash out all the poker games with that face," Ren said as she dialed a number on her phone and placed the call on speaker for Marco to hear.

"Who are you calling?"

"Hello?" Ah-Puch's boyish voice boomed through the speaker. "Hello? Hello?"

"A.P.! It's me, Ren. Why are you saying hello so much?"

"You said I should say hello when it rings, so I thought more was better."

Marco flicked a balled-up straw wrapper across the table and muttered, "You've got to be kidding me."

"Where are you?" Ren asked, grateful that the teenage god even remembered how to answer the cell phone she insisted he carry. She was worried that with his powers diminished she might not be able to reach him any other way.

There were clanking dishes in the background and the low hum of chatter like he was in a crowded restaurant. That was surprising, since the god of death, darkness, and destruction hated . . . well, pretty much everyone. Except for Ren. They were connected. She had saved his life, and he had saved hers.

"Are you in Xib'alb'a?" she asked.

"I'm at a beach," he said. "Hey, waiter," A.P. said, snapping his fingers. "Yeah, you, kid."

Ren winced. She assumed that the waiter was older than A.P. looked, which was fourteen, and probably wanted to vaporize the god for his rudeness.

"Where am I?" A.P. was still talking to the server.

"The Hotel del Coronado, sir," a young man's voice said.

"Yes, I know that, but where exactly is this establishment located?"

Ren winced again. She could only imagine the server's confusion over this young teenager who sounded so old and so arrogant.

"Coronado, sir."

A.P. must have given him a dumb look because the server clarified, "San Diego, California. Would you like some more soda?"

"I didn't ask for any," A.P. said. Then to Ren, "I'm in Coronado."

Marco frowned, whispering, "How can he not know where he is?"

"I thought you were in SHIHOM," Ren said.

"I did a search like you showed me on my phone and googled the finest establishments with an ocean view and delicious cuisine."

Marco rolled his eyes. "Cool. While you were stuffing your face, Ren was almost killed in a Kansas-cornfield shadow prison by some teeth-gnasher who called her queen!"

"Oh," A.P. said calmly. "You're with the ill-tempered son of war?"

Marco started to argue, but Ren shushed him with an outstretched palm.

A.P. asked, "Does he speak the truth?"

"Not a teeth-gnasher. A teeth-*clicker*. Maybe a lord of some kind? Does that sound familiar?" There was a stretch of silence as if the call had gone dead. "Hello? A.P.? Are you there?"

"He probs muted you," Marco said, "so he could scarf down a lobster whole." He grabbed the pen the server had left on the table with the bill. Then he reached over and took hold of Ren's wrist.

"What are you doing?" she asked. "I have to call A.P. back."

"Just hold still."

"Marco!"

"Admit it, Ren," he said. "You don't always make the right call. And it's not because you're not smart. You're sort of a genius. But your heart...it's too..." He hesitated before saying, "Too nice, too trusting. Always getting in the way of the hard stuff. Ya know?"

What was he, A.P.'s spokesperson?

The son of war wrote four letters across the inside of her wrist: *WWMD*. Then he sat back and smiled. "What Would Marco Do?" he said, looking smug and way too satisfied. "A reminder to be more threatening, to do the thing that equals victory, Ren. No matter what."

Ren thought that was such a sad way of looking at the world. But maybe Marco and A.P. were right. Maybe she needed to harden her heart just a tiny bit.

Ren was about to call A.P. back when the air in the diner felt suddenly charged, electric with the sense that something was coming. The gold chain around her throat pulsed like a steady heartbeat, slower and slower, until the buzzing neon commotion of the room wound down to an abrupt standstill. No sound, no movement, no ... anything. "Marco?" Ren's voice was little more than a whisper as her gaze darted around the frozen diner. The son of war was motionless, too, in mid-bite, a french fry hanging in the air.

Ren's chest caved. *What the ... ?*

That's when she saw her. The translucent girl from Waco. Over there by the Monopoly slot machine. This time she wasn't flickering.

And unlike everyone else, she was moving. Toward Ren.

9

Tezcatlipoca

You would've had to be deader than dead not to feel the earth shudder and quake.

Not to see the lightning rip the black sky into bits, not to feel the writhing, whirling wind charged with electricity. There was a loud clap of thunder just as the ancient energy bled from the moist Yucatán earth.

The second Lord of Night, the Smoking Mirror, opened his eyes, black and glittering like obsidian.

His voice, dark and dripping with shadows, whispered, "Finally."

10

Ren felt a spark, a flicker of heat deep in her bones.

As the girl came closer, Ren could see that her mouth was moving: *Help me.*

Her dark eyes were wide, darting back and forth, like she was surprised that she found herself in this place. She wore a pair of jeans and a sweatshirt with a glittery, loopy word Ren couldn't make out.

"Stay right there!" Ren jumped up to meet her halfway across the room, weaving between the creepy mannequin people as she rapid-fired questions. "Who are you? How can I help?"

But with each step Ren took, the girl vanished a little more, like a thinning cloud. Or a ghost. Ren came to a halt about fifteen feet away, trying to bring her breathing under control. She couldn't lose it and black out. Not now. Not when this apparition was trying to tell her something.

A shadow wall rose between Ren and the girl, a shadow Ren hadn't created. She tried to will it away, but it only expanded and thickened, blocking her view.

"The Lords of Night," the girl said in a faraway voice.

"Lords?" Ren echoed, pressing her hands into the shadow, which felt like a wet sponge. "Who are they?" She called up her magic. It started deep in her chest and pulsed at the edges of her fingertips with an unexplainable all-encompassing power. In an instant, she smashed the shadow wall until it looked like a heap of black ash disintegrating into the orange carpet.

The girl spoke again, some of her words lost in maddening gaps. "Wake . . . Lords . . . Hollywood . . . help."

In her eagerness for answers, Ren made the terrible mistake of taking another step forward. In that single motion, the translucent girl evaporated completely. And the world around Ren spun back to life.

The diner buzzed with noise and energy. Through the crowd, Ren saw Marco shoving fries into his mouth as he peered around for Ren. She half wondered how it must have looked to him. One second she was there; the next she was gone.

Clutching her gold chain, Ren took a second to process, to think, to try to figure out what the heck had just happened.

Time stopped. But who stopped it, and why? Why did her magic pulse? Where did that shadow come from? And who was that girl? What was she trying to tell me?

Wake . . . Lords . . . Help. Hollywood?

Marco's eyes locked on hers. She started to make her way back, and a firm hand gripped her arm from behind. She whirled around to find Ah-Puch. The immediate smile that formed on her lips died the second she saw his stony expression. Even though he was now only a teen, Ren sometimes caught glimpses of the god who had once inspired terror.

"We need to go," he said tightly, "and we need to go *now.*"

When the god of death, darkness, and destruction tells you to get a move on, you do it without question. Unless you're Marco, son of war, whose blood is made up of equal parts stubbornness and suspicion.

"I'm not going anywhere with you," he said, crossing his arms tightly over his chest. "Not until you tell us what's up."

Ah-Puch's nostrils flared. "Not here. Not now." He inched closer to Marco, coming face-to-face with him. "Unless you don't care what happens to *her.*"

Those must have been the magic words, because Marco stood down with a single (albeit begrudging) nod.

Outside, the street bustled with hordes of people and music and lights. Ah-Puch went to the edge of the curb and let loose a sharp whistle.

"A.P.!" Ren's voice rose. "What's going on?"

Before the god could answer, an old-fashioned black car rolled up. "Get in," he ordered as he hopped into the front passenger seat.

Marco said, "This thing looks like a hearse, if you ask me." He gagged the second they were inside the vehicle. Okay, it did smell worse than rotting demon flesh masked by cheap perfume. Maybe that's because a demon, dressed in a gold Adidas jogging suit, was driving. Her silvery-blue skin glistened under the neon lights outside.

Marco screwed up his face. "Dude, this hearse reeks!" He started to roll down his window.

"Don't do that," Ah-Puch warned. "And it's not a hearse. It's a 1955 Rolls-Royce Silver Dawn. It has carried individuals far superior to you, godborn."

Ren had had enough. "What's going on, A.P.? Why are you here? And since when do you have a chauffeur?"

"I didn't even know that demons could drive," Marcos muttered.

"We can do a lot of things," the demon said in a youngish, sultry voice, like she was auditioning to be the latest Bond girl. Then her shimmering blue eyes flicked to the rearview mirror, where she studied Marco. "Nice hair."

OMG! She's flirting. Over his hair.

Marco grinned.

So gross!

A.P. spoke to the demon in a language Ren had never heard before. What didn't he want her to know? Her stomach twisted into knots.

"What are you telling her?" she asked, leaning forward.

The demon accelerated, weaving in and out of traffic like they were in some high-speed chase. For an old car, the thing moved like lightning.

"A.P.," Ren tried again, "what *is the deal*?"

"The deal," the god said, "is that we are going to a gateway—a very old, *untraceable* gateway."

"Gateway to where?" Ren asked. "And why does it need to be untraceable? Is someone following you?"

"Hey, man," Marco said, shaking his head, "I've got a game tonight. I need some sleep and—"

"You can sleep when you're dead," the god said. Then to Ren, "SHIHOM. And no, but someone is following *you*."

Ren's eyes went wide. "Do you mean the ghost girl?"

"What ghost girl?" Marco and Ah-Puch asked at the exact same moment.

"The one back at the diner..."

Marco dragged both hands down his face. "You are a total magnet for the weird and awful and things that could give me a stroke."

"Are you scared of ghosts?"

"Uh, negative! Do I look scared of *anything*?"

"Yeah. You look scared of the *word ghost*," Ren said. "Your nostrils flare every time I say it."

"I'm allergic to demons, okay?"

"Enough!" Ah-Puch twisted his thin torso to face Ren, his eyes nearly black.

"Hey, news alert, dude," Marco said, popping his knuckles. "I don't take orders from washed-up gods."

Ouch.

Even for Marco that was harsh. And Ren hated all things harsh, especially words that were meant to stab someone in the gut. It immediately made her think of the cyberbullies and all the cruel things they'd said to her. Even though they weren't true, they still hurt.

"Marco!" Ren socked him in the shoulder. "That was a low blow. He can't help that he doesn't have any powers."

In an uncharacteristic move, A.P. turned to stare right at Marco. Uh-oh. He was wearing that lethal glare again. "You're right," he said. "And if you knew how many comebacks I've had, kid, you'd shut that trap of yours, because I have a long memory. And I really don't care who your daddy is. War may be powerful, but death is final. Just remember that."

"Guys!" Ren said. "I will seriously trap you both in a shadow box if you don't chill out."

"Fine," Marco said. "I guess your car is cool. How fast is this thing flying? A hundred miles per hour?"

Ah-Puch laughed lightly. "Try one fifty."

"Dude! That's insane."

Oh, okay, they're bonding over the lightning-rod car now. Cool.

"A.P.," Ren said, "I want to know who's following me."

"Don't say anything else," the god commanded. "Not until we're out of here."

"Why not?"

"Do you trust me?"

Without hesitation, Ren nodded. She would trust A.P. with her life.

Marco chuckled. "Nope."

"Yeah, well, I don't trust you either, kid."

"Because I'm the son of war, right?" Marco's chest puffed out an inch, maybe two.

"No," A.P. said, "because the blue stripes in your hair are quite uneven."

"Don't disrespect the hair, man."

"Can't we let Marco go home?" Ren suggested. "He has a huge game, and he should get some rest."

But Ah-Puch was already shaking his head. "Once we get to SHIHOM and kill our trail, he can do whatever he wants."

"I'm getting bad vibes," Marco groaned as the demon turned into the desert. There was no road. No lights. No civilization. Dark rock formations took strange shapes in the distance. The car flew across the sand as if the tires weren't even touching it.

Marco leaned close to Ren. "You ever see that gangster

movie where they took the prisoners out to the desert and made them dig their own graves?"

"Marco," Ren said under her breath. "This isn't a movie."

"It totally could be," he whispered. "We *are* with the death god, and just so you know, I'm not digging my own grave."

"It should be another three miles ahead," A.P. told the demon. That's when Ren noticed how tightly the god was gripping the door handle. He was nervous, worried, but about what? What had made him come to Vegas and haul Ren away to the middle of the desert? And who was following her?

Ren was wading through her questions when she heard it.

A wave of distant static.

She didn't think too much of it until it was followed by a chilling whistling noise like wind blowing through a tunnel. It triggered a memory. She had heard the haunting sound before.

"Do you hear that?" she asked, wondering why no one else was reacting.

Marco turned away from the window to face her. "Hear what?"

"Seriously? How can you not?" Ren said. "It sounds just like this recording of Saturn's rings I listened to one time on YouTube. Like a high-pitched whistle and—"

A.P. was speaking in that strange language again. The demon sped up, and the black desert whizzed past outside. But the faster they went, the louder the sound grew.

Ren pressed her hands over her ears.

"Hey," Marco said. "You okay?"

Don't do that, came a low, gruff voice. Not the same one as in Kansas, but similar and far more dangerous sounding.

Ren jumped in her seat, throwing her gaze in all directions, looking for the source.

You can't find me unless I want to be found, the voice said.

"Stop!" Ren screamed.

Everything happened all at once. The demon came to an abrupt halt just outside a dilapidated shack silhouetted against the night sky. Marco tugged her from the car. A.P. shouted orders she couldn't make out. And a blacker-than-black darkness swelled from the earth. Rising and rising. Taking shape a mere twenty yards to their right.

A.P. yelled a command in the strange language. Up ahead, a wall of shimmering orange lit up the night. The gateway.

Ren and the three others ran toward it. Pounding feet and panting breaths and the voice. It was there. It was everywhere.

You can't escape, my queen.

"Stop calling me that!"

They were almost at the portal. Just ten more feet to go.

The rising dark shapes were fully formed now.

Three enormous panthers towered two stories above them. Yellow fanged, red eyed, and with foaming mouths. They were all that stood between the quartet and the gateway to safety.

The godborns, demon, and god stopped in their tracks. Unexpectedly, A.P. backed up, shaking his head. "I'm really not equipped for battle. And I'd rather not die in this body. But . . ." He shrugged off his coat and took a defensive stance. "A god's gotta do what a god's gotta do."

The demon roared, baring claws that dripped a thick clear substance.

"You think a few kitties are going to stop us?" Marco shouted into the night. He really had the worst timing for his outbursts.

Ren drew up a shadow circle that dissipated the moment it came to life. Shock waves rolled through her entire body.

A.P. said, "We really need some cover to get to the gateway. So . . . anytime now, Ren."

"I'm trying!" But no matter how hard she focused, the shadows vanished as soon as she created them.

The ginormous jungle cats hissed and sneered. The voice spoke in whispers now. *If you give up, I won't kill your friends.*

"Who are you?" Ren asked, remembering her SHIHOM training. *Never face an enemy you don't know.*

Come and I'll show you.

The cats were crouched low, balancing on their back paws, ready to pounce.

Ren whipped the time rope from her throat and lashed it out in front of her. The golden chain stretched and grew, glowing with power. Maybe not time-stopping power, but the power to scorch, slash, and destroy. "Let me see you!"

You know who I am. You've always known.

Marco and the demon charged the cats at the same moment that A.P. grabbed Ren and dragged her along the perimeter of the battle toward the gateway.

"No, wait!" she screamed, breaking free as Marco launched himself onto the back of one of the panthers. The demon slid between the legs of another and slashed its gut with her poison claws.

A horrific yowl echoed across the desert as the beast turned to ash.

And then, as if in slow motion, the third cat flew through the air toward Marco. Ren quickly snapped the chain across the distance and roped the creature around its neck. Its flesh smoked and burned, but Ren wasn't strong enough to drag the monster to the ground. Her muscles ached and her fingers cramped. She didn't think she could hold on much longer.

A.P. grabbed hold of the rope, adding his power to the haul. The chain burned through his hands.

"A.P., no!" Ren screamed, trying to shove him out of the way.

But he didn't let go. The smell of his singed flesh was unbearable.

It was enough. The cat stumbled, then burned to ash. A.P. stumbled, too, clutching his hands to his body and grimacing with a pain she had never seen in him.

Marco's panther reared, knocking the godborn off its back. And just as Ren was about to lunge, the panther retreated. Its eyes glowed as its chest heaved.

Why was it just standing there? It stared at Ren with what looked like a sneering grin.

In the next breath, the beast evaporated.

No way. Ren had never been in a battle where the enemy backed down. *Ever.* Something was so wrong about this.

Ren snapped the chain back into its necklace form around her neck and quickly wrapped an arm around Ah-Puch as she guided him to the gateway. It smelled of rust and rot.

"Why would you do that?" she scolded. "You know no one can touch the time rope but me. Are you okay?"

"I really hate the human condition," he said with a moan.

Marco was busy high-fiving the demon. "Did you see that? Coward. It knew it was outnumbered."

Maybe, came the voice as they stepped into the gateway.

Or maybe I now know your strengths. And weaknesses.

11

The sun crept over the horizon, coloring the sky orange and pink with wisps of purple.

The black asphalt shimmered as if tiny diamonds were embedded in it.

Ren blinked. This definitely wasn't SHIHOM. Had they taken the wrong gateway? Ah-Puch had said it was an ancient and untraceable portal. And Ren had heard that those couldn't be trusted, so it was totally possible. . . .

And where were her friends?

She glanced around. She was in the front opening of an airplane hangar where a sleek jet was parked. Beyond her the tarmac was filled with small airplanes taking off, their engines rumbling and roaring as they vanished into the hazy sky.

Out of the corner of her eye, she caught movement over by the jet.

She turned her head to see A.P. descending the plane's steps. It was only now that Ren got a good look at the god of death in his teen form—skinny frame, long arms, and black hair tied back neatly with a leather rope. And even though he looked kind of like a skater dude, he wore, in typical Ah-Puch fashion, a dark fitted suit that appeared to have been tailor-made for him.

When he got close to her, a giggle bubbled out of Ren, but the god didn't notice. He was too busy making his entrance.

"I'm not one for drama," he said, "but I needed to meet you where no one else could follow or listen."

"But Marco and . . ." Her eyes scanned the area again.

"It's only us two," the god said. "You're in an in-between place of my creation." With these words he might have stood a little taller.

Ren remembered reading about Zane's in-between space at the top of an ocean cliff. He and Hurakan would meet there privately, away from godly eyes and ears. "But that means my body isn't here, at this . . ." She glanced around. "Airport, right? I'm, like, asleep somewhere?"

With absolute concentration, A.P. watched the planes lifting into the air. "It's actually a perfect simulation of demon flight school. And you're really here."

"But how?" She hated reminding the god of his not-so-powerful form. Unless . . . "If you transported us here, does that mean your powers are coming back?"

A.P. clenched his already rigid jaw. "The ancient gateways," he said, "the ones no longer used—they bleed old magic, so I used a bit of it."

"Old magic." Ren echoed the words calmly, but she didn't feel so calm. She actually felt like freaking out. Not because she had just battled a monster panther when she was without shadow magic, but because that voice—the one that felt like it was everywhere and nowhere—wasn't going to leave her alone. She knew it would persist and it would keep its promise. *You can't escape.*

"But why meet here? I thought SHIHOM was safe and protected."

"Even SHIHOM's magic can be breached, Ren. Or don't you remember?"

How could she forget that just a few months ago their enemies had broken through SHIHOM'S enchanted borders using the underworld and the World Tree as access?

Ren glanced down at the god's hands, searching for the burns from touching the time rope. "Are you okay?"

He threw her a side glance. "My godly powers might be compromised at the moment, but I still have divine blood running through my veins. So, tell me, Ren. Tell me everything."

Ren scanned the in-between world with the thick, shadowy jungle on both sides of the tarmac. The same airplanes that had taken off a few minutes ago had returned to zoom across the runway again.

"If it's so safe here, then what's with all the noise?"

"Let's just call it a frequency that will keep others out."

"How do you know?" She wondered how any place could be safe if SHIHOM wasn't.

"Can we get to that later?"

"How about now? I have to be sure."

The god exhaled sharply. "Fine. A long time ago, before the beginning of history as humans know it, I created a spy network. The gods liked the idea because we could train the spies to use dreams to send secret messages. And dreams are impenetrable, Ren. Well, mostly."

Mostly meaning with the exception of the godborn Adrik, who was a dream walker and could pretty much infiltrate *anyone's* dreams.

"I know all the tricks because I came up with them," the god went on. "But then we were forced to shut down the whole system when the spies tried to use it against us. And we couldn't afford to have anyone else communicating in secret."

Ren remembered hearing about the network from Zane. At the time, she had thought it was pretty unfair, but then again, she wasn't a paranoid god.

"Your turn." A.P. turned to face her. "Start at the beginning, and don't leave anything out."

As the sun continued to rise and the planes continued to loop, Ren told the god everything, from the strange symbol to the cinco to the ghost girl. She finished it up with the creepy voices.

A.P. paced in front of her, listening intently. His already-deep frown deepened with every few steps.

"Ungrateful godborn scoundrels," the god said. "I look forward to the day they are servants of death in Xib'alb'a. Better yet, perhaps an afterlife of grinding bones into dust with their teeth will teach them."

Ren cringed. "That seems kind of harsh. I mean, maybe we should hear their side of the story?"

Ah-Puch eyed her with a tense gaze. "Story? There is no story that would ever exonerate them for trying to overthrow the gods. To assume power for themselves."

Ren didn't subscribe to A.P.'s one-and-done belief. To her, the world wasn't so black-and-white—it was full of pockets of gray where there was plenty of room for mistakes. "I know it seems really awful, but we have no clue what their lives have been like up to now, or if they're sorry, or why they were in Kansas. Maybe they now realize they were wrong, but they're scared to admit it to the gods because they know they'll never be forgiven."

"They made their choice!"

Ren knew this was an argument she was never going to win. The cinco's betrayal hurt her, too. She felt just as stung that they could be so cold and calculating in their grab for power. But she knew people could change. The god of death was a perfect example himself. He had once been a bloodthirsty scoundrel hell-bent on destroying the world. And if he could change, couldn't Serena and the others, too? Ren wanted to point out the irony, but A.P. was already asking, "Can you tell me more about the ghost?"

"She looked young . . . like our age." She winced at her choice of words. "I mean *my* age. I think I've seen her before, but it was hard to tell because of her being see-through-ish and everything. And like I said, she seemed scared, which is kinda weird. I mean, I thought ghosts were the ones who made everyone *else* scared and—"

"I don't think you saw a ghost."

Ren felt a jab of surprise. "No offense, but, uh, you weren't there. She definitely looked like a ghost."

"She sounds like an astral traveler."

"An astral qué?" Somewhere in the back of Ren's memory, she *sort of* remembered reading about astral travelers in one of her space books.

"It's the ability to separate your soul from your body—"

"And travel somewhere else," she finished. "That should for sure be a class at SHIHOM."

"Ren, very few people can do it well. We gods keep records of such things."

"Why?" Ren shook her head. "Wait. To protect the gods, right? To make sure people aren't communicating in secret?" There was a razor-sharp edge to her tone, but she couldn't help it. She was tired of these power plays, and the constant spying and logging of magic. Why couldn't the gods just chill the heck out?

"That, and other reasons I won't go into now."

"But why would she ask *me*, a stranger, for help? And how did she even find me? And what's with 'Hollywood'? Such a weird thing to say."

For once, A.P. didn't have an answer. He gave a halfhearted shrug. "Maybe she's connected to the Lords of Night."

Ren froze. Alarm bells blared in her head. "How did you know she mentioned them? Are the voices coming from them? Do you know who they are?"

A.P. studied her.

A moment passed. Two. Three.

"Well?" she said impatiently.

"It's a dark, sordid tale, and you aren't going to like it." It was hard to take him seriously with that boyish voice and scrawny face. But underneath all that was still the god of death, darkness, and destruction. And behind those eyes was a story Ren was dying to hear.

12

They made their way along the perimeter of the runway to the edge of the jungle.

Blasts of exhaust from the jets' engines bent the treetops this way and that. A.P. gestured to the planes, and the noise level dropped a couple of decibels. Enough so that they could have a convo without shouting.

The god pulled in a breath like it was his last. And then he began. "There were nine Aztec gods. Each ruled over a designated night—the first, the second, and so on. They were associated with certain fates, good or bad. And they were powerful."

Were.

Ren knew the history of the Aztec empire, how the Spanish explorer Cortés and his crew had waged war against the Indigenous people and killed them off. She'd been told that when the sacrifices to the Aztec gods stopped, the gods grew weak and died off, too.

Then she remembered the devourer, the Mexica earth goddess Tlaltecuhtli, who could both give and take life. The one Camazotz and Ixkik' had resurrected so she could gobble up the Maya gods. And when the devourer barfed them up, some were teens—like Ah-Puch.

Ren's pulse quickened as excitement surged through her body. She was on the verge of solving a great mystery. "So, these

Lords of Night—are they being resurrected like the devourer was? Is that what the cinco are up to?"

Ah-Puch slowed his pace and turned to Ren. "If I were a true human, I would say something entirely useless like *That would be my guess.* But gods aren't in the business of guessing, Ren. We're about absolutes."

But Ren wasn't a goddess, and she knew only one way to get to *absolute.* She had to begin with educated guesses, hypotheses, and theories. Her mind stumbled from one conclusion to the next, each idea dawning like the morning sky. "The cinco wanted to overthrow the Maya gods, and when that didn't work, they thought they could resurrect the Lords of Night. But why? I mean, I don't think these lords—at least the ones I've heard from—are very friendly, and for sure they're not lining up to give away their power to a bunch of Maya godborns."

The sun floated at the edge of the horizon as if it had stopped moving in order to listen to the conversation unfold.

"Do you know them?" Ren asked. "Like, personally?"

"Let's just say we've had dealings, and so I know they're not bound to wake up in very good moods. But you should know that they'll be most powerful when together. The third lord will likely be roused from his slumber tonight, and then the fourth tomorrow, and the next, until they're all awake."

Oh, goody. The more the merrier. NOT! It was bad enough to deal with one or two, but nine? Ren wasn't sure she could stomach meeting another every night for the next week.

"Which means we need to figure this out before the last one opens its eyes," Ren said, gripped with a fear she didn't understand. "That only gives us seven more nights."

"Yes." A.P. went on to tell her the first three lords' names, starting with Xiuhtecuhtli, the Fire Lord; Tezcatlipoca, the Smoking Mirror; and Piltzintecuhtli, the Prince Lord. She learned that the Fire Lord was sometimes called the Old God, and the Smoking Mirror had a bigger reputation for viciousness.

Ah-Puch said, "The Smoking Mirror was—is—the Aztec god of war and strife, among other things. He's also associated with the night sky, the north, jaguars, obsidian, sorcery, and some other things too insignificant to recall. And he had quite a reputation for being repugnant."

"And the Prince Lord?"

"Sun god, healer." He shrugged casually, like the Prince Lord wasn't worthy of a longer description in the encyclopedia.

"Do you think they're waking in the order of their days?"

"They are rather unimaginative, so it's likely, but one can't be certain."

That meant that the teeth-clicker could be the Fire Lord and Mr. *You-Know-Who-I-Am* might be the Smoking Mirror.

Ren drew up short and turned to her friend. "And why are these lords talking to me and calling me queen? Maybe being resurrected made them loopy or something?"

You've always known, the Smoking Mirror had said.

Ah-Puch furrowed his eyebrows. "We need these answers and more. It's all connected—the lords, the astral traveler, the cinco."

"And the symbol. That seems super important, too." She drew out her phone and showed A.P. the pictures she had taken in Kansas.

Ah-Puch stared at them.

Ren's heart jumped from side to side. "You've seen it before?"

"No."

"Then what's wrong?"

"Hmm?"

"Right there..." Ren pointed. "Under your eye... It's twitching." He was hiding something.

"Is not."

"A.P., it's totally twitching. Are you holding out on me?"

The god cupped a hand over the entire right side of his face. His shoulders sagged. "It's all this teen torment. It's dreadful, Ren, living in this... this lab of hormones.... And have I told you that I'm always hungry? Sometimes I even have nightmares... and just the other day I felt fear. FEAR! My whole reputation will be destroyed if it's discovered that the most fearsome god of all is afraid. And now I have a twitching eye, and it feels like the world is coming to an end!"

The guy looked like he was going to melt into a puddle of tears if Ren didn't intervene.

"We're going to get you back to your death-darkness-and-destruction status pronto," she said with as much confidence as she could muster. And then an idea struck her hard and fast. "Wait! What if the time travel wasn't what turned you guys into kids? What if it had something to do with being trapped inside the devourer?"

"We've already been over this," A.P. said glumly. "No way could a resurrected Mexica goddess have that kind of power."

Logically, Ren understood as she patted A.P.'s back. But a

flicker of doubt vibrated under her ribs. And she had the feeling, especially now, that there was more to the Mexica connection than anyone had first believed.

While A.P. was recovering from his teen meltdown, taking in deep but panicked gulps of air, shaking his head and muttering incoherently, Ren brought her magic to the surface, changing the sky to utter darkness with an enormous shadow, leaving only the distant light of the hangar for the landing planes.

A.P. perked up, glanced around. "What . . . ?"

"I thought the darkness might calm you down."

The god's eye was no longer twitching. He nodded solemnly and stood up straighter. "That was rather embarrassing. Every once in a while, I lose myself unexpectedly and . . ." He hesitated, shaking his head. "It won't happen again."

"I could probably teach you some breathing exercises, or there's this thing where you tap your fingertips on certain meridian points." Ren tapped her eyebrow, then under her eye to demonstrate. "It really works and—"

"I decline. But there is one thing you can do."

"What?"

"Don't ever tell anyone about this."

Ren laughed and gave him a dap, trying to lighten the moment.

A.P. turned to her. The darkness behind his eyes shined dangerously. "I won't let them hurt you, Ren."

And yet Ren knew deep down that she couldn't really rely on him since he was without his godly powers. Then, as if he knew what she was thinking, he added, "I am not in my finest form. And that means you need protection from other sources."

"A.P.," Ren argued, "I don't need protection. I'm the most powerful godborn—"

"Whose shadow magic failed her back in Vegas."

Heat spread across Ren's chest. Ah-Puch was right—her shadow magic had proved useless more than once. But why? A worry vibrated deep inside her, one that told her *you really are a fake*. She gripped the necklace around her throat. "I still have this, and you know it can burn like the sun. Maybe I can get it to actually work, like stop time and stuff."

"Ren, we cannot operate on *stuff*. This mission must be precise, thought out to the smallest detail, which is why..." A.P. cast his gaze toward one of the colossal black mountains. "I want you to meet someone."

13

Meet someone?

"Who is it?" asked Ren.

"You'll see," said Ah-Puch. "Take down the shadow, please."

"A.P. . . ." But she did as he asked, mostly because she was dying of curiosity.

The god smiled, slinging his arm over Ren's shoulders. "One of my best-kept secrets."

A guy close to her age approached. He wore tan cargo pants, a gray T-shirt, and a small black hoop earring in each ear. And Ren definitely didn't think he owned a brush—his dark hair was short on the sides and longer on top, where it just kind of flopped over his forehead.

A.P. was still wearing that devilish grin. She leaned closer. "Is he, like, a dream creature, or for real?"

"Oh, he's all real."

"Is he a godborn?" Ren asked. "A teen god? A supernatural?"

The guy stood in front of A.P. and Ren now. He was a lot taller up close. And his attitude was a lot bigger, too. It wafted off him like bad cologne. But it felt fake, like whatever he was presenting wasn't the *real* him. It was more like he was playing a role in a movie.

He shook the god's hand, lowering his gaze respectfully.

"Ren," A.P. said, "this is Edison. Edison, this is Ren."

"The shadow witch," the guy said flatly, but there was a sparkle in his eye and a tremor of his jaw, like he wanted to break into a smile and ask for an autograph or something. But he didn't, which left Ren feeling like she had imagined it.

But she wasn't imagining the magic she sensed floating all around him. "And you? What are you?" *Oomph.* She hadn't meant for it to come out that way. But if it irked him, he didn't show it.

His gaze flicked to A.P. for a split second, like he was looking for permission.

"You can trust Ren with your life and the next," A.P. said. She felt an instant jab of pride.

Edison said, "I'm a demon."

"A demon named Edison?" The words had flown out of Ren's mouth before she could weigh their effect.

"Yes, I know. It's tragic," the god said, rubbing his brow. "But he named himself when he was only five, and it's a long story we don't have time for right now."

His mom didn't name him? What was he called for the first five years? Ren was dying to ask, but when A.P. says *It's a long story,* what he really means is *I'm not interested in telling you more.*

Ren vowed to find out later, but for now she said, "But . . . you aren't blue." *And you don't smell like death.* "Are you wearing a disguise?" Demons were known for being able to change their skin. Literally. Although most of them were allergic to human skin, and he wasn't scratching.

Edison tilted his head and narrowed his eyes like he was trying to figure out Ren, or maybe whether he was going burn a hole through her with laser eyes or something. "No disguise," he said. "This is how I appear . . . most of the time."

Most of the time?

"Let me clarify," the god said. "Edison's mother was a demon. His father is of undetermined origin."

Ouch. Something about that last part daggered Ren in the heart. Undetermined origin? They weren't talking about UFOs! But Edison didn't seem to mind. Ren remembered how Ixkik', part goddess, part demon, had conceived the dreadful hero twins when a skull spit into her hand. So maybe Edison's dad was a skull, too, Ren thought. *I guess anything is possible.*

And did A.P. say his mom *was* . . . as in past tense? As in dead?

"When he was born fourteen years ago," the god went on, "his mother hid him in a dark corner of Xib'alb'a, afraid of what Ixtab might do if she found out that one of her elite soldiers had kept a secret like this."

Ren's heart felt double daggered. She thought about how hard it had been to grow up with secrets, without knowing who her mom was, or what powers she possessed. But at least she'd had kind of a normal life with her grandpa. Hanging out, going to school, running her alien blog . . . *not* hiding in a dangerous pocket of the underworld.

"Um . . ." Ren hesitated. She hated to ask the most obvious question, but she had to know. "I thought demons didn't . . . couldn't . . ." This was coming out all wrong, and neither the demon nor the god was rushing to fill in the blanks. *Yeah, thanks, guys.* "I thought Ixtab said her demons *couldn't* have kids."

"Well, the facts say different." Ah-Puch snorted. "Ixtab lives in a world of her own making with rules that exist in a warped reality. But that's what happens when you bite off more than you can chew."

"My mom vanished a few months ago," Edison said, changing the subject.

Vanished? So she was only maybe *dead?*

"Oh," Ren breathed. "I'm sorry. I hope she's okay."

Edison merely nodded.

"Hey," A.P. said, shaking his head guiltily. "Don't look at me like that, Ren. I'm a hundred percent innocent. I had nothing to do with anything." He looked at Edison. "Tell her. Tell her how I rescued you, trained you, helped you hone your powers, took you out for the best meals...And the flicks—tell her how I let you choose what we watch." The god turned to Ren. "I've done my best to teach him about humans and how they act. I mean, the kid grew up with only old ghosts for company. He was saying things like *shucks* and *golly*, Ren. No one talks like that anymore, and it was too humiliating to bear."

Ren squinted at A.P., wondering what his angle was. Because there was *always* an angle. No way would he rescue and train a demon without a reason that likely involved his own self-interest.

"Except last night," Edison said to the god. "You didn't let me pick the movie."

Ren's heart did a little dip. She felt sorry for this demon who had named himself and learned about being human from ghosts. "So, you've been living with the god of death, darkness, and destruction since your mom left?"

Edison said nothing, just gave Ren a blank stare.

She stared back expectantly.

"Oh, is that a question?" he said. "Uh, no. I've only been in SHIHOM for the last two weeks. Before that he put me up in a hotel. It was really nice and had so many more shows than the underworld. And the room service was bad." He tilted his head closer. "Is that the right word for saying it was good? Doesn't sound right, but I heard it on a couple of different programs."

Ren nodded and then glared at the god. "You left him in a hotel?"

"A five-star hotel," A.P. said.

"And Ah-Puch visited a couple of times a day," Edison added. "And maybe it sounds weird to live with the god of death, but he's a kid, too, so it's all good . . . or bad. . . . You know what I mean."

A.P. cleared his throat. "Please do not discuss me as if I am not here. And I will not be a kid forever. Mark my godly words."

"So, why are you training him, A.P.?" Ren asked, suspicious.

Edison's expression shifted to one of confusion. "Who's A.P.?"

The god cleared his throat and waved a hand through the air. "Code name, and it doesn't matter. What matters is that Edison is now assigned to protect you, Ren."

"Protect me?" Her laugh started as a small thing and then bubbled into near hilarity. A.P. wanted the teen demon who'd been raised in the underworld to protect *her*? "I mean, no offense, Edison. I'm sure you're powerful and cool and all that, but, um, I've got A.P. and Marco—wherever he is right now— and . . . I'm the daughter of time and also a shadow witch."

"Yeah, I know all about you. I read Ah-Puch's report."

Prickly heat crawled up Ren's neck, spreading across her face in what were probably huge blotches.

"This is a waste of time," A.P. put in. "I still need to teach you the rest of the lords' names, Ren. Their powers. You must understand your enemy!"

"Look, Ren," Edison said. "I get it. You don't want me around. You don't know me, which means you don't trust me. But my agreement isn't with you—it's with Ah-Puch. And you don't even know what I can do yet."

All the demons Ren had ever met were epically strong, and they could vanish in a column of smoke only to reappear elsewhere a second later. They were sort of like underworld genies without the wishes. So, maybe she *did* have an idea of what he could do.

And Ren knew what having a "protector" meant. It meant giving up her own control, doing what she was told. *No thanks.* "This is my quest," she said as gently as she could manage. "It doesn't matter what your magic or powers or whatever are. I can take care of myself."

The guy's very thick eyebrows came together in a tight frown.

A.P. took Ren by the arm and guided her a few feet away, out of Edison's earshot. "You're being entirely unreasonable."

"I'm being myself," Ren argued. "And I don't need protection."

"You do."

"Do not."

A.P. grimaced, cast his gaze at the ground. "Ren, I can't... I don't have the same strength and power I once did, and if anything happened to you on my watch..." He let out a long breath and looked up again.

"I don't even know him," Ren said, suddenly missing her godborn friends. "Has he ever been on a quest?"

The god leveled her with an unyielding gaze. "Everyone has a first quest, Ren. I would think you would remember that."

Ren felt a pang of guilt. Maybe Edison would be fine. Maybe he wouldn't get in the way. Or say all the wrong words. Maybe he might actually help. Or maybe not.

"How about this?" A.P. said. "We won't call him your protector. How about guardian?"

"Tagalong."

"Sentinel."

"Subordinate."

"You are very stubborn."

"Like you."

"Call him whatever you want, but do we have a deal?"

"He won't try to boss me around?"

"Never."

With a resigned sigh, Ren gave a small nod.

"Good. Now are you ready to see what this kid can do? Training arena, SHIHOM, first thing tomorrow morning."

14

Ren woke totally rested, as if she hadn't spent the night in a dream world having cloak-and-dagger convos with the god of death and some teenage demon.

She sat up and looked around her room, the one in her familiar SHIHOM tree house. Bits of sun filtered through the shutter slats. Everything was the same as it had been a few weeks ago—a white linen comforter painted with silver stars, fluffy purple pillows, a telescope by the window.

Everything is the same.

Nothing is the same.

There were so many nuggets of information that Ren needed to sort through. The astral traveler, the symbol, the Lords of Night...But perhaps the heaviest thing on her mind was *Why didn't my shadow magic work earlier?*

She realized that both times her magic had failed her, a Lord of Night had been hanging around. Testing her theory, she flung an arm toward the ceiling, easily creating a shapeless shadow. On the one hand, she was relieved; on the other, her heart contracted with terror at the thought that the lords had somehow hindered her magic. She bounced the shadow from one side of her room to the other like a ball. Easy as breathing.

Disappearing the sombra, she replayed last night in her head, reviewing each piece of the puzzle and always landing on

Edison—the teen demon who wasn't supposed to exist and who was now her . . . what? Teammate? Helper-outer? Well, whatever he was, he was *not* her protector.

Are you ready to see what this kid can do? Ah-Puch had asked.

It was so typical of Ah-Puch to dangle a carrot, she thought as she washed up. She found her SHIHOM uniforms still folded neatly in the dresser. After throwing on a pair of black leggings and a gray tee, Ren hurried across the intricate bridge system that connected all the godborns' tree houses, tucked in the shade of the thick jungle. She had so much to tell Marco, so she headed to his tree house first.

Bursting through the door, she hollered, "Marco!"

There was no answer.

She hurried down the small corridor to his bedroom only to find an unmade bed. Morning shadows crept up the walls. And she heard slow breathing, as if someone else was in the room. She quickly looked inside the closet and under the bed. Empty.

Ren felt a strange burning in the center of her chest, an added pressure she had never experienced before. It spread beneath her heart and across her ribs. Forcing her into absolute stillness.

The breath was everywhere—in the breeze, the walls. And then came that spine-chilling *click, click, click.*

The teeth-clicker! The Fire Lord.

Ren wanted so badly to run, to never look back. But if she did that, if she let her fear win, would she ever be able to face *any* of the Lords of Night?

He can't be here, she told herself. *I'm hearing things.*

Click. Click. Click.

There was one way to be sure. If a Lord of Night really were here, her shadow magic wouldn't work. Swiftly, she grew a tall shadow. Spun it into the shape of a tree. Relieved, she relaxed her shoulders and vanished the shadow. The room went silent.

A memory of her grandfather bloomed.

After she'd returned home from saving the Maya gods, she'd had trouble sleeping. She kept hearing the monsters she had encountered, like the huge bats that had originally forced her to flee. Abuelo had said the sounds were nothing more than "fear echoes."

He'd told her, *Sometimes, when something really bad and scary happens, we carry the fear deep within us for a long time. So long that it begins to come to life all over again, and it feels more real than the ground you're standing on.*

Was that what this was? A fear echo?

Thinking of her abuelo made her realize she hadn't checked in with him today. She pulled out her phone and sent him a text update so he wouldn't worry. Thankfully, the phone had plenty of juice thanks to a charger she'd left in her tree house. Ren glimpsed another text notification from Marco. Just as she was about to open it, the sound of footsteps startled her. She whirled to find Ah-Puch standing in the dim morning light. "You look rather pale this morning, Ren."

"I'm ... I'm fine." She inhaled and exhaled, pulling herself together. She didn't want the god to worry, to think her fear echoes would keep her from completing this quest. Then she remembered what Sir Switchblade had said back in Kansas: *Kick fear in the teeth, and be great every single day no matter what.*

She wasn't a loser or a liar or a fake. And she was going to prove it. "I was just looking for Marco," she said.

The god's eyes darted about the space. Maybe he could sense the fear echoes, too.

"Have you seen him?" she asked.

"How did you sleep?" he asked. "I hope you rested. We have a lot ahead of us today."

"Right. You were going to show me Edison's powers," Ren said. "And you didn't answer me."

"Neither did you."

"Yes, I slept okay. Now tell me, have you seen Marco?"

"I'm not his keeper. Or his messenger, but . . . check your phone."

She opened the unread text from Marco.

> Hey had to bolt. Sorry, but we can meet up after game if you want.
> No quests. Gotta protect the throwing arm. Break a leg . . . but not
> really

Ren's heart sank as she texted a response.

> No biggie. Go win your game.

She knew he had to go back, but she'd been hoping she could have talked to him first, could have told him about her chat with A.P. and picked Marco's brilliant strategizing brain now that she had new intel.

A.P. said, "Don't tell him about Edison."

"Why not?"

"If anyone finds out he's a demon, he'll be in grave danger."

"Then why did you bring him here?" Ren asked. "Maybe it was better for him to stay in the underworld."

The god said, "Because *you're* in danger, and that matters more. And why do you keep glancing around this dreadful room? Are you looking for something?"

"A.P., you can't throw everyone else under the bus to protect me."

"What bus?" Ah-Puch narrowed his eyes. "Are you sure you're all right?"

Ren wanted to tell him about the pain in her chest and the bizarre breathing she'd heard, but a small voice inside stopped her, urged her not to make a big deal out of it.

We already have enough mystery to deal with, she told herself.

A few minutes later, the two of them grabbed some breakfast burritos and headed to the training arena. All the equipment from the summer had been put away, even the ropes for the climbing wall. Edison was already there, walking around the edge of the field and muttering to himself. About what, Ren couldn't hear.

She wadded up the burrito wrapper and tossed it in a nearby trash can. "What's he doing?"

Throwing his head back to catch the last of the eggs spilling out of his fifth tortilla, A.P. said, "He's studying the perimeter."

"For what?"

"Making sure his powers don't go beyond the border, because even though that would be wildly entertaining, it would be very bad."

"So he can't control his powers?"

JUST PERFECT! she thought.

"I never said that."

"Is it fire? Are you afraid he'll burn down the jungle?"

Ah-Puch laughed. "I wouldn't care if he burned down the whole world. But no, it's not fire."

Just then, the demon jogged over. He was wearing the same cargo pants and tee he'd had on before, but here in the real world, he seemed... Ren searched her brain for the right adjective—taller? Thinner? Darker eyes? Bigger nose? But her brain landed on only one: *Cute.*

She cringed at herself, glad that Edison's attention was focused on the god. Ren secretly prayed Edison's magic power wasn't mind-reading.

"Are you ready?" A.P. dropped his voice down to some weird baritone level. Was he trying to sound authoritative?

Edison nodded. "The perimeter is secure."

Ren felt like she had just joined the CIA.

"Ren." A.P. gestured to the center of the arena. "Would you like to take your place?"

Ren considered herself a pretty chill person, but all this hype and drama was irking her, especially when two Lords of Night were running around and another was getting ready to wake up tonight. She did *not* want a repeat of teeth clicking or creepy whispered warnings.

"Shouldn't we be preparing or strategizing or something?" she asked.

"You need to know the strengths and weaknesses of your comrades," A.P. said, "just as much as those of your enemies."

"Then shouldn't he be taking *his* place?" she argued. "I thought you wanted me to see his magic."

"It requires both of you."

"Why?"

"You and Edison are going to do battle."

WHAT?!

"I won't go too hard on you," Edison said, offering an awkward but genuine smile. "I promise."

Ren could feel her face getting hot and itchy. "Hard on *me?*" She fought the intense urge to roll her eyes or to laugh or to shove a shadow ball down his throat. Twice. She didn't want to be rude to this guy/demon/whatever, but didn't he know that she could snap him in two with a shadow dagger or the time rope? Not that she would, because she seriously hated unnecessary violence, but he was very quickly helping her change her tune.

Edison was nodding way too excitedly. "This is going to be awesome. You'll be my first real-world practice. I mean other than Ah-Puch and some simulations that felt super real." He clapped his hands together and jogged to the center of the arena followed by a very reluctant Ren. She took back her *cute* assessment and quickly replaced it with *annoyingly upbeat*.

They stood about thirty feet apart, her seething, him bouncing on the balls of his feet.

He bowed slightly and said, "Hit me with all you've got."

"Oh, believe me, I will, *Eddie*," she muttered, clenching her fists as she brought her shadow magic to the surface. Its heat pulsed in her fingertips, dying to break free.

"First move is yours, Ren," Ah-Puch called from the sidelines.

She groaned. "This isn't chess."

"Isn't it?" the god said.

Ren glared at A.P., who was now surrounded by air, earth, and mountain spirits. The little beings were munching on popcorn, gabbing as they passed some kind of coins back and forth. Were they taking bets? A strange anger pulsed in Ren's chest, dark and demanding, like it was trying to tear its way out. She didn't want to be on display, to compete for someone else's entertainment. And just like that, her readers' bullying comments washed over her in a giant swell of shame.

Get a life!

You're a fake!

You're a loser!

Ren took a few deep breaths, whispered a calming mantra, and dug her heels into the earth.

What shall I throw at you? she thought as she studied Edison. *A shadow dragon to swallow you whole? Or I could go easy on you and begin with a shadow snake just to scare you.*

Edison didn't even get into a defensive stance. He just stood there like he didn't have a care in the world. Like he wasn't even remotely afraid of Ren's powers.

Shadow dragon it is.

Ren's good nature and even better heart wouldn't allow her to unleash a giant dragon (betting or no), so she cast one the size of a lion. With glowing satisfaction, she watched the dragon swoop and soar before she willed it to charge the demon.

The spirits cheered things like "Go big or go home!" and "Is that all you've got?"

Edison's gaze flicked to Ren. Was he going to smile? He

lifted both hands in front of him like he was about to catch a ball. She felt a chill as he seemed to bend and twist the very air, forming an iridescent surface with swirls of pink and yellow and blue. It was like looking through a giant soap bubble.

Eddie was a bubble maker?

Ren didn't know how wrong she was until she watched her shadow dragon slam into the shimmering wall that protected Edison and vanish on contact.

The spirits' applause grew louder. Laughter filled the air.

"I was being nice!" Ren called out.

The demon just laughed. "I told you... give me all you've got."

Okay, she thought, *you asked for it.* She launched a hundred shadow daggers at him. They zinged across the field, dying the moment they touched Edison's shimmering barricade.

A spirit shouted, "Unleash your magic!"

Determined not to let him win, Ren freed the time rope from her throat, snapping it across the space between them.

As soon as the rope connected with the wall, there was a bright electric flash of lightning, jagged and angry. It sizzled with a powerful energy. Edison's expression tightened as he thrust his hands forward again.

There were some boos and jeers.

"Come now," A.P. called out. "Let's put in a little more effort, kids."

Ren wanted to glare at the god. She wanted to send a dozen shadow hands to clamp over the spirits' mouths. But she couldn't break her concentration.

A great wind swirled through the field now. Ren could practically taste the magically charged air.

"You're really strong," Edison shouted through another laugh, which made it sound like more of a snort.

Was he goading her?

Ren pulled back the rope, steady, focused, trying to keep it from whipping around in the gale. The longer she had possessed the rope, the more it had come to bend to her will, until she felt she was practically one with it. Even though it still wouldn't allow her to control time.

She flung it out again with an even mightier thrust than before. The gold chain expanded and grew, curled and looped like a slithering snake, untouched by the wind. *If I can't go through the wall, I'll go around it.*

The gold glimmered, reaching higher. But with every inch it won, the demon grew his barrier by two inches.

The rope struck the wall with so much intensity that streaks of lightning bled down the translucent side in great bursts of light. And with crushing disappointment, Ren realized that she—the strongest godborn of them all—wasn't powerful enough to break the demon's magic.

Just then, an arrow with a bright blue feather whizzed across the field, right through Edison's shield.

Spirits fluttered into the air in all directions and then vanished.

The arrow hummed past the demon and straight toward A.P.

Ren screamed, "A.P.!" She started running to her friend, throwing up shadows to catch the arrow, but they weren't as fast as the streaking weapon.

Everything was happening so quickly. Too quickly for Ren to think, to process. Why wasn't Ah-Puch moving out of the way? "A.P.!" she screamed again. Edison was shouting and running, too. He threw out his hands. The air shimmered and shifted, swelled and surged into a wave of energy that rushed at the god.

And Ren realized with a terrible and sudden agony that they were both too late to save him.

15

Too late.

Until . . . Ah-Puch raised a single hand and snatched the arrow out of the air. Okay, so he definitely still had some godliness in him. Edison's force field came to an abrupt stop at the edge of the arena. Right. Edison had set the perimeter.

Ren halted, vanished her shadows, and gasped. Her chest heaved with the horror of what might have been. Tears pricked her eyes.

The god stood and smiled. Smiled!

She wanted to wallop him. Well, after she hugged him.

A.P. was heading over, gesturing to someone behind Ren. She whirled to see a girl on the other side of the arena. Her curly black bangs hung over one eye while the rest of her hair was tied into a braid. She wore a purple puff vest, star-printed leggings, and white-and-pink unicorn Converse high-tops. She was younger than Ren and Edison—maybe ten or eleven. And she was gripping a bow.

She shot the arrow?

The crowd of nature spirits returned only to boo and shout things like "Rip-off!" "Worst battle ever!" and "Waste of time!" Then they vanished again.

"A.P.! What's going on? Who is that?" Ren cried, trying to make sense of the previous minute. "She shot at you!"

"And did you see how I snatched that arrow out of the air like a true champion?"

"A.P.!"

"It was really impressive," Edison said to Ren, which she ignored because she couldn't trust the adrenaline coursing through her—it made her want to smash something.

The god rolled his eyes. "She wasn't shooting *at* me. Do you think she would still be standing if she had?"

Maybe... Ren thought. Ah-Puch so often forgot that he no longer held his divine invulnerability.

"She was targeting Edison's magic," A.P. went on. "Making a point that no matter how strong you think you are, there is always someone stronger, someone willing to destroy everything you've got."

By the look on Edison's face, Ren could tell he didn't know who this girl was, either, or how her arrow had penetrated his magical barrier, especially when Ren's shadows and time magic couldn't.

"Montero," Ah-Puch called out as he gestured for the girl to join them at the edge of the field. As she came over, Ren noticed the leather strap of her bow across her chest and the quiver of blue-feathered bows on her back.

Edison and Ren shared a confused glance.

"Hi, Ren, hi, Edison," Montero said with bubbly excitement. "Ah-Puch told me all about you two. And I can hardly believe I'm *here*. I mean, I never thought I'd get summoned by a Maya god. I'm not complaining or anything. Just, you know, like wow."

"Who are you?" Edison said, his gaze on her arrows. Nine, to be exact.

"You can call me Monty. I'm a descendant of the great Aztec king Itzcoatl. I'm here to help you. And to earn my place as a Jaguar Warrior. The most elite. Well, the Eagles are, too, but . . ." She leaned closer, her eyes dancing. "Between us, Jags are way cooler." She gave a determined nod as Ah-Puch returned her arrow, which she slipped into the quiver on her back.

Edison was silently appraising Montero. His thick dark brows lifted in what looked like surprise or admiration or both.

Ren was still tripping over the girl's words, especially *I'm here to help you.*

I didn't ask for any help! she wanted to shout, but she wasn't about to hurt Montero's feelings. Instead, she forced a grin. "Nice to meet you."

"It's better than nice," Montero said, her face glowing. "This is my whole future! And the great Ah-Puch has already told me everything. And don't worry—I'm homeschooled, so I have as much time as you need. And I am super excellent at keeping secrets like yours." Her eyes flicked to Edison.

"How old are you?" Ren asked.

Montero lifted her chin higher, giving the illusion of another inch on her small frame of maybe five feet. "I'll be twelve next month, but I've been training for this my whole life, so I'm not too young. Swear."

"Montero," Edison repeated. "That's a surname that comes from *monte*, which means *mountain* in Spanish. It's also an occupational name, right? Assistant at a hunt or something like that?"

Monty was already nodding while Ren stared at the demon like he had just grown two heads. "How do you know all that?"

"I read a lot."

Right. Because what else is there but ghosts and books when you're in hiding in the underworld?

Edison said, "So, uh, Monty, what's your first name?"

"Can't tell you."

"Why not?" Ren said, not sure if Monty was kidding or not.

A.P. said, "It's a well-guarded secret, a power passed on from her parents, and it's where much of her magic resides. If she were to tell you, you would have access to her power. Only her family knows her true name."

Wow. Ren was impressed with all the legendary magical history Monty clearly came from.

"And you're a trained warrior," Edison said like he couldn't quite believe it. Ren wasn't sure she did, either. No offense or anything, but Monty was eleven years old and small for her age. But she was large on personality and confidence, so that had to count for something, right?

"She's a hunter," A.P. corrected.

Monty smiled, revealing a small gap between her two front teeth. "Everyone in my family is, or was, a trainer warrior. But some of us got the gift of the hunt. Not animals. I mean, I guess I could use my magic for that, but why? I'm one hundred percent vegetarian. Have you ever seen a cow's big brown eyes or—"

A.P. cleared his throat.

"Right," Monty said with a small giggle. "And I can find anyone or anything you want me to. Amazing, right? And if I succeed at this quest, it'll be a great honor to my family and I'll get to keep these magic arrows forever."

"What happens if you don't?" Ren said.

The girl's face fell. "Then I'd have to give up my magic, and my name, and pass these"—she pointed over her shoulder—"to the next warrior or hunter or whatever."

"That's terrible!" Ren cried, wishing the information hadn't come out oozing so much drama. She was the leader of this quest, and she had to start acting like it. She needed to be more serious, more in control, more poker-faced. Zane used to tell her she was very easy to read, to which she had replied, *I like that about myself.* But now she realized that she didn't have the luxury of being herself.

"Seriously," Edison muttered his agreement. "But there will be other quests, right?"

"I only get one shot." Monty rubbed her chin. "That's the way it's always been. For five generations, no one in my family has won a quest. Some have never even gotten a chance to try. So I'm super grateful for Mr. Ah-Puch here."

The god squeezed the bridge of his nose as Monty blew her curly bangs off her forehead. "I really have to make this work," she said. "And I promise I won't get in your way or anything."

Ren finally understood. A.P. had brought Montero here so she could track down the next Lord of Night. And locate the cinco.

Ren shook her head. "Hold up, A.P. How do you know Monty?"

The god's nostrils flared. "I make it my business to know people with specific skills and talents. Especially now."

He didn't have to clarify what he meant by *especially now.* Pointing out his own weaknesses had to be hard for him, so Ren let it drop. She didn't want to shine a light on his deficiencies.

She turned to Monty. "You said magic arrows. What kind of magic?"

Monty counted on her fingers. "First, they never ever, *ever* miss their target. Second, they return to the quiver on their own. Third, they glow when I'm in really bad danger, and fourth, they can either slay or paralyze. All I have to do is think which result I want, and *bam!*"

"That's amazing." Ren's mind was already cycling through all the ways that kind of magic could be useful.

"What's their range?" Edison asked like he was some kind of weapons expert.

"About a mile, but I think with more practice they can go farther."

"Ren, she is necessary and our best chance," A.P. put in, as if she needed convincing.

Monty stared at Ren with wide brown eyes like she was waiting for her to say yes to a question no one had asked. Ren knew the feeling. She remembered when she was the new girl trying to fit in with Zane and his friends. They'd been so nice to her, and of course she would do the same for Monty because she would never want anyone to feel unwelcome.

"I'm really glad you're here." Ren smiled. "But are you sure? Quests might sound all exciting and fun, but they can be really scary and dangerous and—"

"Puh-lease. Danger is in my blood." Monty stood straighter and saluted Ren. "I won't let you down. Swear."

"You really don't have to salute me."

"But you're the captain."

Ren felt her chest puff up a little. She wanted to say, *Tell Eddie that.*

Edison, still frowning, said to Monty, "How did your arrow cut through my magic? It's impenetrable."

"Because you were so focused on Ren you didn't see it," A.P. said. "Your magic is powerful, but it's only as good as your awareness of other threats in your vicinity."

Edison's frown deepened. His eyes darted back and forth across the ground like he was trying to figure out what he could have done differently, to guarantee he never made the same mistake again. But how could he be prepared for every single threat?

"Hang on," Ren said to the demon. "What exactly *is* your magic?"

He shot her a confused look. "Uh—I just showed you."

"You make walls to block magic." But she had a feeling there was something else. No way would A.P. let this demon join their team unless he had something seriously powerful to offer that was off-the-charts destructive.

"Yeah and no," Edison said. "I mean, I create energy from different sources, like light or heat, or even super-intense emotion, like fear. But I can do more than block magic. See that tree over there?" He lifted his right hand and thrust it forward with a little twist of the wrist. A hollow iridescent sphere flew out of his palm, expanded into a wave of energy, and like a strong wind, bent the tree to a forty-five-degree angle.

"Whoa!" Monty said, twisting one of her gold-star earrings. "That's so cool! You're like a human . . . er, I mean a demon weapon. Could you demolish that tree if you wanted to?"

"And the entire jungle," A.P. confirmed. Then he sighed. "Now that we've had this nice little meet and greet, can we please focus on the matter at hand?"

"What about a god?" Ren asked Edison. "Do you have enough magic to block their powers or knock one of them down? Because that's what might be called for." As much as she wanted to be awed by his abilities, she couldn't let her amazement influence her role as "captain."

"Let's not get carried away," A.P. said with a devilish smirk.

"But I knocked *you* down," Edison reminded him.

"I let you!"

Ren bit back a laugh. "And why couldn't my shadows or the time rope break through it?"

"I knew the force of your magic," Edison replied. "Ah-Puch told me what to expect, and I ramped up my powers."

Right. The report. Ren really needed to get her hands on that thing.

"How do you ramp up power?" Monty said, adjusting her bow.

"By making sure I'm at least eighty percent 'hydrated.'"

Ren wasn't sure she had heard him right. "Hydrated?"

"Yeah, you know, like you drink water." Edison had a way of saying things that could come off as arrogant, but his friendly good-natured tone managed to smooth them over.

"Okay, so we have to make sure you never get thirsty," Ren said. "And what if there isn't any light or energy source nearby?"

Ah-Puch sighed again. "Why does this matter?"

"You said we had to know each other's strengths and weaknesses," Ren said. The words echoed those of the Vegas Lord. *I now know your strengths. And weaknesses.* The memory made her shudder.

"I didn't think it would take all morning," A.P. spat. "So hurry it up. We have runaway gods and malefactors to contend with."

Edison scratched his cheek as he responded to Ren's question. "Well, it has to do with wavelengths and frequencies and stuff, and I can usually find something, but if I can't, then there is no vanquisher." He gave a sheepish smile. "That's what I call my power. I thought about *eliminator,* but that sounded like a toilet or something."

"And without your vanquisher, you're a sitting duck," Ren said. If there were going to be times when he wouldn't be able to use his powers and her shadow magic was limited, what chance did they have against a bunch of newly resurrected gods?

Edison looked confused. "Duck?"

"It's like if an enemy is coming at you, you're in big trouble."

"Oh yeah . . . No. I guess in that case I can always vanish."

Monty squealed. "Show us!"

"Okay, that is enough interrogation," Ah-Puch growled.

"One more question, A.P.," Ren said. "How did you know about Montero and her family?" She didn't add, *They aren't of Maya magic,* because that might make Monty feel bad.

Ah-Puch threw back his shoulders. "You forget I know the greatest secrets of the universe. Now, we must find the next Lord of Night's place of slumber before I die of boring conversation and he awakens."

"How will you find the third Lord?" Edison asked Monty. "He could be anywhere."

Ren's keen mind jumped into action. *Wake ... Lords ... Hollywood ... Help.*

Ren's theory flew out of her mouth in a flurry of excitement. "A.P., maybe that's what the astral ghost girl or whatever was trying to tell me. Hollywood! That must be where the Prince Lord will wake up."

Edison perked up. "Hollywood?"

"Or it could merely be where the astral traveler is," A.P. said to Ren like they were the only two in this conversation. *Why does he always have to be such a buzzkill?* "And, as I told you, I deal in absolutes. So, we must be sure."

"Then we find the cinco first and follow them," Ren offered. The moment she made the suggestion, she knew she was on the right trail because A.P. was grinning that wicked *way-to-go* grin.

"Do you have anything that belonged to anyone in the cinco?" Monty asked Ren eagerly. "Anything I could use to track one of them?"

Ren nodded. "The rogue godborns' tree houses are filled with their things."

Monty started toward the jungle as if she knew the way. Edison followed. "We are going to be the best team in the history of the world!" she cheered as she leaped into the air.

"And once we find the location of the third Lord?" Ren asked A.P. as she fell into stride with him.

The god sneered. "We make sure he stays asleep. Forever."

"How? Do you have a magic sleeping pill or—"

"I'm still thinking about our options."

"Let me guess," Ren said. "We don't have a lot."

The god stopped and faced Ren. Fear reflected in his eyes, making her pulse jump. "It's okay," she assured him. "We've faced monster situations before."

"I was a god then. And, Ren, even with the demon and the hunter, this isn't like our other quests—this is well beyond our Maya world." He shook his head and looked away. "I need you to know that this isn't just another challenge. . . ."

His unspoken words hung in the air. *This might be impossible.*

16

The door to Serena's tree house was locked.

"Well, well, well," Ah-Puch said. "Untrusting, just like her capricious mother, Ixchel."

"That's the Maya moon goddess, right?" Monty chewed on a fingernail.

"She has other names, too, but yes," the god said, pressing his hands against the door with an irritated sigh. "And if I had my godly powers, I could blow down this hunk of wood with a single breath."

"I've got it," Ren said, shouldering her way past A.P. She created a key out of shadow and the sombra inserted itself into the lock before vanishing in a wisp of smoke. Frowning (and kind of embarrassed), she tried again with the same frustrating results. She felt a sudden sense of despair. If she couldn't count on her magic, who was she? She glanced at A.P., realizing she wasn't the only one struggling with her identity. She made a vow right then and there to help him return to his godly status when this was all over with.

"Let me try," Edison offered as he thrust out his hands, creating a surge of iridescent magic that reminded Ren of the northern lights. But even with the vanquisher on duty, the door didn't budge.

"You're like a walking light show," Monty uttered to Edison.

"We are not going to let a pathetic godborn-enchanted door keep us from this quest," A.P. growled.

Ren spun toward the hunter, an idea blooming with each heartbeat. "Monty, your arrows are an ancient Aztec magic and Serena used *Maya* magic, so maybe..."

Edison was nodding and grinning. "You're right, Ren. Serena's enchantment wouldn't protect this door from *other* sources of power. That's really brilliant."

"How did you know that's what I was going to say?" Ren asked, hating how much she liked his mind... and his smile. It made his whole dumb face light up.

Monty reached for an arrow. "Ah-Puch was right. You guys are, like, smarty-pants!"

"I said *intelligent*," the god corrected as he and the others moved aside to give her space. "No one with any ounce of pride or decorum would use *pants* to illustrate such a point."

Monty stepped backward, creating a space of maybe twenty feet. She planted her feet and nocked the arrow as her tongue poked out of the side of her mouth. Then, with careful precision, she pulled the bowstring taut and let the arrow fly. The thing whizzed by so fast it was nearly imperceptible except for the *whoosh* of air.

The tip of the arrow pierced the wood, springing the door open with a tired groan.

"Neato," Edison uttered, nodding his appreciation. Ren nearly laughed but didn't want to make the guy feel self-conscious. It wasn't his fault he grew up watching ancient TV shows.

"You're awesome," Ren told a beaming Monty as they entered the all-too-orderly tree house.

The white sofa looked like it had never been sat on. The floors didn't have a speck of dust. The linen drapes were pressed, and the wood tables were polished to a shine. Ren knew Serena was a control freak, but she had never taken her for a neat freak, too.

Monty went hunting in the bedroom and emerged with a perfectly pressed tee Serena had left behind.

"So, are you supposed to smell it or something?" Edison asked.

Monty frowned. "I'm not a wolf. I don't track by scent—I track by energy. Everyone leaves some behind wherever they go, and on everything they touch. You can't see it, but I can feel it."

"Feel it how?" Ren said, intrigued.

Monty walked in a slow wide circle, observing the place. "Like, I can feel that she was once here." She toed the sofa, holding her sneakered foot there. "She laughed here. And she had some bad dreams here, too." There was a sudden pause. "She didn't like this place."

"Ingrate," Ah-Puch growled.

Monty knelt on the floor and removed an arrow from her quiver. She set the arrow down delicately on the shirt like it was a live bomb. While her hand floated over both objects, she held an expression of total focus, and sweat broke out on her forehead.

The arrow's blue feathers fluttered. Sparks flew. The air sizzled.

Closing her eyes, Monty stiffened.

She stayed like that—all zombielike—for a good thirty seconds. Then her arrow floated up and, in an instant, the T-shirt burst into a small flame. Monty jumped up and stomped it out with her shoes, leaving behind a pile of white ash. Strange, garbled whispers circled the room as the arrow returned itself to the quiver. Ash swirled into the air before vanishing with a *pop*.

"Thank you," Monty whispered to no one in particular. And then she passed out.

Ren acted fast, breaking the hunter's fall. "She's burning up!"

"It's the effects of the magic," A.P. said casually.

Edison blew out a long breath and knelt next to Ren. "I've never seen anything like that, and I'm from the *underworld*."

Ren could feel Monty's gentle pulse in her palms as she cradled the hunter's neck. "We can't do this," she whispered. "She's just a kid. We can't let her get sick—it's not fair."

Monty's eyes popped open. The heat rushed from her body as if she'd never had a temperature. "I can do it!" she said, bolting upright. "The fever—it's part of the magic. It's how I talk to my ancestors. They're the ones who guide me. And now I know where Serena's going."

A.P. rushed to Monty's side. "Where?"

"Hollywood."

Ren groaned as she felt a swell of annoyance combined with *I-told-you-so* pride.

Ah-Puch shot her a shushing look as he said, "Good. Now we have our confirmation."

"But that's a huge place," Ren said. "How will we ever find her?"

"Hello? You've got a natural-born hunter," Monty said, giving a thumbs-up. "Just get me there and I'll track her down. Swear."

Edison exhaled. "So now we go to Hollywood and have a . . . What's it called? Knock-off?" There was no mistaking the excitement in his voice, even though Ren could tell he was trying to keep his cool.

Monty whispered out of the side of her mouth a bit too loudly, "I think you mean face-off?" She clapped. "Wow—my first real hunt. Woot!"

"I really hate excessive displays of emotion," A.P. muttered.

"Before we go to Hollywood," Ren said, throwing her gaze at A.P., "we need to know more about these Lords of Night, yes?" She had already been on two missions, and so she knew the first guiding principle of all quests: Be prepared. "I mean, what's the point of hunting down Serena and hopefully following her to the next lord's resting place if we can't keep the god in Snoozeland?"

"But we can't waste time and lose this lead, either," Monty argued.

A.P. exhaled sharply. "Ren, you and the others go find Serena, see what she's up to. I'll meet you along the way." And before the godborn could ask, he added, "*Before* the next lord awakens."

"But that could be anytime!" Ren cried, hoping she didn't sound overly dramatic. She probably did.

"Ren," Ah-Puch said calmly, "he will likely awaken close to midnight—it's the time of in-between, when the gods' powers are at their peak. So we have about ten hours."

Ren was about to ask how he could be so sure when Edison said, "You're not coming?"

A crooked smile spread slowly across the god's face. "I have somewhere else to be. And don't call me; I'll call you."

Ren knew what he was up to. The god of death was going to find out exactly how to keep the rest of the Aztec lords asleep for good.

17

"We have a *three*-hour layover?" Edison asked disbelievingly as they hiked through the lush jungle toward the gateway located by Ren's watch. Spider and howler monkeys swung from the trees, trailing the trio with their beady eyes. Probably looking for something to swipe, Ren thought.

"Yeah, portal travel isn't always as instant as everyone thinks," Ren said with a sigh.

Edison frowned. "Doesn't that kind of defeat the purpose?"

"Where's the layover?" Monty skip-shuffled alongside them. "New York? DC? Paris? That would be so amazing. Did I tell you guys I want to be a travel blogger? Go round the world and get paid—what could be better? And, Ren, you have a blog about aliens, so maybe you could teach me the ropes."

"Uh-huh." Ren felt a sudden jab under her ribs at the reminder of *Eyes in the Sky*.

"*That* wasn't in your report, Ren," Edison said with an almost smile. Or was it a smirk? Either way, Ren didn't want to talk about her blog. It only reminded her of the tormentors filling her in-box with their poisonous words.

"Well?" Monty said. "Where's the layover?"

"The next gateway to Hollywood is in Boring, Oregon."

Monty chuckled, then scowled, then chuckled again as Ren

double-checked her watch. "Like, is that its actual name?" the hunter asked. "Or is it a code name?"

Edison was already nodding. "That's the real name, and if I remember right, it was named after some William guy. I think he was a Union soldier."

"How do you know something so rando?" Monty asked.

Ren said, "He reads a lot," at the same time Edison offered, "I read a lot."

"Maybe you should go on *Jeopardy!*" Ren suggested to the demon. "I bet you'd win."

"I don't like cameras."

"Hey, guys," Monty said, strolling ahead, "you think it'll be *boring*?" She cracked up at her own joke.

Her laughter echoed through the trees as a monkey tail emerged from above, swooping through the air toward Monty's arrows. It all happened so fast Ren barely perceived Edison hurling his magic in an enormous gust of power that sent the monkey flying before setting him down gently with a soft thud.

"Whoa!" Monty said, readjusting her quiver. "That was some choice magic. Thanks!"

Choice magic resonated with Ren. She could see now that A.P. really *had* created a stellar team.

An hour later, they sat at a pizzeria in Boring, Oregon, chowing down an extra-large pepperoni pizza and spicy wings. The wings were Edison's idea. The only other people in the restaurant were a group of cyclists still wearing their helmets. A gloomy country song played on a nearby jukebox.

It was five o'clock Pacific Standard Time. And if all went well, they would set foot in Hollywood at precisely 8:00 p.m.

Ren picked at the crust of her pizza, her stomach in knots. None of her calming breathing/tapping/positive thinking exercises had helped. All she could think about was what would happen if they failed. It would mean more power to the lords, who were clearly up to something she wished she didn't have to think about.

The fear of the unknown was wearing on her last nerve. Would the next Night Lord be worse than the teeth-clicker who'd told her to go to sleep? Or the Vegas creeper who'd sent humongous jaguars to test her strengths and weaknesses? But it wasn't even the visits from the supposedly dead gods that unnerved Ren so much. It was not knowing what would happen if all nine of them woke up.

And then there was Serena.

The last time Ren had seen her was in Montana, when she and some of the other godborns had rebelled.

Ren would never forget the way Serena had challenged Zane. *The gods are the ones who abandoned us, never cared about us in the first place. They wanted us dead! Why should we care about them now?*

It was true the Maya gods had never expected or wanted offspring, but not all of them wanted the godborns dead, either.

Serena had wanted revenge then, and she still wanted it now. And somehow she was using the Night Lords to exact it.

Ren's plan was simple: Find and follow Serena, hoping she would lead them to the Prince Lord. And if all went perfectly,

Ah-Puch would arrive just in time with the intel about how to keep the guy asleep for the long haul. Aka forever and always, amen.

"So, Monty, I have a question," Ren said.

"And I have an answer."

"How long will it take you to find Serena once we're in Hollywood?"

Monty chewed an ice cube, casting her gaze upward like she was doing some mental calculations. "Uh—maybe like twenty-two and a half minutes."

"That's pretty precise," Edison said.

"It's my record, and tonight I'm going to beat it." Monty took a bite of pizza. "I read Serena's whole report, but what else do you know about her that maybe isn't in there?"

Ren frowned. Did A.P. have a report on everyone? "She's really good at illusion and has this snake she can make out of mist. I've never seen it but a godborn friend of mine said it's humongous and terrifying."

"I hate snakes," Monty said, screwing up her face. "Does it bite?"

"I'm guessing yes," Ren said, wishing the truth didn't suck so bad.

Edison tapped his fingers on the table in time to the country song. "Right. But how do her illusions work?"

Ren stretched her memory back to SHIHOM, to the training she'd had with Serena every day at dawn. "The bigger the illusion she creates," she said, "the more it drains her. Once I saw her change our entire training stadium into a Hawaiian beach, and when everyone went running for the water, it looked and smelled super real. Then her magic ran out, and they all face-planted in the dirt. It was humiliating. Oh, and she can command moonbeams, too."

"What good is a moonbeam?" Edison asked.

"Yeah, well, if you were in the bottom of a darker than dark pit with black widows spinning poisonous webs around you, I bet you'd like a moonbeam," Monty said.

"Yeah, because *seeing* the spiders is going to help."

Ren laughed, but Monty did have a point. Even though Ren had never been afraid of the dark, she disliked it because no light meant there could be no shadows.

Monty scratched the tip of her nose. "I meant the *real* stuff about Serena, Ren. The personal stuff that no one else might know." She side-eyed Edison. "Like our friend here . . . He likes old movies from waaaaay back in the eighties and nineties, reads too much, and he's obsessed with technology and invention. . . . See? Personal."

"That was in my report?" Edison asked with a quirked brow that told Ren he was either entertained or confused. "And for the record, I like some stuff from the early two thousands. Anything after that is kind of derivative."

"Deriva-que?" Monty asked.

"Unoriginal."

Ren wanted to know how come *she* hadn't gotten to read *their* reports. She said, "Other than being a control-slash-neat freak and that she didn't like her tree house?" Ren swept her bangs out of her face. "I don't know, Monty. Serena wasn't very friendly or talkative. Kind of kept to herself."

"Except when she was organizing an overthrow of the gods,"

Monty said, suddenly sounding older than her eleven years. Maybe it was a warrior/hunter thing.

Edison shoved the last bit of crust into his mouth and talked around it. "I saw this movie once about some robbers who weren't hitting up banks because they wanted all the money—they just didn't want these rich dudes to have it. The robbers wanted to prove that they could outsmart them, to send a message that the richies weren't as good as they thought they were." He threw a side glance at Monty. "And no, it wasn't from the eighties *or* nineties."

Ren knew what Edison was getting at. Maybe Serena's intentions weren't to keep the power for herself but just to take it from the Maya gods, to hurt them where it counted. And if that were the case, maybe she could be negotiated with. "That's a really good point," she told the demon, her heart fluttering as she weighed the possibility and what it might mean to the quest. "She's vengeful, yes, but that may not be her only motivation."

Monty picked a crispy pepperoni off her slice like it was a dead moth and flicked it onto the table. "She could want something more than revenge and power."

"Like what?" Ren liked the way Monty thought—it reminded her of Marco's twisted strategic brain.

"*That* wasn't in her report."

Within the hour, they stepped through the magical gateway into an itty-bitty space with a full-length mirror and a chair piled with discarded clothing.

Thankfully, the dressing room was empty, because the

horror of popping in on some half-naked person was enough to give Ren heart palpitations.

A couple of women gabbed outside the door.

"That dress is the best revenge."

"Yeah, but it's *expensive* revenge."

Edison pressed his hands against the walls and mirror. "Uh, hey . . ." he whispered. "Where are we?"

"In a store," Monty whispered back. "Where people try on new clothes and decide if they're going to buy them."

"How are we going to get out of here without being seen?" Edison asked, looking frantic.

Ren cracked open the door and peered out to see the two women standing in front of a three-way mirror. She closed it again and turned the lock.

"Ren and *I* are stuck, but *you're* the vanquisher," Monty reminded him with a grin.

"My *magic* is called vanquisher."

"Mm-hmm . . . Well, whatever. You can just vanish out of here. Lucky duck."

"We're back to ducks?" Edison said.

"It's not the same as a sitting duck," Ren put in. "Monty's right. Best if you aren't seen in here."

"Okay, but uh, can you guys turn around?"

"Seriously?" Monty said. "You're going to have to vanish in front of us sooner or later."

"Later sounds good. And no peeking," the demon ordered.

"Wait!" Ren whisper shouted. "Where will you go?"

"Somewhere with more air and space." He raised his eyebrows and gestured for them to turn. "I'll find you, don't worry."

Monty and Ren did as he asked. Ren felt a pulse of buzzing energy down to her toes, and in the next instant, there was a blue flash of light. She spun around. Edison was gone.

Monty was grinning ear to ear. "Wow—he's supercool, right?"

"Uh-huh." Ren inched the door open a second time to see if the coast was clear yet. It was.

"And he's kinda cute, too."

"Monty..." Ren said, turning back. "You need to focus. And...there are rules." She concocted the best one she could think of in the moment. "You can't crush on someone on your team."

There was no such rule. After their last adventure, her friends Zane and Brooks had gotten together. Not to mention Hondo and Quinn. Still, it made good sense, and since this was *Ren's* quest, she got to establish the boundaries.

Monty scrunched up her face, still managing to hold her smile. "I said *cute*, not *crush*."

They stepped outside the dressing room and hadn't gone four feet when they walked right into the scowling gaze of a tall, skinny girl in unimaginably high wedges, tight red pants, and a cropped sweater. She wore a gold-colored name tag that said BECCA.

"What were you two doing in there?" Becca's tone wasn't inquisitive. It was totally accusing, and it made Ren's skin itch with annoyance.

"Uh, just..." Ren's brain swam in a thick fog of zero answers.

But Monty? She didn't miss a beat. "I had a wedgie, and she was fixing it for me," she said cheerfully. "We didn't think it was a good idea to pull down my whole jumpsuit in front of everyone."

Oh gods, Ren thought. *Becca is going to call security. She's going to see those arrows on Monty's back and think we're armed robbers or something.*

But Becca didn't move an inch or scream. She just huffed and said, "No children are allowed in this area."

Ren bit back a laugh that threatened to explode as she and Monty rushed out of the dressing room area. Once they were in the clear, Ren let it out, and it felt great.

Monty chuckled. "What's so funny?"

"Becca's reaction..." Ren started.

"She wasn't funny, though," Monty said, getting serious.

Ren wiped her eyes, took a deep breath, and confirmed what she had already guessed. "She couldn't see your arrows, could she?"

"No unmagicked can." Monty touched every blouse, sweater, and jacket they passed. "That's what I call anyone without powers. Pretty good, right?"

"Very original."

"Yeah, it's a Montero thing."

The department-store floor was spread out in sections, filled with racks and racks of clothing. Customers milled about. Some fiddled with their cell phones, others traveled in pairs, conversing about what was worth trying on, what was priced too high, and how the store really should invest in better lighting.

After a quick search and no Edison, they cut through the athleisure and hopped onto the escalator, figuring he was downstairs.

Monty started to take off down the steps. "I'll call you when I find Serena."

"Whoa." Ren tugged on her sleeve, holding her in place. "We aren't in Hollywood yet."

"Where are we, then?"

"Century City, about seven miles away. This was the closest gateway."

"These gateways are kind of a rip-off."

Monty had barely finished her sentence when suddenly the air felt charged with high-voltage electricity, like it had back in the Vegas diner. Ren's chain pulsated . . .

Thud

    Thud

        Thud

"Ren?"

The escalator, Monty, the music . . . everything came to a sudden halt.

Ren shook the hunter's arm, but there was no response. She sucked in a sharp breath, her eyes darting back and forth.

And then Monty's arrows began to glow a pale blue.

18

If Monty's arrows were glowing, that could mean only one thing. Danger.

What had the hunter said? Oh yeah. "Really bad danger."

Perfect.

Ren quickly scanned the floor below. Everyone was frozen, in mid-blink, mid-stride, mid-comment.

But where was the danger?

That's when Ren saw her.

The astral traveler stood below, near a pink-and-gold perfume display. As before, the girl's form faded in and out. Honey-brown hair hung around her face, and she wore a darker-than-night green sweatsuit. Her eyes widened as she glanced around. This time Ren didn't hesitate. She slipped past a frozen Monty and eased her way down the stairs with the stealth of a jaguar on the hunt.

With each step Ren took, the girl vanished just a little bit more. Ren slackened her pace and finally came to a standstill ten feet from her.

"You said you needed help," Ren said in a low but inviting voice. "Are you with the cinco? I mean Serena?"

The traveler blinked quickly, looking from side to side. Then, tipping an inch closer, she whispered, "Stay away."

Ren's pulse quickened, and in between each beat, she felt

frustration, anger, and uselessness. "But you told me to come here! Well, Hollywood, not Century City. And how can I stay away *and* help you?"

"The Prince..." the girl managed. Her voice was small and distant, like a brewing storm. And while her mouth was moving, trying to communicate something, Ren only caught two words. "Trap..." The girl looked stricken, horrified. "Don't..."

"Don't what?" Ren cried. "What trap?"

The traveler began to step back, visibly trembling.

"Are you okay?" Ren spoke softly, afraid to break their connection.

The girl's eyes widened.

And then she was gone.

It took Ren three, maybe four seconds to process what the astral traveler had told her.

Prince. Trap.

Maybe she was trying to tell Ren that the Prince Lord was trapped? He was the last one A.P. had mentioned. So the girl was definitely connected to the Lords of Night and very likely the cinco, too. But Ren still didn't recognize her or understand why she was trying to communicate with *her.*

Wait. Why was everything still in freeze-frame mode? She glanced back up the escalator. Monty's arrows were no longer glowing. Ren could only deduce two things from this. Either the girl had posed some sort of threat to the hunter, or time did. Ren looked at her watch. The hands were making tiny jerky motions as if they didn't know whether to go forward or backward.

Tick. Tick. Tick.

I am so not going to live in a time warp with a bunch of mannequins, Ren thought as she pressed the watch's side dial, half expecting, half hoping it might work to start time again. But she knew it was futile. She had already used the threads that had once given the watch its time-manipulation powers.

Ren needed to remain calm. She breathed in, then out. Who was she kidding? No amount of breath work was going to calm her down. Marco had once told her that adrenaline is to the warrior what chocolate is to the Maya gods. *Just drink it in, chica.*

Easy for you to say, Marco. You're throwing around a dumb pigskin right now.

Her heart beat wildly, hopefully.

It was a long shot, but she had to try. . . .

Ren removed the golden chain and wrapped it around her wrist so its magic could touch the watch. There was a spark.

The overhead lights flickered.

Once.

    Twice.

        Gone.

Ren was plunged into immediate darkness.

A voice echoed across the space. *Are you here to play a game?*

It was the Smoking Mirror. Again.

Ren didn't know how to answer, worried that anything she might say would be used against her in another one of his dumb strength/weakness assessments. So, being that she was pretty strategic and happened to be BFFs with the god of death, who

had taught her all the villain moves and countermoves, she
threw the question back in his face. "Are you?" Okay, it had
sounded a lot better in her mind.

The Smoking Mirror let out a slow laugh. *Games have rules.*

Ren stood her ground even though her legs were wobbly,
and her insides felt like they were going to disintegrate. "I'm
not playing by your rules."

Aren't you?

Ren clutched the time rope, which was still around her
wrist. The Mirror's sandpaper voice was all around her, bleeding into the space between his darkness and her fear.

I knew you'd come, he said.

Ren glanced down at the letters Marco had written on her
wrist: *WWMD. What Would Marco Do?* For one, he'd want to
throw blows. But he'd know that was impossible, so he'd show
a fearless front by probably . . . what? Ugh! It really didn't pay
to be nice, did it?

But it did pay to gather intel.

"How did you know I'd be here?" *Did it have to do with the
astral traveler?* Ren wanted to ask, but something told her this
could put the girl in danger.

I already told you, Queen. I know you.

Not true, Ren thought. *He doesn't know anything about me.*
He was just trying to get under her skin, trying to get in her
head with his bogeyman tactics. Well, it wasn't going to work.
And yet . . .

And yet . . . she felt something unfold inside her.

"How come you're here?" Ren asked. "What happened to
the teeth-clicker?"

The Smoking Mirror was silent. Was he puzzling it out, googling *teeth-clicker*? But he didn't respond.

"I know about the Prince Lord," Ren blurted.

And?

Marco's voice popped into her head as if he were right there with her. *Go big or go home!* And in this case, Ren thought she might as well ask, "Where is he?"

The Smoking Mirror sighed. *If I told you, where would the fun be in it?*

"I don't want to play your stupid games!" Ren cursed herself the second the words flew from her mouth. She had shown anger, an emotion that gave away too much and won too little. She wrapped her hand around Marco's message as if his strength and courage could somehow bleed into her.

I take it back, the lord said. *You don't have what it takes to be a queen. No composure. No grace.*

Harsh!

"You know what I think?" Ren said bitterly. "I think you're a coward who won't show his face."

A couple of moments passed before she heard, *I thought we were talking about* you.

Ren changed the subject. "What does Serena have to do with this?"

Nothing.

There it was—the chink in his armor Ren had been looking for. He'd answered too fast, like he wanted Ren to think Serena didn't matter. Not knowing what his angle was, Ren didn't know how much she should say. Surely he was using the godborns, or maybe the other way around. But if that were true, then why

did he want to play games with Ren? What card was *she* holding that he needed?

Ugh! Think, Ren. Think.

Had Serena and the others woken up the first lord? And the
symbol—it had something to do with all this. But what? And
how did the Smoking Mirror find her here? Or in Vegas?

Now, he said, *let us ring the bell, roll the dice, deal the cards.*

Ren held her breath. She unwound the golden chain slowly.
One loop . . .

Shall we begin? he asked.

Two . . . three . . . four . . .

She snapped the chain out in front of her, casting a golden
stream of light, enough to see that the Smoking Mirror wasn't
in plain view. So why the darkness? A mind game, she thought,
remembering her training. This was a way to intimidate her,
to create fear, because fear can create missteps. Missteps, or at
least enough of them, make you the loser.

The Smoking Mirror laughed, a satisfied purring sound.
Ready . . .

"You think you're so tough—but you won't even show your
face!"

Set . . .

Light flooded the store.

A guy a little older than Ren stood there. Black hair, bronze
skin, glistening obsidian eyes. He wore a dark button-down
shirt and pair of slacks. With a smile, he said in a low voice,
"Go."

And before Ren could blink, he and all six-ish feet of him

had vanished. *He,* the guy who looked like he was trying out for the lead role in a vampire movie.

Ren swallowed. *He* was not at all what she had been expecting.

It didn't matter. Ren *was* going to play the game. And she was going to play to win.

19

Everything around Ren in the department store thawed back to life at an agonizingly slow pace, as if an invisible puppeteer's hand was winding the world's clock one click at a time. And then, before Ren could take another breath, the world returned to normal. Her knees went weak with relief.

Ready. Set. Go.

The Smoking Mirror had looked so pleased, so eager. Like those boys at school who get everything they want—student body president, team captain, leading man.

Ugh! Ren already couldn't stand him. She watched as Monty descended the escalator wearing an expression of utter confusion. "Hey, what happened?" she asked, coming over. "Why are you...?" She paused, glanced around suspiciously. "You were just up there and...Whoa, can you vanish, too?"

"No. Time stopped for everyone but me."

Without even a shudder, the hunter said, "Sick. For how long?"

"A few minutes."

"Did *you* stop it?"

Ren twisted her mouth. "No."

At the same moment, Edison appeared by her side, startling her. She couldn't be sure whether he literally appeared out of thin air or had just snuck up on her like a super ninja. Whichever it was, it was bizarro.

"I've been waiting for you guys by the shoes," he said. "I kept telling them I was just looking. Is that not a thing? Anyhow, it was stressful. They kept coming at me: 'Can I help you?' 'Can I help you now, sir?' 'What about *now?*'"

He was stressed?!

"Can you give me a heads-up before you just appear out of nowhere?" Ren said. Her voice hinted at an anger that she felt way down inside, but why? Edison had done nothing wrong. And yet there it was, bubbling beneath the surface.

"You mean like a signal?" Edison asked like the good sport he was.

"Hey, time stopped," Monty announced. "Ren didn't do it."

"Huh?" Edison's and Monty's eyes swiveled to Ren. They were looking for answers but she didn't have any, and it made her feel like the *fake* those cyberbullies had labeled her.

Ren started to unfold the story when Monty held up her hand. "We really gotta get to Hollywood if I'm going to track Sara."

"*Serena.*" Ren reclasped the chain around her neck before checking her watch. "It's already eight thirty. Come on. I'll explain in the Uber."

"What's an uber?" Edison whispered to Monty while Ren tugged her friends out of the store and into the outdoor mall. The sky was midnight black.

The trio made their way to the main road, where Ren ordered a ride. As they stood on the curb, watching the cars zip up and down Santa Monica Boulevard, Ren spilled the story, leaving out her face-to-face meeting with the Smoking Mirror. She needed more time to sit with that, to wrap her mind around it before she explained it to anyone else.

"Pretty funny timing, if you ask me," Edison said, crossing his arms.

Ren looked up at him. "What do you mean?"

"I mean the astral traveler paid you another visit like one of those Dickens ghosts, right? And at the same exact moment, time slows. So obviously she has something to do with it."

If only it were that simple. Nothing Ren had seen could be taken at face value. Not the symbol, or the lords, or the astral traveler.

Was that even the Smoking Mirror's real face? Of course not. Just another game. He probably picked it out of a magazine.

"Did the Smoking Mirror really challenge you to a duel?" Monty's voice carried a note of dread.

"Pretty much," Ren said as a white Toyota pulled up. "This is us."

"And my arrows glowed?" Monty chirped, climbing into the backseat ahead of Ren and Edison.

"Yeah." Ren's mind whirred in seven different directions all at once. "And now he knows I'm here. Maybe the astral traveler was trying to warn me, to tell me that this whole thing is a setup. And *not* to come here. That's why she called it a trap."

"The Smoking Mirror..." Edison muttered, keeping his gaze out the window as they swept through pristine Beverly Hills with its swaying palm trees and glittering buildings. "But how would he even know you were coming?"

I know you, Queen.

The driver's eyes found Ren's in the rearview mirror. But the fortysomething didn't remark on their convo—she just shook her head and turned on the radio.

"Maybe he has some kind of tracking system or something," Ren guessed. "Let's face it—he *is* a god." A second, very depressing option made its way into her mind: *What if he anticipated my next move?*

"Is *that* why my arrows glowed?" Monty asked. "Because the second lord was there in the store?"

"Except I don't think he knew you were there," Ren replied. "And they stopped glowing the second the traveler vanished, so I don't think so. Maybe the arrows got confused?"

"Ha. As if." Monty shook her head vehemently. "The arrows don't lie."

"That's what we want," Edison put in.

Monty said, "To be in danger?"

"Think about it. If the Smoking Mirror or the other teeth-clicker dude, if they don't know about me and Monty, that's a point for us. Right?"

"Ooh—good thinking," Monty said. "We're the secret sauce."

Edison threw her a confused look. "Sauce?"

"You guys are right," Ren said. "And now we have to use it to our advantage."

"Are we still talking about sauce?"

"No. We're talking about a surprise attack!" Monty squealed. She gestured like she was launching arrows. "Bam. Bam. Bam."

"I thought *bams* were for bullets," Edison said.

"They're for hits!" Monty countered. "And I'm so fast with the bow they'll never even see 'em coming."

"We're not shooting anyone," Ren insisted. "Not yet. The mission is simple: we find and follow; *do not* engage. Got it?"

The driver said, "Are you guys playing that Pokémon game or something?"

"Yeah, it's a thing all the kids are doing," Ren told the driver. This seemed to satisfy the woman.

"Maybe the astral traveler is a ploy, to distract you," Edison suggested, like he was going back through the story, scene by scene.

Ren repositioned herself in the crammed middle seat. "You mean distract me from keeping the Lords of Night in snooze mode?"

Except I have no idea how to do that! Where are you, A.P.?

"Could totally be a thing," Monty said.

"If that's true, then . . ." Ren's whole body zipped with excitement as the idea bloomed. "That's super-good news."

"It is?" Edison said.

"That means they think I have the power to hurt them." *That I'm holding a card that they need.*

The three stared straight ahead as if there was a horizon beckoning them. But there was only the Dream Factory buzzing with neon lights as they made their way up Hollywood Boulevard. Throngs of people cruised the streets, sidewalk merchants peddled their wares, and billboards with beautiful faces towered above. For all its splendor, Ren sensed there was also a cold and empty darkness lying beneath.

A.P. had once told her that beautiful things can't be trusted. *Ugly things, misshapen things, they are what they are. They can't lie. But the beautiful? You never know what's really inside.*

Edison craned his neck to watch the world pass by, and Ren wondered what it was like to be in his mind, to see this kind of glitz for the first time. Not that Xib'alb'a wasn't its own kind of amazing, but the underworld feasted on death. This place? It wanted your life.

"Can we drive any faster?" Monty asked, already clutching the door handle.

"See that traffic?" the driver said. "Can't fly over it, now can we?"

"I could run faster than this car is going," the hunter whispered as she sank lower in her seat.

"And what did the traveler say about the trap?" Edison said.

"Only that there is one."

The demon let out a low, devious kind of laugh.

"What's so funny?" Ren asked.

"It's only a trap if you don't know about it ahead of time."

20

Hollywood Boulevard felt like an explosion of rainbow confetti: bright glowing lights, street performers, a bustling crowd, and the sound of dance jams coming at them from all sides.

Edison turned in slow circles, absorbing it all. He had the look—the one everyone gets when they go to Disneyland for the first time. Except this wasn't the happiest place on earth. This was Tinseltown, La-La Land, El Lay.

"This is going to be tough," Monty said, scanning all the activity.

Not exactly the words Ren wanted to hear. "Define *tough*."

"I have to pick up Serena's energy print." And before anyone could ask, Monty explained, "It's like a fingerprint—unique to you." She toyed with her jumpsuit zipper. "It's kinda complicated. And I need space. I gotta track her on my own. No distractions."

"I can't let you go off on your own," Ren said, making a solid captain choice in both body and spirit. And she wasn't going to back down no matter what the hunter said.

Monty looked up at Ren with liquid-brown eyes that conveyed *I'm not a regular eleven-year-old kid from the Bronx. I'm one hundred percent pure Aztec hunter.* "I have to do this by myself," Monty said. "And I don't care how hard it is, I won't let you down. Swear." Then she saluted.

Ren's dam of *No way*s cracked, split in two. "Fine, but once you find her, only follow. Do not—"

"Engage. Yeah, got it."

"And call me the second you've got eyes on her."

"Yup."

Monty took off into the crowd. Ren watched the hunter go until the last bit of her was swallowed up, and she thought two things: *I really hope A.P. knows what he's doing.* And *Being responsible for others on a quest seriously sucks.*

A pink flashing sign across the street caught Ren's attention.

"Now what?" Edison said.

"I have an idea." Ren led the demon into the souvenir shop, which included props from the movies: monster masks, fake daggers and swords, even Hollywood clapboards. But it was the hats and wigs that had caught Ren's attention and far-flung hopes.

"I didn't even think of it until now, but I need a disguise," she told Edison. "I can't risk Serena or any of the other godborns recognizing me."

"Should I use a disguise, too?" Edison asked.

Ren was about to say no, but then she thought of Marco. He would tell her to assume nothing about the enemy, including what they knew and didn't know. If the cinco really were in cahoots with the Lords of Night, there was a solid chance they knew Ren was here, but could they possibly know about the hunter and the demon, too? He might as well wear a disguise just in case.

She turned to show Edison a fake mustache when she saw his gaze land on the stormtrooper costume standing in the corner. "Aren't you a little short for a stormtrooper?" he said, quoting the movie.

Ren had seen the old-school Star Wars movies a million and one times, always wishing they had included more aliens and fewer droids, but whatever. She snickered, holding out two options. "Mustache or wig. Take your pick."

"Which is your favorite?"

"I guess the mustache?"

"Not those," Edison said. "The Star Wars movies."

Ren smirked. "How do you know I've seen them? Please tell me that wasn't in the report." *Because that would be way disturbing.*

"You told me you like space and aliens, so of course you saw the movies. I mean, right? You seem like that kind of girl... person."

"Edison, how many girls have you known?" Ren asked respectfully, hoping he didn't take it the wrong way.

The demon looked like he was doing some mental calculations before he said, "About a hundred and three."

"Seriously?"

"I mean, they were all ghosts. Does that count?"

Ren laughed. "Yeah, I guess that counts."

Edison looked pleased... or was it relieved? Either way, he grinned and said, "I'll take the hat since I can't pull off that 'stache."

Ten minutes later, Ren and Edison walked out of the shop. He sported a Jurassic Park baseball cap (even though he, a demon, said the movies were unrealistic and the special effects were subpar). Ren had opted for a short blond wig. She'd almost bought some Harry Potter glasses, too, but they made her look like a fly. Plus, she'd never really ever been impressed with the wizard.

"You look really..." Edison almost smiled. "Different."

Heat rushed to Ren's cheeks, and she hoped it didn't show.

"And don't worry," Edison added. "I can always vanish or change my look if..." He stopped. Looked around. "I mean..."

The echo of his words filled the silence.

Ren remembered what he had told her when they first met. *This is how I appear...most of the time.*

Edison's eyes scanned the other side of the street like he was trying to direct his attention anywhere but at Ren. And as much as Ren wanted to know what he *could* look like under that human skin, she didn't want to embarrass him.

"Map to the stars!" a vendor shouted, shoving a flyer at Edison. "See their homes, their lives, their secrets."

"No thanks." Edison maneuvered his way out of the vendor's reach. Then to Ren he said, "You know what the movies don't teach you?"

"What?"

"How things smell and taste and feel. Like, this place is unbelievable. It smells sweet and spicy all at once. And the air is thick but thin, cool and warm. And the people...Wow! Nothing like the ghosts in the underworld."

"You mean the hundred and two girls?"

"Hundred and three, and no, nothing like that."

"Have you never been around this many people?"

"You mean living humans? Nope. But I like it. I think..."

Ren chortled. "Well, sometimes this kind of chaos is fun and other times not so much."

"Must be easy to be human."

"Ha! Is that what the movies have taught you?"

"No, I just mean that human lives seem simple, straightforward." Ren read the subtext to mean: *Easier than being a demon.* Because let's face it, demons were at the bottom of the supernatural ladder, at least in terms of likability, trustworthiness, and niceness. But Edison had all three. And bonus: he was easy to be around.

"Can I ask you something?" Ren said.

Edison threw her a side glance. "Er...okay?"

"Why did you name yourself Edison?"

His shoulders sagged. Was it relief or...?

"I mean, did you see it in a movie or something?"

"A book—well, lots of books. About invention."

Ren's lightbulb went off. "Oh, so after Thomas Edison, the inventor?"

"Not just him," Edison said. "He's a symbol, you know? To remind me that I want to do something important, something useful."

Ren soaked it in, the words, the dream. It only made her like Edison more. She could appreciate someone with a dream and someone who was willing to name it.

"I want to go to space," Ren blurted, and the moment that the words were floating between them, she winced. She had never admitted this to anyone. Sure, she loved space and the

idea that aliens existed, but she wanted to actually see it...
beyond Earth's atmosphere.

Edison stopped walking. He looked up at the night sky. He
said only one word. "Imagine."

Ren felt a swell of emotion: happiness, gratitude, and pride,
and she found herself nodding as that word grew inside her:
imagine.

They sidestepped a crowd of tourists in HOLLYWOOD T-shirts
and UNIVERSAL STUDIOS caps. "Since I've never been in a crowd
like this," said Edison, "I should test something."

"Should I be worried?" Ren teased. "You're not going to do
anything to get us on *TMZ*, right?"

With an intense gaze focused ahead, he said, "No idea what
that is." Then, slowly, he raised his hand to chest height and
circled a single finger in the air. A woman's straw hat flew off
her head, spun in three tight circles, and plopped back down.
Her expression was one of astonishment as she clutched the
brim and increased her pace as if worried a ghost was on her
trail.

Ren chuckled. "What was that for?"

"Just making sure the vanquisher works with all these
humans around. You never know. I mean, magic has all these
strange rules, and there's an order to it—or at least to each
person's own brand of magic—and I've never used mine in these
conditions."

Ren added *prepared* to her running list of Edison adjectives.

"Great, so the vanquisher is locked and loaded, but..." Ren
hesitated, then realized she had to ask, "Have you ever had to

use it in, like, a do-or-die situation?" Or had it all been simulations? In which case maybe the vanquisher wasn't so crushing after all.

"Yeah, once a few ghosts threw me into Pus River in Xib'alb'a."

Ren gasped. "That's so mean! Did you blow them away?"

"Nah. They were just playing around. But I stunk for days. I had pus coming out of my ears and everything. And oof, the taste?" Ren must have looked completely grossed out because he quickly added, "Anyhow, as I was floating to a vile place downstream, I realized I could use the vanquisher not only to destroy things or blow them around but to do something else. So, when I saw a canoe on the riverbank, I released my magic and instead of launching that thing into the air, I brought it to me."

"Oh, that was smart," Ren said, but she couldn't shake the most critical part of his story—the meanie ghosts who had thrown him into the pus in the first place. Apparently, bullying wasn't limited to the human imagination.

But how could Edison be so chill? So forgiving? Ren felt like she used to be more like the demon, but then those horrible emails changed everything. They held a mirror up to her and insisted that she take what they were serving. Ren tried to convince herself that they were only false accusations. She wasn't a fake or a liar or a loser. And winning this quest would prove that—at least to herself.

Just then, Ren's phone buzzed. It was Monty.

"Eyes on target," she said. "I repeat, eyes on target."

Ren's heart started to jump around in her chest. "Where?"

"Madame Tussauds Wax Museum, 6933 Hollywood Boulevard. She's just standing outside, glancing around like she's waiting for someone."

"We're on our way," Ren said, checking the location on her watch. "It's only a mile from here."

"Roger that."

"And stay where you are!"

"Unless she leaves . . . Then I'll follow."

After a seven-minute sprint, Ren and Edison found Monty on the opposite side of the street from the museum, ducking behind a car.

"You guys need to up your speed game," Monty said, pushing Ren down and out of sight.

Catching her breath, Ren clutched her sides and glanced over the car hood at Madame Tussauds. There was Serena, standing outside the museum with two of the five rogue godborns. Kenji, son of Ah-Muzen-Cab, the god of bees; and Diamante, daughter of Akan, the god of wine and art. But he was killed in the battle with Ixkik' a few months ago.

"What's she waiting for?" Ren whispered as if she was in danger of being overheard by Serena.

She couldn't shake the astral traveler's warning: *trap.*

Edison said, "Uh-oh."

Ren's stomach plummeted. "What's uh-oh?"

"See that bald man in the baggy yellow T-shirt who just arrived? He's a demon in disguise, and in about ten seconds, he's going to catch my scent." Edison made a sound in his throat that sounded like a growl.

Monty leaned closer to the demon and took a whiff. "You don't smell to me."

"But I will to *him*." Edison adjusted his cap. "Listen, he'll sense your magic the second you get within ten yards. You'll never get past him."

"Have you not seen my arrows?" Monty said. "I'll paralyze him real quick."

"Or I could create a diversion," Edison said.

Ren considered the options. Diversion or paralysis. She usually opted for the less violent route.

"How long will he be paralyzed, Monty?"

The hunter waggled her eyebrows. "How long do you want him to be?"

"Is there a way to knock him out, too?" Ren couldn't risk him seeing them.

"Yup. I call it Combo Number Three."

Ren knew that whichever choice she went with, it would reveal either the demon or the hunter to the enemy.

If anyone finds out he's a demon, he'll be in grave danger, Ah-Puch had said.

"Monty, you're up." Ren turned to Edison. She couldn't risk the demon's olfactory system being off-line just because he was going to be lights-out. "Just in case, stay clear of the smell range but close enough so you can keep your sights on the museum."

Monty handed him her phone from her back pocket. "Know how to use one of these?"

"Nuclear launch codes," Edison teased.

Monty frowned.

"We'll call you if we need you," Ren said.

Edison looked disappointed, but he nodded, then cut loose, vanishing into the crowd.

Ren kept her eyes on Serena and crew, who were now surveying the people in line. What were they up to? But before she could answer her own question, the entrance began to shimmer, spark, and hiss. The Madame Tussauds sign crackled with enough magic to light up every grid in Los Angeles.

"What the heckster?" Monty said.

Ren realized a second too late that Serena was creating an illusion—a fake museum for the crowd so she could do whatever she wanted in the real one. And that meant that Ren's ridiculous disguise was worthless. No "unmagicked," as Monty called them, would be able to get past the illusion.

But what about the people already inside?

Then Ren understood. The other two godborns must have been evacuating the real museum somehow.

"We have to get inside before the wall of magic disappears," Ren said as Serena and her crew stepped across the threshold. "Take down the demon, now!"

Monty drew an arrow with the speed of light and sent it flying.

The arrow hit its clueless target in the center of his chest, creating a cloud of pink smoke, and by the time the shaft circled back to Monty's quiver, the demon had collapsed like an empty pillowcase.

"Out for the count," Monty shouted as she spun toward Ren. "You coming or what?"

The two bolted across the street, dodging traffic, horns, and some very choice words from drivers. The magic wall was shrinking into itself.

"We have to make it!" Ren cried as she turned up the gas to catch Monty.

"Hurry!

As the opening narrowed to a mere few feet, Ren somersaulted through the wall. She landed with a painful thud on thin red carpet. Rolling to her feet (of course Monty was already on hers), she glanced around. They were in a dim chamber with a wax statue of Kevin Hart. It was eerily silent.

"What now?" Monty whispered.

Just then, Ren's phone buzzed.

It was Zane Obispo.

21

Zane had the worst timing in the universe.

In ten universes.

But Ren couldn't waste this opportunity, because who knew when she might be able to talk to him again? "Zane?" she whispered.

"Shhh!" Monty warned.

"Ren!" Zane's voice was loud but not as loud as the music playing in the background. "Finally! Did you get my pictures? Man, I have so much to tell you, but I gotta hurry."

"I'm busy. Text me about the symbol."

"What? Speak up. I can't hear you!"

"The symbol," Ren said more forcefully this time.

"Yeah, cool, right?"

She was going to create a shadow octopus to strangle Zane the next time she saw him.

"I think it's related to aliens, Ren. Aliens! You were spot-on! But I'm not supposed to tell you, or *anyone*, so don't text me about it or, you know, put anything in writing."

Ren wanted to scream his name, and if he had called just forty seconds earlier, she would have. "Zane!" she hissed.

"I can tell you this," he said, his voice suddenly serious. "Ah-Puch knows. He has to. It's one of those big fat ancient godly secrets. Ask him. If anyone can get the truth out of him, it's you."

Then the connection died and so did Ren. Or at least that's how she felt. She went as still as Lady Gaga. Even with the connection lost, she couldn't bring herself to lower the phone from her ear. In case there was more.

"Are you going into shock?" Monty whispered, shaking her head. "I don't do shock. That wasn't part of my training."

All Ren could do was nod. Had she even heard the question? Aliens? The symbol had to do with aliens? But what did that have to do with the Lords of Night, and Serena, and—

"Uh, can you do the shock thing later?" Monty said, adjusting her bow. "Like after we get out of here alive?"

Ask Ah-Puch.

Is that why he freaked when I showed him the symbol? Ren wasn't sure whether she wanted there to be a link or not. If there was, the god had lied to her. If there wasn't, she was back to square one.

Forcing herself to return to the moment, Ren quickly texted A.P.

Where are you?

She sent him their location, knowing full well he was never going to be able to get through the now-closed magic perimeter. Which meant she and Monty were on their own to figure out what Serena was up to.

She had to go with plan B: Make up a better plan than plan A.

Slowly, carefully, they crept through each chamber of the

shadowy museum. The place was disturbingly quiet, no movement or other signs of life. Just the staring glass eyes of famous
people in wax form. Who knew Kevin Hart could look so terrifying? Monty was crouched low, stalking like a cat ready to
pounce. "This way."

She must have picked up Serena's energy print again.

They cut through two more chambers before they heard
voices in the next room.

"Everything is all clear." That was Diamante.

"Good," Serena said. "This is the spot."

Ren and Monty were on all fours now, crawling across the
grimy red carpet, making their way to the corner so they could
peer into the next chamber and finally see what the rogue godborns were up to, see if they were in fact the ones who were
waking the Aztec lords. And with each move, Zane's voice
echoed in Ren's mind: *I think it's related to aliens.*

But there's a difference between *think* and *know.* Maybe
Zane was wrong. It wouldn't be the first time. And Ren couldn't
pin her quest and hopes on *think.*

Peering around the corner of the divider wall (did Monty
really have to breathe so loud?), Ren spied the three godborns.
They were more or less facing her direction, so she quickly cast
a small shadow to make sure she and Monty stayed hidden.

Heart thudding, she watched as Diamante and Kenji stood
motionless while Serena thrust out her hands, palms up.

"Is this like a weird séance?" Monty whispered, wiggling
herself into a better position.

Ren blinked, fought to find air, to make sense of what she
saw next.

There in the middle of Serena's palms was the symbol—it looked burned into her skin. The same exact tight spiral made up of dozens of little circles. The image glowed for a long enough moment that Ren could see what was at the center, a seven-pointed star.

Instantly, a brilliant shaft of light appeared from a skylight above, illuminating her flesh. And the godborns' chamber faded away until all that remained was a dreary desert, a long narrow basin of nothing but sand. The air was thick with dust.

What was with the illusion? Ren wondered.

Monty sucked in a breath like she might sneeze. Ren pinched the hunter's nose closed, urging her with desperate eyes not to blow their cover.

A tiny squeak emerged from the girl. Ren winced. Thankfully, the godborns hadn't noticed.

They were too distracted by the emergence of a figure from a cloud of dust.

It was the astral traveler—this time in the flesh. She must have been waiting in the museum. Maybe she was part of the advance team that had evacuated the place. The other godborns acknowledged her with nods.

Seeing her now, fully formed, fully human, Ren remembered her from SHIHOM. When they were there together, Ren had barely noticed her. The girl had just sort of blended into the background.

Now Ren struggled to remember her name. Something that started with an E . . . Elizabeth? Erin? Ernestine?

Kenji and Diamante stood side by side, waiting. And judging from their relaxed expressions, Ren could tell they had done this ritual before. She didn't know if that made her feel worse or better.

A thread of light separated from the beam, wiggling across the space until Serena took hold of it, extending it so she could lay it on the ground like a piece of yarn. Ren watched as she created a circle no bigger than a dinner plate.

The air was charged with so much magic, Ren could barely breathe. She sensed its current coursing over her skin, felt its heart and hands and teeth.

"Want me to shoot her?" Monty whispered. "I could take them all out in four seconds flat."

Ren threw Monty a scowl and shook her head as Serena dropped to her knees and pressed her palms into the sandy circle.

A hot wind rose, spinning like a tornado, kicking up sand, swirling the girl's dark hair in every direction.

There was a tremble, slow and rising, from the earth as Serena continued pressing down. Her body was stiff, rigid, determined. The earth shook harder and harder. The circle grew bigger and bigger. And then *cracckkk*.

The earth ruptured along the circle's edge. Smoke rose.

The smell of burning flesh and hair touched everything in an instant. Ren wanted to gag.

Instantly, the world became still again.

And then . . . Serena extended her arm to her friends, smiling. There, right above her wrist, was a third symbol.

For the third lord, Ren guessed. Tremors of shock rolled through her. Where had Serena gotten this kind of power?

Ren's gaze diverted to the ground, where the glowing red symbol began to breathe, pulsing like it was alive.

Serena stepped out of the circle. "Ezra," she said.

Ezra. That was the astral traveler's name.

The name flooded Ren with memories from the ceremony this past summer when the gods came forth and either claimed or disavowed their children. If they claimed someone, they offered them a gift of amazing magical proportions. That was how Ren had ended up with the watch that was now of *zero* magical proportions.

Confidently, Ezra stepped into the circle, clutching something close to her body. Something small and . . .

Monty gasped. Ren threw a hand over her own mouth, wanting desperately to gasp, too, as Ezra set an eyeball in the ring's center and began to roll it over every line of the symbol.

Wait. Ren peered closer, realizing that it wasn't a *real* eyeball. One side of the small sphere was painted to look like an eyeball, but the other side was a brilliant azure, a night sky dotted with tiny golden stars.

The little globe was actually . . . beautiful. But what exactly was it? What magic did it possess? If only Ren could remember Ezra's godly parent . . .

And then she finally did. A cold shudder ran down her spine.

Ezra was the daughter of the goddess of spells and magic. A newer god with a name Ren shouldn't have forgotten—Yohualli, which simply means *night*.

22

Piltzintecuhtli

First there was absolute quiet. Then the stillness of death. Next came the need, vicious and hungry, to fuel the heat and the fury. A light, more dazzling and blinding than the sun, exploded with unimaginable force, propelling him outward to devour and destroy.

The third Lord of Night, the Prince Lord, opened his eyes.

He shook the dust from his long black hair.

And then he waited.

23

"All done."

Serena's desert wasteland vanished the moment Ezra spoke.

Ren's heart sank. Even though there was no visual proof, she could feel it deep in her bones—the Prince Lord was awake. But if that was true, where was he? She scanned the dim museum chamber but didn't see anyone new.

Ren bolstered herself with this thought: *Well, at least the remaining six are still asleep. That has to be good, right?*

Crouching, she glanced at her watch. It was ten p.m. Hadn't A.P. said the lords were likely to wake at midnight? And speaking of the ill-informed god, where was *he*? Had he found anything that would keep the rest of the lords asleep? Anything to counteract that creepy magical eye Ezra was using? That had to have been Yohualli's gift to her. But did it really have the power to wake dead gods? And if it could do that, could it also knock them back into their slumbers?

Maybe not. Ren knew enough about magic to understand that the rules weren't cut-and-dried; they weren't always logical. If that orb had the power to send the lords back into dreamland, Serena would want it for herself, to wield power over the newly awakened gods.

"The illusion is collapsing," Serena said. "We have to go."

Ren's heart was in shreds. She desperately wanted to confront Serena, but she knew it wouldn't do any good. The godborn would give up nothing. And Ren would only throw away her chance to exploit the element of surprise.

There was a faint buzzing. Kenji whispered something in Serena's ear. Ixchel's daughter glanced around, forcing Ren and Monty to duck out of view.

And then the chamber was plunged into darkness.

Ren's ears pounded. Her throat swelled. She inched back, reaching for Monty's hand. In the space of two heartbeats, there was motion, footsteps, breath. Monty's hand was ripped from hers. And then came the hunter's scream.

"Ren!"

"Monty!" Ren turned, groping air, cursing the uselessness of her shadows in the dark. As she bumped into a wall, she saw the blue glow of the magical arrows being carried away.

Ren raced forward, never taking her eyes off the beacon of light.

Don't disappear. Don't disappear.

But within ten steps, the glow vanished. Ren spun around, fumbling, desperate for even a glimmer. But there was only darkness.

The time rope!

She yanked off the necklace and whipped it in front of her. A golden gleam of light lit up the space, guiding her to the museum exit.

As soon as she stepped outside, she returned the time rope to her throat. Gasping the fresh air, she scanned the street. *Where did they go?*

That's when she felt someone grab her arm and begin dragging her down the road.

It was Edison. "This way!"

"How do you know?" Ren's heart was beating out of control. *Ba-boom, ba-boom, ba-boom.*

"I smell her."

Right. How could Ren have forgotten that demons had the most advanced tracking system in the universe? For half a second, she wondered why Edison hadn't found Serena himself, and then she remembered he was only half demon. And that probably meant his olfactory sense wasn't nearly as precise as Monty's.

Together they sprinted down the packed street. They cut around tourists taking selfies, hamming it up, laughing, acting as if nothing in the world was wrong. Just for funsies, or maybe to let off some steam, Ren wanted to shout, *Demons and godborns and lords of night are in your midst—take cover!* But this was Hollywood. No one would probably even blink an eye.

About a quarter mile later, Edison came to an abrupt stop at the edge of a building.

Ren was sucking wind, but the demon hadn't even broken a sweat. While pressing Ren behind him, he carefully peered around the corner.

"What are you doing?" she asked impatiently.

"I'm making sure it isn't a trap."

Trap. There was that word again—so small, but it carried a lot of weight. Ren hated it.

"This is weird," Edison whispered, turning back to Ren.

"That's not what I want to hear right now."

"I can smell her, but I can't see her."

Ren took a look for herself. Edison was right. The dead-end alleyway was empty except for some crates and trash cans. She scanned the scene, carefully, deliberately. There. A tiny blue glow near a stack of boxes. Monty's arrows!

She was still in danger.

There was no thought, no consideration, no planning, only a deep-rooted fight-or-flight response. Ren bolted into the alley.

"Ren!" Edison shouted. She could feel the rush of his movement behind her.

She stopped suddenly. The air vibrated. It looked distorted and warped, like when heat rises from asphalt in the afternoon sun. Ren understood too late.

The net sprang from nowhere, lifting her and the demon up in one fell scoop. Ren struggled against the glittering silver ropes, which were strong despite being an illusion.

"One wrong move, one ounce of magic," Serena said as she and Kenji stepped out of the wavy air, "and your little friend gets hurt."

Desperately, Ren scanned below, searching for the glow of Monty's arrows. But she didn't need to. She could now see the hunter in Ezra's grasp. And worse, the daughter of spells and magic was wearing Monty's bow and quiver. The arrows' color had deepened to a midnight blue.

"Monty!" Ren cried, suddenly realizing that she was asleep.

Edison was still, his gaze zeroed in on the godborns below. His arms and legs were tangled up with Ren's, and she felt his warm skin vibrating with an energy she hadn't felt coming from him before. And his pulse was steady and powerful, as if a huge lion's heart was beating inside his chest.

Do demons have bigger hearts? she wondered.

Edison gripped her hand. "Stay calm."

Was he joking? They were suspended fifteen feet in the air by a sparkly illusory net, two godborns were sneering at them, Ezra had Monty's magical arrows, and the hunter was down for the count!

"Let us go!" Ren cried.

Kenji covered his mouth like he was going to bust up laughing. "You make everything so easy. Man, didn't all your SHIHOM training teach you anything? You walked right into it!" He sucked his teeth. "Guess you picked the wrong team to play for, Rennnnn."

Every inch of Ren felt like it was on fire. Her shadows thrashed within her, demanding to be set free. But she couldn't risk them hurting Monty. She shoved them down, her chest aching with the effort. She glanced toward the end of the alley. Kenji might've been trying to make Ren think this was an intentional trap, but now she was sure that wasn't the case. Serena had taken a wrong turn, and now she had no choice but to face off.

Ren's mind did double-time calisthenics, racing through every scenario, every possibility. Serena had run into a dead end. She couldn't maintain her illusion forever, and even if she could, it didn't conceal the arrows, for some reason. Serena was just as caught as Ren and Edison were. And even if she tried running away, she knew Ren and Edison would follow as soon as she was out of range and the net disappeared.

What to do? What to do?

Edison said, "You touch one hair on her head and I promise you'll answer to me forever and even after that."

"Harsh!" Serena smiled, an eerie, otherworldly smile that would have looked more realistic on a monster. The godborn's voice was even, controlled, an octave lower than normal. "I have something you want, and you have"—her eyes met Ren's—"a wannabe loser who gave up time control for a bunch of Maya gods who don't care about her or anyone else. What a joke!"

Ren felt a flare of heat in the center of her chest. What if Serena was right? Maybe Ren *had* squandered her time-control power on a god who still hadn't answered her messages, a selfish god who had left her to figure this all out on her own.

"Serena..." Ren said, hoping she could appeal to the godborn's innate goodness. It had to be in there somewhere. "Please, just let Monty go. We won't follow you."

"As if we believe that," Kenji said.

"You don't make the demands here, Ren," Serena said angrily. "You got that?"

"Then *I* will," Edison said with a weird authority that reminded Ren of a cop...or no, a principal. Maybe an elected official with a lot of power. He leaned into the net, fingering it like he was looking for a weak point. "Here's how this is going to go: You're going to give us Monty and her arrows in the next two minutes."

Boom! He threw down the gauntlet like a boss. That was

all he said. No *and*, *but*, or indication that he was going to give anything in return. Except that he wasn't the boss, Ren realized. He was a demon trapped in a net.

Serena said, "I don't think you're listening very well."

Edison sighed. "And I don't think you have any idea what I'm capable of."

Ren stared at the demon in awe. Who *was* he? And what had he done with the awkward nice guy?

"Except that we have the girl," Kenji snarled.

"I don't care how many threats you throw at me," Serena warned. "You try anything, and she'll be the first to get hurt." Her cold gaze cut to Ren. "And I know you'll do anything to make sure that doesn't happen, bruja."

Ren had always felt pride in her Mexica heritage, her bruja magic, but hearing the word coming from Serena's lips filled her with a weird sense of shame that quickly turned to anger.

"You don't know me like you think you do," Ren fumed, feeling her dark shadows growing within, pressing against her bones and flesh, wanting out.

Serena and Kenji laughed.

In a tiny whisper, Ren said, "Don't do anything dumb, Edison. I know Serena better than you do, and she's not bluffing. We have to listen to her . . . for now."

The demon traced his finger along the net's thick shimmering rope. Then his eyes met Ren's. He gave her a wry smile. "I've never been good at following other people's rules."

Ren didn't know Edison well enough to predict whether his threat was empty or locked and loaded. But she knew she was about to find out.

24

"Sixty seconds," Edison said calmly to his captors.
Serena's eyes glowed with the light of the half-moon hanging low in the sky. And in the span of a single blink, they flashed red—the color of a blood moon. "Don't threaten me!"

Kenji was still smiling, Serena was still glaring, and Monty's arrows were still shimmering. *Monty*, Ren told herself. *Focus on Monty.* Except that Ezra had lifted Monty into her arms and was creeping down the alley.

Ren panicked. "What do you want?"

Serena rolled her eyes and pushed a strand of hair away from her face. "I want the hunter and her weapon. I mean, you can feel the magic from here. Props to you for finding her."

Ren froze. She was stunned speechless, but she couldn't let it show.

Ezra was nearly right under them now.

Edison said, "Thirty seconds."

Casually, Serena drew a piece of bubble gum from her pocket, unwrapped it, and popped it into her mouth. A couple seconds later, she blew an enormous pink bubble. "I'm super scared."

Ezra spoke for the first time. "I can cast a spell over the hunter that would give her scales for skin or worse," she warned as she passed. "So no funny moves."

"Guys," Ren said, digging deep for her better, kinder side. "We don't have to fight each other. It doesn't have to be like this."

Serena rolled her eyes. "You're always so innocent and unrealistic, Ren, so . . . what's the word?"

Kenji said, "Dumb?"

Ren's cheeks burned with a heat that quickly coursed through her entire body. No way was she letting Ezra out of here with Monty.

Ren's shadows thrashed inside her, yearning to get out, to do damage and cause pain.

It was in this moment, this exact second, that everything felt like it had been balanced on the tip of a needle, like things could go either way, and now there was no stopping the momentum, the force of anger that had been unleashed.

"Follow my lead," Ren whispered to Edison.

He squeezed her hand. "You got it!"

Ren reached for the pulsing shadows within her, the dangerous ones that lingered in her chest, waiting, heaving. Then, in a rush of speed and power, she released them from her body. The sombras wrapped tightly around the hunter, keeping her safe in a shadow cocoon for now and instantly severing Ezra's hold on her. But the godborn still possessed the arrows.

"NO!" Serena shouted.

At the same moment, Edison burst through the net, arms extended, throwing his magic at the enemies with such force that they stumbled back.

He and Ren drop-rolled to the asphalt.

Everything happened so fast—too fast. Serena flung her hands in front of her, forming a cloud of mist from which a red-scaled snake emerged, ten feet to start and growing faster by the second. Its forked black tongue stabbed the night air. Edison retreated, sending the power of the vanquisher at the serpent, forcing it to recoil with a warning hiss.

While Serena was focused on Edison, Ren saw her chance. She raced past them toward Ezra and the arrows.

Kenji grabbed hold of Ren's arm, dragging her back with the strength of a two-ton ox. Ren spun and swept his leg with her foot while simultaneously throwing an uppercut to his ribs, bringing him to the ground with a loud *thump*. Adrenaline took over, all thoughts gone. She was operating on pure instinct now.

Kenji jumped back to his feet, a flash of surprise crossing his face, just as Ren caught sight of the arrows' blue light. She raced toward it. Kenji followed. Over her shoulder, she threw a web of shadows at him.

She was only two steps ahead, and soon he'd be on her.

One...

"Monty!" Ren screamed, hoping beyond all hope that her voice could reach past Ezra's spell and wake the hunter.

Two...

A sudden force catapulted Kenji into the air, and he spun, windmilling his arms and legs against Edison's magic, which was holding him in place.

Serena screamed. The snake hissed.

Ren didn't look back. She didn't need to. Edison was buying her time. It was then that another demon appeared—the one Monty had paralyzed outside the wax museum. Gone was his scrubby tourist look. He was in full demon mode now: blue skin, sharp teeth, long claws dripping with poison. And he was all that stood between Ren and Ezra. Ren had to get the hunter's weapon back.

Ren tumbled across the ground, out of his reach, before she unleashed the golden time rope and whipped it through the air, making contact with his face.

A painful howl echoed across the alley. The demon recoiled, grabbing hold of the rope. Its magic burned through his flesh, bringing him to his knees on the concrete, where he melted into a sizzling heap of nothingness.

Ezra kept running, but Ren was on her, throwing long shadow arms hoping to knock the bow and arrows out of her hands. Before they could, Ezra managed to nock an arrow. She aimed it at Ren.

The magic shaft flew.

The arrows never miss, Ren remembered Monty saying. Ren cast a shadow of protection over herself and cringed.

But it wasn't necessary. The arrow missed her by a wide margin. *How...?*

Ezra growled, clutching another arrow, and Ren thought she was going to let that one fly, too. Instead, she snapped it in two. Sparks flew. Screams echoed across the night.

A vicious anger grabbed hold of Ren—a hate so deep and dark she could feel it taking root in her, giving her strength. She screamed, and from her mouth emerged a shadow with the intensity of a thousand waves. There was no shape to it, only darkness. Ren let the fury fly.

The shadow engulfed Ezra. Swiftly, Ren lassoed the time rope around the girl's now-blistering ankles, bringing her down with a hard *thwack* while the sombra kept her pinned. Then Ren reeled in the rope, snatched up the bow and arrows, ran back for Monty, and lifted the shadow-protected hunter into her arms. She hurried in the opposite direction of the battle, still going on behind her.

Then came the buzzing.

Edison. Was he okay? She made the mistake of glancing over her shoulder. Kenji must have broken free of the vanquisher because he was right behind her. His mouth was open wide in a silent scream. And then Ren realized it wasn't a scream—it was an exit for the thousands of bees swarming from the deep cavern of his mouth.

Ren's legs burned as she pumped them faster and faster. Her arms ached with Monty's deadweight. In two seconds, both of them would be consumed by stinging pain.

The buzzing penetrated her ears, her mind, her bones. She couldn't fight and carry Monty. She had to choose one or the other.

At the same moment, she felt Edison's magic pulsing, growing. *We're going to make it,* Ren thought. *We're going to—*

Edison threw up a wall of protection shielding Ren and Monty from the bees, but it was too late. A swarm had gotten through. Ren felt the stingers as they entered the skin of her arms and legs, face and neck. She collapsed. The unconscious hunter tumbled from her arms onto the ground.

Edison stood between his friends and the godborns, the last shield. "I'll hold them!" he shouted, his voice strained as errant bees stung him all over the face. "Get her out of here!"

"What about you?" Ren cried. She could see, feel the break in his power.

"Go!"

But Ren couldn't move because, in that same instant, Edison started to transform. The bee stings had split open his skin to reveal an ugly, slippery, infected-looking second skin.

This is what I look like . . . most of the time, he had told her.

Ren lifted Monty again, pushing through the unbearable pain of the stings, knowing they were venomous, knowing she and the hunter had little time . . .

With every ounce of strength she had left, Ren staggered forward, holding tight to Monty. The hunter's face was pale, and beads of sweat rose on her forehead. She was burning up. Tears pricked Ren's eyes. "You're a Jaguar Warrior!" she cried.

Her right knee buckled. She stumbled, collapsed. The hunter rolled from her arms again.

Get up. Get up. GET UP!

The venom leaked into her. Her vision went fuzzy around the edges.

"Hello, Queen."

And then the world went black.

25

Ren wasn't sure if she was dead or alive.

She was lying in a bright and sunny landscape bursting with leafy green vines. Orchid-like white flowers drooped from the ends. She could hear the burble of a gently rolling stream nearby. Sleepily, she sat up, half remembering. . . .

And then the memory of her efforts to save Monty overwhelmed her.

She got to her feet clumsily, feeling like she'd just run a marathon. She glanced around while concentrating on her breathing. Inhale, exhale. The air was thick with the scent of vanilla.

"I know you're here," she said, waiting for the third lord to appear.

A figure emerged from a thick curtain of vines. He didn't look older than sixteen, had dark hair that hung to his shoulders, and his dark eyes sparkled like they were made from the sun.

What was the deal with all these lords being teens? Or did Aztec gods just age super well?

"You're the Prince Lord," Ren said, half expecting him to start glowing.

He was barefoot and wore faded jeans and a white T-shirt.

Where's the surfboard? Ren nearly asked.

Unlike the Smoking Mirror, the Prince Lord was only a few inches taller than Ren. "Do you like vanilla?" he asking, lifting a flower to his nose and inhaling slowly. "We call it Black Flower for its pods. The darkness is where all the flavor comes from."

"Great. Congrats," Ren said, her head still too foggy to trust her own thoughts. "Can I go home now?"

"Those bee stings are quite perilous." He inched closer.

Ren stepped back. "What do you want?"

"I am Piltzintecuhtli, the Aztec god of the rising sun, and of healing." Aka the Prince Lord.

His voice was sort of hypnotic, like an app that tells you stories to help you fall asleep. Calming. Soothing. He also sounded bored, as if he'd made this introduction a million times before. "Would you like me to make it all go away?" he offered.

It? The garden? The bee stings? Her quest?

Ren shook her head, glancing around. Okay, this place was way better than the teeth-clicker's shadow prison, but still, she couldn't rely on her eyes, only her heart, and right now it was screaming *trap!*

Where's Monty? Lying on the asphalt where I left her? Has Kenji caught up to her?

Ren felt like she had been turned inside out. Just thirty minutes ago, she'd been in the museum with Monty, and now she was in this sunny Garden of Eden–like place with a surfer-dude god.

"If you don't accept my help," he said sadly, "you'll die."

Lies. Her dealings with the Smoking Mirror had shown her that she held a card they needed. And that meant they wouldn't let her die. Not yet.

"You used Ezra," Ren said, totally guessing but wanting to see how much he might reveal. "The Maya daughter of spells and magic. She woke you guys."

"Yes."

That one word nearly knocked Ren over. She had expected him, like most gods, to lie and cover up their plot.

"And once you're all awake, you're going to destroy the Maya gods and take over the world." Ren had seen and read about this kind of plot a million times. "And Serena is cutting a deal with you for some control, right?"

"That would be wholly unoriginal," the Prince Lord said.

Ren waited, holding her breath, but he didn't say more. *Why* didn't he say more? *The silent type is the worst!*

The sun rose high in the sky, a white ball of heat that made her feel all warm and fuzzy. But she didn't want to feel warm and fuzzy. She needed to be alert, on guard, ready to charge.

"The hunter will die soon," he said softly, kindly.

Ren could feel tears threatening, but no way was she going to let them spill in front of this guy. He wasn't telling her anything she didn't already know. He was telling her he wanted to cut a deal. "What do you want?" she asked again.

The prince smiled. He really did look like someone who could be crowned a king. But Ren wasn't sure if that made him more dangerous or less. Probably more, she thought. Kings always got what they wanted. And didn't all princes become kings? Well, mostly...unless you were William, Duke of Cambridge. She forced her dumb stream of consciousness to come to a halt.

"It's easy," he said. "We want you to come home."

"Have you hit your head? Been asleep too long? I'm Texas born and bred, and it's the only home I've ever known."

"Are you sure about that?"

Yes. A thousand times yes. And yet there was a flicker of doubt in some unknown recess of Ren's heart. "Well, if you want me to be queen, or . . ." Ren pressed her lips together. "Then you won't let me die, will you? You have to save me."

"True. But what of your friend? Would you gamble with her life?"

Ren found herself shaking her head and hated how easily she showed her emotions.

"Then all you have to say is *I am your queen.*"

"You want me to say four words?" Ren couldn't hide the incredulity in her voice. "And then you'll heal me and Monty?" *Mm-hmm . . . Yeah, right. NOT!*

"Not words," he said unfazed. "A promise, a fulfillment of your destiny. A destiny written so long ago."

Ren wanted to laugh. She wanted to tell Mr. Sunshine that he had the wrong girl. But that wouldn't do her any good. If Ren was going to make a deal, she might as well get more than her life and Monty's out of it. She might as well get intel. "First, tell me why all you lords keep calling me queen."

"That's who you are."

Bzzzz . . . wrong answer. Or at least not one that offered anything new.

Ren moved on. "And what do you mean by *destiny*?"

"It means that you will accept your calling," he said in that velvety voice.

"I'm only fourteen . . . I don't want to be queen."

"Don't you?" The Prince Lord hesitated, smiled slightly like he knew everything and Ren knew nothing. She hated that smile. "The queen has access to all knowledge. Your questions about who you are, your magic, your family history, about the universe *itself* will all be answered. Isn't that what you want? To know why? Why you search the skies, why you believe there is more than what you see? Why you have never felt like you belonged?"

Whoa! Had he read her report, too? Ren found herself nodding, found herself *wanting* to know. And then her mind's gears started turning, clicking to a rhythm that made sense, that felt right. *It's just some words, and queens can quit. No one said I have to STAY queen. And besides, I'll take these guys down, put them back to sleep before any crown touches a hair on my head.*

A heartbeat echoed across the garden. Slow. Weak.

"Do you hear that?" the prince said. "The hunter is losing her life."

Thump.

Thump . . .

"Save her!" Ren shouted, terrified of the awful silence between the beats.

"Say the words."

Was this his card? The words? Panic rose thick and heavy inside Ren. She couldn't breathe. Suddenly she hated the smell of vanilla. "How do I know you're not lying?"

Thump . . .

"You don't, but if it makes you feel better, I have never felt the need to lie."

"You promise she'll be okay? You swear?"

"You have my oath."

Thump...

"And you'll let us go?" The last thing Ren wanted to do was strike a deal and then wake up in a shadow prison with some dumb crown on her head. (And if you think queens don't do time, read the history books.)

"I will let her go. You...Well, you can go for now, but soon you will return."

Scowling, Ren said, "You mean you're going to make me. You're probably going to kidnap me in the middle of the night or something."

The Prince squinted against the bright sun. "You will come of your own accord."

"No way."

"Mark my words."

Never. Never. Never. Mr. Sunshine is for sure off his rocker, which means my statement would be meaningless. Probably. But even if it wasn't, she couldn't let Monty die.

Ren drew closer. She knew a deal with a Maya god was binding, and she hoped that was the case with Aztec gods, too, because it would force him to keep his promise to save Monty. She thrust out her hand. "Shake on it."

Thump...

The prince looked amused as he glanced down at her hand and took it in his. His dark skin was warm, pulsing with light and energy like the very sun coursed through his veins. It probably did.

"I will save her life and yours," the Prince Lord said again.

Ren kept her gaze on the vanilla flowers. What had he called them? The Black Flower.

She smashed one beneath her shoe, drew in a breath, and whispered, "I am your queen."

26

There were no fireworks, no explosions, no creepy coronation, no catastrophic anything. Only the awful words ringing in Ren's head: *What have I done? What have I done?*

She opened her eyes. The first thing she saw was a bear's head, its mouth open in a roar, revealing gleaming fangs. Its glass eyes stared at her from the wall above the stone fireplace. And the first thing she thought was *Pobrecito*. The second thing she thought was *Where the heck am I?*

A.P.'s face loomed large above her. She let out a startled gasp, grabbing her chest.

"Finally!" he shouted. "I've been pacing all night, worried, all tangled up." He fluttered his arms to demonstrate but ended up looking like a really bad traffic cop. "And you just lay there sleeping! You are the worst! How dare you do this to me? It's been eight hours! Eight, Ren." He pointed to a clock on the mantel. It was seven a.m.

"Monty! Where is she?" Translation: Did the Prince Lord save her?

"She's fine," the god said. "It's quite strange how quickly the two of you healed."

So the Prince Lord had kept his promise. Ren scanned her

own arms and hands—no welts, no evidence that she'd ever been stung.

She didn't know where to begin, or *how* to begin. *Hey, A.P., I totally agreed to be queen of the Lords of Night. Ha-ha! Me, a queen. Funny, right? But don't worry, I will one hundred percent no way in a million universes ever go to their side.*

The same four words pounded away at her mind: *What have I done?*

"Seriously, Ren?" a familiar voice said. "After one day you're already in this deep?"

Ren sat up and swung her legs over the edge of the cowhide sofa. "Marco! What...? What are you doing here?" She didn't know why that question came to mind, but she was very curious. "Did you win your big game?"

Pointing to his grass-stained jersey, he said, "Can't you smell the victory?"

"As if football is hard," A.P. grumbled. "They wear pads and helmets, Ren! Try playing some Maya ball. Now *that's* hard!"

Marco glared at the god so intensely Ren was sure smoke was going to come out of his eyes. But he didn't throw any shade—he just shrugged it off.

Happy to change the subject, Ren said to Marco, "So why are you here? You said no quests."

Marco shrugged. "I'm on a winning high, okay?"

"He's the one who found you in LA," A.P. said with a tightly clenched jaw like it killed him to admit that.

"You weren't answering your phone," Marco said, "and you know how much I hate that, so..."

"But how did you find me, and how did you get to Hollywood? You broke your gateway map."

"Location share, remember? And turns out I didn't break the map—I found it in the bottom of my gym bag, stuffed in my cleats. It reeks pretty bad, but hey, it works."

Ren jumped up and pulled Marco in for a big hug, the kind he hated most. She had no words. He had come all this way. The son of war had a rep for being cold as ice, but Ren knew there was a pinch of sunlight underneath. She leaned back and socked him in the chest. "And just because you saved me, don't think you're getting any more essays out of it."

Marco smiled. "Yeah, well, it was a team effort. That Edison dude came through in a big way." He then acknowledged Ah-Puch with a barely-there nod. "Him, too."

Ren turned to A.P. "Thanks, but . . ." She paused. How do you thank someone for saving your life and in the next breath chew them out for not keeping their promise? Gently. So she ignored what she really wanted to say—*You were supposed to meet us at the museum!*—and went with "Didn't you get my text?"

The god rolled his eyes. He was for sure getting the whole teen vibe down. "How do you think you ended up here? When Marco found you, he called me. I was already in Hollywood, so I got to you in two seconds."

"Ten," Marco coughed.

For once, the god let it go and added, "The others had already fled, so Edison and I carried you and Monty through a gateway to the nearest safe house."

"That half-demon dude wouldn't let you go, man," Marco

said. "He stayed here all night. Kinda weird, Ren. You don't even know the guy."

But I know what his dream is.

She took in the grand room with its sweeping windows that looked out on a lush forest. "Did you say *safe house?*"

A.P. leaned against the fireplace mantel. "You heard me loud and clear."

Why was the god being all stuffy and serious? He was acting like a dad, not a friend. Maybe some humor would loosen him up. "Am I in a witness protection program now?"

The joke flew over the god's head. "When you're the god of death, you keep a few of these shelters just in case."

"Smart move," Marco said, "when everyone wants your head and your spine, too."

Ren mouthed, *Be nice.*

"This one is near Lake Tahoe," A.P. went on, "and tended by twin mountain spirits—retired, but efficient." He tapped the ornately carved wooden mantel. "And it's guarded with old magic so no one we don't want to can get in or out."

Old magic. That was one of Ren's favorite classes at SHIHOM, but they'd only been able to cover its origins (not of this world) before the summer session ended. And mountain spirits? They were Ren's least favorite, mostly because they were so much more temperamental than spirits of air (bossy) and earth (paranoid).

A.P.'s gaze pierced hers. Yup, the god of death was still in there, behind those boyish eyes and baby face. And then came the question she'd been dreading: "Where have you been?"

Ren tried to shrug it off until she could pull the truth apart and put it back together. "Asleep."

"Renata Santiago, do not play games with me!"

"Why are you acting so weird?" Ren's voice rose. "Like an angry dad or something."

"You're deflecting."

"Am not."

"Kind of are," Marco said.

Ren glared at him and took in a deep breath.

"Hey, uh," Marco said, "I'm gonna get cleaned up . . . unless you need me here for the showdown."

"It's not a showdown," Ren said.

The godborn walked out of the room mumbling, "Right. Sure."

Ah-Puch crossed the room and sat in a plush green chair across from Ren. It was so hard to take him seriously when he looked younger than she was, but underneath that facade was still a ruthless deity. And he was likely to combust once he found out about the deal she had made. Even though it probably meant nothing. It could've just been the Prince Lord's way of messing with her head. A voice rose inside her: *No reason to tell A.P.*

A more logical voice countered, *Friends tell each other the truth even when it hurts. Even when it's a bomb ready to detonate.*

"Why are you looking at me like that?" Ren said, suddenly feeling self-conscious.

"I know about the Smoking Mirror's little visit in LA."

Ren nodded. Of course, Monty and Edison had told him. It wasn't like it was a secret, so why did Ren feel so exposed?

"Monty told me about Serena and the astral traveler waking the gods."

"Ezra's the daughter of spells and magic, so I guess it makes sense that she would have that kind of power," Ren said, wishing she had connected the dots sooner. "She tricked me—I see that now. But then why give me the clue to go to Hollywood?"

"To lure you in," A.P. said. "To force your hand. She took advantage of your trusting nature, which is why I have told you a million and one times that you need to harden you heart, learn to be shrewder."

Doesn't that defeat having a heart at all? Ren wanted to say. But then she remembered the darkness that had stirred in her. It had given a stunning power to her shadows in the alley, a power she had never felt before.

"Tell me exactly what the Smoking Mirror said to you."

Ren gave the god the details—the Smoking Mirror's denial that Serena mattered (just like the Prince Lord's), his taunting her to play a game, his insult that she didn't look like much of a queen.

A.P. closed his eyes and inhaled. "He actually showed you his face?"

"Yeah, why?"

"He doesn't do that often."

Ren didn't really care about the Smoking Mirror right now. She wanted to be on the other side of all this, making plans, figuring out how they were going to fix everything. "So, what did you find out?"

"Very little," A.P. admitted as a lady with spiky silvery hair came in with a wooden tray. She was slim and wore brown yoga pants and a T-shirt that read GO GREEN. The mountain spirit was about five feet tall, but her swagger made her seem taller. "I don't cook," she growled. "So here's a bologna sandwich. Take it or leave it."

Bologna for breakfast? Ren didn't care. She was starving. "Thanks." She took a huge bite because the mountain spirit was standing there expectantly like she was waiting for more than a thank-you. The toasted bread was airy; the bologna was thick and salty. It was delicious. "I love it," she said around a mouthful.

"Then you should be telling *me* that." An exact replica of the first spirit burst into the room. "You should be saying 'Citla, you're the best sandwich maker in the world.'"

"*Psh*," her sister said. "I'm Mina, and big deal that *she* can make a sandwich. My part of the name carries all the power."

A.P. sighed. Then, by way of explanation, he said, "Citlamina means *greatest of all the female heroes.*"

"But there's two of us," Mina said. "See the problem?"

"That's why our name got divided," Citla said, "so we wouldn't fight about who really is the greatest." She jabbed her thumb into her chest.

Mina huffed. "If you were the greatest, you wouldn't have to talk about it all the time!"

The house began to tremble. A slow and deep grumble that rose from the floors, shaking some decorative glass orbs on the coffee table.

"Citla, Mina," A.P. growled. "I told you. *No* shaking the mountain."

"But it's *our* mountain," Citla said.

"And I gave it to you."

"Details, details," Mina said as the quaking stopped. Then to Ren, "That's not real meat, you know. It's tofu made to taste and look like bologna."

"We're very much vegetarians," Citla put in. "And we'd never hurt any living thing. That isn't in our nature."

"Unless said living thing was trying to hurt anyone in this house," Mina amended with a deep scowl.

Ren's eyes swung to the bear head hanging over the mantel. The sisters followed her gaze. "Oh, he's not real," Mina said like she could read Ren's thoughts.

Ren liked these sisters. Maybe they were a little rough on the outside, but she could tell they were softies on the inside.

After they left, Ren polished off her tofu bologna sandwich and set the plate on the coffee table. "They're funny."

"They're annoying."

Familiar voices drifted in from another room. Ren was already on her feet when Edison and Monty walked in. Relief flooded every cell in Ren's body at the sight of the hunter. She ran over and threw her arms around Monty.

Monty's small body went stiff at first, and then she wrapped her arms around Ren's waist, squeezing her tight. "I failed," she whispered.

"No, you didn't!" Ren said, breaking free to meet the hunter's gaze, which went from regret to anger in less than a second.

"She broke an arrow," Monty said with a deep frown. "That evil girl snapped it in two."

"I'm sorry" was all Ren could think to say.

Monty snatched an arrow from her quiver and stroked it

like a puppy while she studied its beauty. "She doesn't know what she's done."

"What do you mean?" Ren asked, afraid of the answer. *Please don't let it be some world-ending doom.*

"She only made the other arrows stronger, more lethal," Monty said. "She made them mad, which means I have to shoot them once a day to get their energy out."

"Oh, that reminds me," said Ren. "You said they never miss, but the one Ezra shot at me did."

Monty snickered. "They never miss when *I* shoot them. No way would they work for anyone else. Especially that mean witch girl. Oooh, man, my arrows are going to have it out for her." She practically sang the words.

"Maybe revenge isn't the best idea right now," Ren said lightly. She turned to a silent Edison. "Thanks a ton. You saved us."

"I wasn't fast enough," he grumbled. Edison's eyes swept over Ren's arms and hands. "I saw those bees, the stings, the welts . . . How did you guys"—he swallowed—"survive?"

A.P. was nodding, giving Ren that *I-can-read-your-mind* look. "Kenji's bees are lethal, Ren. So how *did* you and Monty survive? And how did Monty awaken from Ezra's sleep?"

A small, ridiculous giggle escaped Ren's mouth. "Well, it's, um . . . you see . . ." She was stalling, trying to connect the pieces. Should she tell them about her deal with the Prince Lord? If she did, A.P. would come unglued and lock her up in this safe house forever and the forever after that and so on. But she couldn't *not* tell them—it was too big.

Everyone's eyes were pinned on her. "Is it hot in here?"

"Ren..." A.P. said.

In that moment, watching the god in the slanting rays of the morning sun, Ren suddenly remembered Zane's words. *Ask Ah-Puch.*

Ren thought back to when she'd showed the god the symbol from the cave and the cornfield—how he had freaked out and then blamed it on teen hormones. Now she saw his reaction for what it had been—a cover.

Well, guess what? she thought. *No more covers, Mr. God of Death. No more godly secrets while I'm over here drowning in a sea of anxiety.*

Feeling emboldened, Ren said, "Remember that symbol I showed you the pic of?"

A.P.'s dark eyes drilled into hers. "I'd rather not."

"Tell me what you know about it," Ren said, "and I'll tell you how we were healed and where I've been."

"Are you actually trying to make a deal with me?" A.P. drew closer, so close they were practically toe-to-toe. But his intimidation tactic wasn't going to work. Too much was on the line.

She lifted her chin. "Are you going to accept it?"

A.P. never took his gaze off Ren. There was a challenge in his eyes that she didn't like. A challenge that told her Zane was right—the god knew exactly what that symbol was. But the question was, would he tell her?

27

This was going to be a game of Pollo with a capital *P*.

Bock. Bock.

Who was going to cave first? Ren didn't know why it mattered except that the info about her little vanilla-garden visit was all she had as collateral, so if she was ever going to get the truth about the symbol it was now.

Just then, Marco waltzed in smelling like pine soap and wearing a plain gray tee and some jeans that were screaming for a belt. He vaulted himself onto the sofa, clutching a bag of Doritos. "What'd I miss?"

"A.P. was just about to tell us about the symbol," Ren said, wondering where Marco had gotten the threads.

"Ren was just about to tell us where she was while she was sleeping," the god countered.

Marco threw a knowing gaze at Ren, one she didn't have time to decipher right then.

"Sounds like a standoff," he said, tossing a chip into his mouth. "Want me to ref?"

"NO!" said Ren and A.P. at the same time. Then, remembering her manners, Ren gestured to Edison and Monty. "I guess you've all met?"

"Yeah," Marco said. "When the demon dude was carrying you through the gateway."

Edison inhaled a gallon of air. His eyes caught Ren's, and she remembered the peek she'd gotten at his demon skin. It didn't matter to her. He was her friend, and he had saved her life. "I owe you," she told him.

"Jeez, can we ixnay the Hallmark moment?" Marco groaned.

"I still can't believe it!" Monty squealed. "The son of war! I've heard a lot about you, and to be honest, I think you're in the top-ten godborns. Like, if we were forming a godborn band, you'd for sure be the drummer."

Marco's eyebrows shot up. "First, I don't do bands. Second, I'd for sure be lead singer. Now, let's get down to business." He clapped like he was directing a huddle.

Ren turned to Ah-Puch. "Let's start with the symbol."

"Why does it mean so much to you?" A.P. asked.

"Zane told me I was right," Ren said. "Aliens are real, and I don't know how, but it's connected to this. That symbol was in Kansas and in Hollywood and on Serena's arms! It has everything to do with the Lords of Night."

"It was really creepy," Monty said, making a face, "how the symbols were, like, branded into her skin."

"But why?" Edison asked, more to himself than anyone else.

"You talked to Zane?" Ah-Puch hissed the name like he had spit out a cockroach. He and Zane had a long history, and maybe not a great one, but they were on good terms now—or at least they were until a few seconds ago.

"For a quick sec." Ren told the god that Zane had seen the

symbol, too, on an island near Holbox. "And he said to ask you about it, A.P."

The god tugged on his ear, cursing under his breath. He began to pace. "This is ludicrous. Worse than ludicrous! Is there a word for that? If not, someone should create one." He paused, turned to Ren. "You go first."

Ren shook her head. "I'm the more trustworthy one, so you should go first."

"Says who?"

Edison and Monty raised their hands. Marco folded his arms across his chest like he wasn't ready to take sides.

The god threw his hands on top of his head. "Fine! But if I tell you, you will be privy to one of the gods' greatest secrets. All of you will live in danger for the rest of your lives because, as you know, knowledge is power. Is that what you truly want?"

Marco stifled a laugh. Everyone whirled toward him.

"What? Like, come on! Danger is in our job descriptions. Sorry, Ah-Puch, but if that's your best threat, no one's biting." He chomped on another chip and wiped the orange dust off his lips with the back of his hand.

Edison and Monty looked to Ren, waiting for her approval.

The Prince Lord's words wrapped around her: *The queen has access to all knowledge. Your questions about who you are, your magic, your family history, about the universe* itself *will all be answered. Isn't that what you want?*

Whether any of that statement was true, Ren didn't know, but she had a chance to learn the truth right now from the only god she really trusted. She nodded.

"You're sure?" A.P. said. "Dangerous life going once, forever and ever . . . Going twice."

"Sold!" Ren said.

"I liked you better when you were a baby godborn, all innocent and sweet." A.P. snatched a remote control off the table and clicked a button, grumbling insults under his breath to no one in particular. "As you know, my memory is . . . not so great, so . . ."

An enormous light filled the room—taking the shape of a translucent blue globe.

It was Saás, the highly knowledgeable, very salty, giant floating globe that usually resided in the ancient library of SHIHOM. She could answer most any question in the universe, assuming she was in the mood. If there was ever a perfect example of technogics (the combo of magic and technology), Saás was it.

The magical globe was better than Alexa and Siri, better than Google. And Ren was pretty sure Saás hated her. Over the summer, Ren had planted herself in the huge library to ask Saás questions, things like:

1. Is there alien life? *Yes.*
2. Where can I find it? *Your human brain cannot handle this information.*
3. What's inside a black hole? *Nothing you want to find.*
4. Can the golden time rope help me travel into space? *It is a time-traveling mechanism, not a space-traveling one.*

The very last question Ren had asked Saás was this: *Who made you?*

The globe hadn't responded. Instead, she'd blinked off with a flash.

Now the globe appeared like a hologram of itself. "I already told you, Ah-Puch," Saás said. "I am not a trainer of godborns." "I don't expect you to be." A.P.'s voice was strained, bordering on murderous. "That isn't why I've brought you here."

Edison was now studying the orb, walking in circles beneath her, muttering things about hardware, input, and data. *Wow, he really does read a lot,* Ren thought. Marco sized him up like he wasn't sure what to make of the demon.

"Then why am I here?" Saás asked.

A.P. hesitated, glanced at Ren, and then said, "To tell the story of the Time War."

A heavy silence followed. Like dead silence. Deader than dead.

"I do not compute," Saás replied.

Ren had never known the globe to play dumb before.

The god of death wasn't used to asking for favors. He was accustomed to making demands. But that's the thing with technogics—it doesn't always work the way you planned or hoped for. Kind of like smartphones or the internet or Siri. But this wasn't that. Saás was holding back.

"Do as I say," A.P. said with a semi-defeated tone that made Ren want to wrap her arms around him in a bear hug. Or maybe he was just playing her "trusting, open" heart. When the globe didn't respond, A.P. let the beginning of a threat fly. "And if you don't provide the information, I will—"

"What he means," Ren interrupted with a nervous chuckle, "is that if you don't share your amazing wisdom with us, then we can't defeat the Lords of Night, who are waking up, and they'll probably make their own technogic globe, and then there would be two of you."

"WHAT?!" Saás cried. Her floating form swept across the room and back again. "I am one of a kind! No one or no *thing* will ever rival me."

"I beg to differ," A.P. muttered, but thankfully, Saás, in all her hysteria, didn't hear.

"Exactly," Ren said to the globe. "But if you can just give us some intel on this Time War, then maybe we can stop the lords."

"War," Marco muttered. "Always comes down to war."

"You're manipulating me," Saás said angrily.

"No," Ren argued, trying to hide her escalating frustration. "I'm just trying to make you understand."

"Understand?!" Saás hollered. "How dare you! I am the greatest understander of all time."

"But if you don't tell us," Monty threw in as she twirled an arrow between her fingers, "I'll lose my name and my magic."

"And why would I care about—" Saás halted abruptly. "That arrow," she said, her voice now soft. "It isn't of Maya origin. Where did you get it?"

Monty's enormous eyes flicked to the globe. "I'll tell you if you teach us about the Time War."

"Let me scan the arrow," Saás offered, "and then I will tell you whatever you like."

Monty looked to Ren.

"Go ahead," Ren told her.

The hunter held out the blue-feathered arrow while a white beam of light radiated from the globe, scanning the weapon.

"Mmm...Ohhh...I see...Fascinating," Saás kept repeating with a delighted tone Ren had never heard from the globe. When Saás was done, the light vanished, and Monty secured the arrow back in her quiver.

"Okay, subjects, gather around," Saás said airily, like an overly caffeinated flight attendant.

Blackout shades mechanically lowered over the windows, plunging the room into darkness. A holographic screen appeared, revealing a blue-black sky with thousands of distant flickering stars scattered across it.

"The Nine Lords of Night were Aztec gods," Saás reported, "each representing a day that carried either blessing or curse."

"We already know all this," A.P. said. "And what's with the theater?"

"This isn't a story you tell in the light of day. Now, where was I? Oh yes. Before time began, there was a war..." Saás said. "It was between the great Maya gods and a species of being that the gods deemed nothing more than monsters."

Species of being?

The stars on the ceiling took the shape of blocky indecipherable characters doing battle as Saás spoke.

"What happened to them?" Edison asked.

A.P. growled. "We gods annihilated them. We—" He stopped short.

"Ah-Puch," the globe said, "are you sure you want me to tell them the truth? I don't like the idea of getting reprogrammed or tossed into a junk pile in Xib'alb'a."

Ren looked up at A.P. in the dim starlight.

He closed his eyes and said, "Tell them all of it."

28

All of it **turned out to be A LOT.**

"The monsters were called the Unknowns," the globe said. "And yes, the gods annihilated them, sort of." There was an animated explosion in the projected night sky to demonstrate. "The gods allowed a few survivors and cast them into the darkest depths of the earth, as a warning."

"That was probably my dad's idea," Marco said with a twisted grin.

"You're telling it backward!" Ah-Puch snapped at the globe.

"Do *you* want to tell it?" Saás bit back, then quickly softened her tone. "At first, the Unknowns were considered allies of the gods. It was the Unknowns who helped the gods create the Fifth Sun, what we know as human existence today."

"Yeah," Monty put in, "since the gods kept getting it wrong."

Edison snickered. A.P. threw him a side glare as Saás swept ahead. "Pleased, the gods invited the Unknowns to great banquets and allowed them to mingle with the giants, spirits, demons, nawals, and other sobrenaturales."

"Man, I already see where this is going," Marco said, kicking his feet up onto the table.

Ren's heart was racing. She could hardly believe what she was hearing. She thought about the symbol, wondered if it was related to these Unknowns. But she didn't dare interrupt.

"Then the gods found out that a demon secretly married an Unknown," Saás said. "That is what began the war."

"Why would they care?" Monty asked.

"Clearly you don't know the gods," Marco said.

"I'm getting to *that*!" Saás barked. "The Unknowns didn't understand why the gods were so angry until they realized that when their blood mixed with the blood of a demon, it created a powerful force. If left unchecked, the offspring could become strong enough to overthrow the gods themselves."

"Where have I heard this story before?" Marco said in a grating singsong voice. "Oh yeah—when the gods wanted to wipe out the godborns for the exact same thing."

Ren went cold all over. Her mind had stalled on *their blood mixed with the blood of a demon*, then raced ahead to the inevitable possibility, the one she'd been spouting all along. Aliens and demons were related!

"Hold up!" Her voice shook. "How did the gods *realize*? Are you saying that a demon and an Unknown had a baby?"

"Whoa!" Monty chewed her bottom lip.

Edison's eyes were so wide, Ren was sure his eyeballs were going to pop out any second from the strain. Marco just shook his head.

"I am saying no such thing," Saás said. "But it has been surmised."

A.P. cleared his throat. "We have reason to believe, yes, that they had a child."

"And?" Ren said. "Did that child...? Did others...?" She had so many questions she couldn't get out the right one. "Do you think there's a race of demons-slash-Unknowns cruising around?" But she already knew the answer. Deep in her bones, she knew.

"Can I please get to the point?" Saás said. "The gods searched high and low for the couple who had married, but no one ever learned their identities or whereabouts. And the Unknowns were losing the war, so they vanished, never to be seen again. It is rumored that several hundred years ago a few Unknowns came back."

"Why?" Ren asked.

"Probably to check on their great-grandkids," Marco said with a sneer.

Saás went on. "We believe they created an alliance with the Aztec Lords of Night. The lords were already in trouble—their empire collapsing, their people being killed—and they understood that this alliance would mean their death as well."

"But what did the Unknowns get in return?" Edison said.

"We aren't entirely sure. Sources tell us that the Unknowns promised the lords a new world even greater than Aztlán, their mystical homeland."

"Aztlán," Monty said. "That's where the Mexica, the Aztecs, came from."

Saás plummeted ahead. "The Unknowns put the Lords of Night into a deep sleep, promising they would return someday and take them to the new land."

"But why would the lords agree to that?" Edison asked.

"Dude," Marco said, "it was either deep slumber or death. Which would you choose?"

"Aren't they kind of the same thing?" Edison said.

Everyone fell silent. Monty's stomach rumbled. The blackout

blinds rose to reveal a light rain falling outside. Everything felt like it was clicking into place—all except for one burning question.

"If this is such a huge secret," Ren asked, "how could Serena know about the connection between the lords and the Unknowns?"

Saás paused. Ren could tell the globe didn't know the answer and probably hated to admit that fact. "You'll have to ask her" was all Saás said before racing on. "The great calendar K'iin foresaw all this. She looked for the Unknowns across the universe but couldn't find them, so the Maya gods buried the truth. They agreed never to speak of it again, and they made sure their prisoners never got out."

K'iin. The all-seeing calendar Ren had made a promise to on her last quest.

You will repay me with a favor someday, Renata Santiago.

"And the symbol?" Ren asked, trying to stay on track.

"It represents an idea, a phrase—"

Before Saás could go on, A.P. said, *"The initiation is near."*

"Initiation?" Edison echoed.

"Ha!" Marco barked. "That ship has sailed. I'd say the initiation is in the rearview mirror."

Ren held her breath. "And what about a queen?" If Saás knew all this, maybe she knew something about that, too.

"What queen?" Saás said.

"The lords . . ." Ren's voice hitched in her throat. "They called me queen."

"Hmm. I know nothing of a queen, and surely it is mistaken identity."

Ren swallowed the shame she felt. Was it so hard to believe that she *could* be a queen? She began to pace as the rain outside began falling in sheets. "We have to tell the gods about all this, A.P." This was so much bigger than she could have imagined.

Edison was nodding. "What if the Unknowns are back? What if they're working with Serena? What if—"

"I've tried to tell the other gods," Ah-Puch said, clenching his jaw, once, twice. "They won't listen. They're too busy trying to restore their own powers."

Because half of them had never returned to their full glory and were still teens after the whole time-travel disaster. Which made Serena's timing perfect.

Ren paced even faster. "Okay, so we know the lords were aligned with the Unknowns, who are aliens."

"Never said that," Saás put in.

Ren let the shock waves roll through her. The proof of aliens she had been seeking for so long was right here, staring her in the face. Her curiosity was eating away at her. Who were the Unknowns, really? Where did they live? Where were they now? But she had to keep her eye on the ball, as Marco liked to say.

"Everyone here is missing the point," Marco said predictably. "Right now, we need to learn all we can about these loony lords."

"Do you know how to keep them asleep, Saás?" Edison's face looked pale in the gray morning light.

"Finally, the right question, but be patient for a minute, demon." Marco rolled his eyes and got to his feet.

"Tell us about the three who have woken up, Saás," Ren said. "That would be the Fire Lord, the Smoking Mirror, and the Prince Lord."

"Wow, he really goes by 'Prince Lord'?" Marco said. "Talk about an ego."

Ren's heart was thudding. It was like being on a roller coaster in the dark and bracing yourself for the massive drop you can't see but you know is coming. "What can you tell us about them?" she asked the globe.

A thick silence settled over the chamber.

Monty raised her hand.

A.P. sighed, rubbing his brow. "Yes, Montero?"

"I mean, it might not be important, but, um . . ." She cleared her throat and said, "The Fire Lord also likes to click his teeth."

Ren whirled toward her. "How do you know that?"

Monty's eyes scanned the darkened room fearfully, like she had gotten something wrong. "My mom and dad have told me lots of stories." She spoke slowly, carefully. "They made sure I understood my history so I could understand my magic. Stuff that's been passed down forever, since all the real records got burned by that meanie Cortés."

Ren felt a painful pressure in her chest, wishing her dad had done the same for her. And yet here she was still not knowing where her shadow magic came from. "Why didn't you tell us you knew about these lords, Monty?"

"The stuff I know is *not* in the reports," Monty said with a wary smile. "But nothing really stood out. And my stories aren't written down anywhere, so I can't prove they're true." Then with a shrug, she added, "Plus, I didn't think being a teeth-clicker mattered that much."

Ren felt an immediate and frantic need to get inside Monty's head. "What else do you know?"

"The Mirror dude is really awful."

"We already know that."

"He's a real planner, a set-a-trap kind of guy."

Marco sighed. "That night in Vegas, the Smoking Mirror didn't put up a fight to win. He drew us into battle to decide who we really were so he could design the right trap."

"And the third lord?" Monty said. "I heard a story that supposedly Mr. Prince was really stuck on himself and, when he keeled over, he had some last words."

All eyes turned to Monty expectantly.

She deepened her voice, and with dramatic arm-thrusting flair, she spouted, "'I am the sun. I will rise again, and when I do . . .'"

Her voice trailed off into startling silence.

"*When I do* what?" Edison asked.

"That's it. That's all he said."

"Empty, idle threats," A.P. sneered.

Except they weren't, Ren thought, shaking her head. "Even if some of these gods were once good guys, that doesn't mean they still are. Look at bullies. They probably started out nice, too, until someone did some terrible things to them."

A.P. muttered, "The lords deserved what they got."

Ren snapped her attention to the god. "What's that supposed to mean?"

"Not to be glorious gods, not to be revered," A.P. said. "They let all their people perish."

Marco said, "Enough History 101."

Saás was silent aside from the hum of her machine mind turning. Finally, she said, "There is only one way to put the lords to sleep and preserve their slumber. The Obsidian Blade."

Everyone waited for further explanation, and when none came, Ren asked, "What's that?"

"Something that doesn't exist," A.P. growled as he kicked a table.

"Oh, it exists." The globe's voice was like velvet. "You just have to know where to look for it."

Edison exhaled, shaking his head like he didn't want to say whatever words were on the tip of his tongue.

"But if Ezra's orb woke them up," Ren surmised, "couldn't it also put them back to sleep?"

Ah-Puch shook his head. "You can't use the same magic that awakened them to put them back into their slumbers."

"Why not?" Monty asked.

"Because this kind of magic doesn't work that way," Saás said.

"So the Obsidian Blade is our only choice?" Ren asked dejectedly.

Edison exhaled again.

Ren looked over at him. "You know where it is, don't you?"

Edison's voice came out barely a whisper. "Magic that isn't supposed to exist can only be found in one place."

The god clenched his trembling hands. "No. There has to be another way."

What location could be so bad that the god of death was afraid of it? Ren's insides froze. "Tell us, Edison."

The demon threw his gaze to A.P., then back to Ren in the dismal light, and said, "The Dark Mercado."

29

The Dark Mercado had other names: El Maldad,
Shadow's End, the Cursed Dwelling, and more.

Edison rattled off each name casually like they weren't enough to conjure horrendous images of evil, but that wasn't what sent tremors through Ren's body. It was Ah-Puch's response—wide eyes, dilated pupils, sweaty brow, clenched jaw. Uh-oh. He was scared. And it's a really, *really* terrible sign when the god of death, darkness, and destruction gets scared.

Ren was the first to speak. "So, we go to the Dark Market."

Rubbing the back of his neck, Edison said, "There's a big problem."

"We've got more than one," A.P. put in snidely as the sun filtered in through the roof window, throwing long shadows across the floor.

Ren folded her arms over her chest, anticipating the worst. "What is it?"

"The only entrance to the Dark Market is through the Maze of Nightmares."

"Of course it is," Marco said. "Because no quest would ever sound like *Oh, you need a magical artifact? Well, come on in and let me get that for you.*"

Monty was bouncing on the balls of her feet like a runner

getting ready for takeoff. "I love mazes—so mysterious and interesting and—"

"You won't like this one," Edison warned.

"This is a wasted conversation," A.P. growled. "*No one* is going to the Dark Market."

Ren felt a jab of anger. This was her quest, not A.P.'s. "Why not?"

The god was pacing, fuming, exhaling so loud he sounded like a bull.

"It's pretty awful," Edison said.

"Have you ever been inside?" Ren asked.

Edison shook his head. "I've heard stories. Really bad ones. As in not good. Not the other meaning . . . I really need to quit using the word *bad*." He crossed his arms, frowning. "Basically, the maze wants to turn your brain to mush."

A.P. sighed melodramatically. "I *have* been in the dreaded maze, and it is not mysterious or interesting or any other adjective that might conjure false images of an adventure. It is a maze of cruel proportions—its only goal is to make sure anyone who enters never gets to the other side."

Ren's heart was fluttering wildly, making it hard for her to breathe. She'd never lacked courage on other quests, but this one felt different, not only because she was the leader, but because it seemed personal. Like there were answers at the end of this long road she might not like. And promises she didn't want to think about.

"But why make it so hard to get to the Dark Market?" she asked. "I mean, if it's a marketplace, doesn't that mean selling and buying? Doesn't that mean you *want* customers?"

Monty leaned closer to Ren, speaking out of the side of her mouth like a ventriloquist. "I was totally going to ask the same thing."

Edison's whole face screwed up. "Uh—*market* isn't the right word, really. Not sure why they call it that, but it's this really seedy world where bad things are allowed to happen and no one pays any consequences."

"And the hits just keep on coming," Marco said, pretending to throw a football.

"So what do they do with these objects that aren't *supposed to exist?*" Ren asked. "What's their angle?" That's when the lightbulb went off. "Is this like the twisted magic market that the wicked hero twins, Bird and Jordan, used to run in LA?" Ren asked. "Where people had to trade their love and honor and talent—things that really mattered to them—for a magical favor?"

"Exactly," Ah-Puch breathed. "Because the twins are exceedingly unoriginal, and they loved stealing what didn't belong to them—ideas, magic, even histories. But, assuming that any of us could actually get through the maze," A.P. said, standing a bit taller now, "we'd still have to procure the object, and most vendors won't let go of their magical objects without demanding a price that no one is willing to pay."

Why does everything always come down to a price?

"We have to do this," Ren argued. "It's the only way to put and keep the lords asleep, right?"

A.P. didn't need to say yes or no or even blink. Ren could tell by the dark flashes of anger and worry in his eyes that he wasn't even considering this option. "You'd be better off battling

all nine lords than trying to obtain some object in the Dark
Market. And that's *if* you made it out alive."

Ren refused to be dissuaded. She said, "If you've been in
the maze before, A.P., then maybe you can guide us through."

"It changes every new moon," he said miserably.

"How do you know?" Monty asked.

"Because I created it."

30

#$*&!

In the next three minutes and thirteen seconds, Ren and the others learned that (1) A.P. needed air, so they all headed outside to the rain-soaked forest, and (2) A.P. had created this illegal-trading whatever market over a thousand years ago to keep the dark energies flowing. Energies he drew on for his own power.

"Every trade, every sacrifice meant more power for me," he said sullenly as he paced beneath a canopy of pines. "I eventually tried to destroy it, but by then the dark energy had gotten out of control. So I made the maze to keep the market locked away."

"And to keep anyone from ever getting in," Ren said, following his train of thinking. She rubbed the cold off her arms. "So then . . . destroy the maze."

"I don't have my powers anymore, remember?" A.P. shook his head sorrowfully. "Anyway, the darkness has spread—it now connects the maze and the mercado. But at least it's contained."

Marco leaned against a tree like someone posing for a portrait, including the smile. "Since the market is a no go, sounds like we're gearing up for battle."

"Don't look so happy," Ren chided.

"Hey, this is my positive-vibe face," he argued.

Monty readjusted her quiver, nodding. Of course she was nodding—battle is what she had trained for. And she still had a quest to complete if she wanted to keep her arrows, her name, and her power.

Ren felt a surge of frustration. How could Marco side with the god? He didn't even like him! Then she answered her own question. *Because this isn't personal to either of them.* "You'd rather fight the lords and . . . the godborns?" Her voice cracked. Why did everything always come down to violence?

Edison threw Ren a sympathetic gaze, one that said *I'll take door A or B. Just say the word.*

"Battle is the better option," A.P. said. "Before they awaken the others, before they galvanize the lords' strength." Running a hand over his messy hair, he said, "And, Ren, a deal's a deal. I told you about the Time War—now it's *your turn*. Tell us where *you* were."

Ren watched a squirrel clamber up a nearby tree. She took a deep breath and then unfolded the details of her time in the garden of Black Flowers with the Prince Lord. "And he agreed to heal me and Monty if I said some words. See? Not very interesting."

"Heal?" The god's voice was dark, distant, and ancient sounding. The air was so thick with A.P.'s sudden anger, Ren wanted to take back everything she had said and run into the woods.

"I thought you'd be glad we're still *alive*."

"WHAT WORDS?" the god's voice boomed.

"Maybe we should all just take a little breath," Edison suggested. "Or two."

Thunder rumbled in the distance. Once. Twice.

"You need to calm down, A.P.," Ren urged. "You don't even know what I said and you're getting all worked up for nothing. You want to have a coronary?"

"I know you made a deal," he spat. "I see it written all over your face. And *no* god would give away something for nothing." He sucked in a lungful of air like there wasn't enough to go around. "What did you trade?"

"Nothing! I only told him . . ." She hesitated, hoping it wasn't as bad as it now seemed. "'I am your queen.'"

Citla and Mina dropped from the trees, where they must have been eavesdropping. "You did what?!" they said in unison.

Suddenly, the earth began to shake, the trees trembled, rocks tumbled down the hill, and the temperature dropped, like, a million degrees.

Ren was sick and tired of being judged, criticized, and interrogated. "STOP!" she shouted. Indistinct shadows rose up all around her, shadows she hadn't called. They pulsed with sudden power and fury.

The mountain went still.

Everyone stared at Ren and her lingering shadows. Mouths were open. Eyebrows were raised. Her heart pounded and her limbs tingled. "I . . . I didn't call them," she said. "I swear."

At the same moment, Monty's arrows began to glow blue. Ren was lost in a sea of confusion. "Monty, your arrows."

Marco inched closer. "Hey, Ren, just take it easy. Breathe . . . imagine. Or is it imagine, then breathe? Well, whatever, just chill, okay?"

Ren tried to vanish the shadows like she always had, but

they didn't obey. They waited, pulsing. She could sense a hunger in them that she'd never felt before. Cold terror washed over her. And yet . . . there was also a strange new feeling, like she wanted to feed them what they craved. Fury. Cruelty. More darkness.

Edison raised his hands slowly, sending a gentle wave of magic toward the shadows that nearly engulfed Ren. There was a spark, a flicker—a hum of warmth and calm.

Ren sensed a struggle between the two magics, and then . . . they seemed to merge. One second passed. Two. Three.

Ren could feel the shadows' anger and hunger subsiding. And then they vanished as quickly as they had come.

"What just happened?" Ren was shaking all over.

"Dude, that was some serious shadow bruja power," Marco said. "Even *I* was scared. And I never get scared. Well, not usually."

The light around Monty's arrows blinked out. "It's okay," the hunter said. "I know your shadows wouldn't hurt me."

Tears pricked Ren's eyes. "Then why did your arrows glow?" She threw her gaze at A.P., who had been quiet all this time. His fury was gone. For a split second, he looked like a regular teen boy with messy hair.

"I need to talk to Ren alone," the god said quietly.

No one argued.

Except Marco. "Everyone but me should leave, right?"

"It's okay, Marco," Ren said. "Just give us a minute."

Marco looked like he was struggling to get to a yes, but then he nodded and wandered off with the others.

"Ren," the god said when they were alone. "You have agreed to the one thing they wanted."

"I didn't agree to anything. I just said the words. I didn't have a choice!" Ren cried. "I couldn't let Monty die."

"Listen." Ah-Puch rubbed his forehead vigorously and took a deep breath. "We have to go somewhere. Now."

"Now? Where?"

"The only place where we have half a chance of discovering the truth."

A.P.'s safe house came with a magical portal. Well, the mountain did, and it was a good two-and-a-half-mile hike to the top of a steep slope that overlooked a lush valley. If Ren hadn't been so panicked, she might have appreciated the tranquil view.

"Where are we going?" she asked for the fiftieth time.

"You'll see."

She grumbled, kicked at a rock. Why were the gods so secretive? Why not just say *Hey, we're going to Disney World*?

"I hope it's in working order," A.P. said, coming to a massive pine tree that leaned a little too far to the left. With a single touch from the god, the trunk began to sparkle pink and blue with flickers of white. Then the air shifted, swirling into a rainbow gateway. Not at all what Ren expected the god of death to have created.

As if he could read her mind, he said, "It was a gift from Ixchel."

Serena's mom, goddess of the moon.

"It takes you anywhere you ask," he said.

There was a strange whirring sound, like a dying computer, and then the gateway went ... kaput.

"Hey!" A.P. banged on the trunk. "Open up." And when that didn't work, he kicked it. Then he spit on it.

"Maybe you should try being nicer."

"Stupid old magic, rotten godly gifts!" he growled. "I knew I shouldn't have trusted Ixchel. And not everything is about being nice, Ren! Rainbows are supposed to be nice, but this one ..."

A.P. pouted and kicked the ground like a toddler. Just when Ren thought he was going to throw another tantrum, he straightened up, took a deep breath, pressed his forehead gently against the trunk, and said, "Listen, ancient gateway, I really need this right now, okay? So ... if you could do me a solid and just take us to Seven Death, I'd really appreciate it."

Ren had just started wondering about that name when the gateway flashed, and before it could change its mind, A.P. pulled her inside.

31

The world was all ice.

A harsh glacial landscape. A bitter wind careened off a jagged white mountain, threatening to swallow Ren whole. She hugged herself tight, bracing against the gale as A.P. tugged off his thin jacket and placed it on her shoulders.

"Is this the North Pole?" Ren managed through chattering teeth.

"Not exactly," A.P. said. And then he dropped to one knee and pounded the icy earth with his fist. Once. Twice. Three times.

The *CRACCCKKK* was deafening as the ground split open.

Ren's heart was kick-kick-kicking against her chest and ribs as if to say *Let me out!*

A dark swirl of smoke rose from the crevasse.

"We're going in there, aren't we?" she said. Her lashes were freezing over. She couldn't blink. Could barely breathe.

And instead of answering, A.P. took her hand and threw them both into the fissure.

Dropping through an icy hell wasn't as bad as it sounded. Not when the god of death had your hand firmly in his and the fall was only ten feet. They drop-rolled onto some fluffy white carpeting.

Soft was Ren's first thought. Then, *Warm*. Then, *Are those cats?*

Her senses thawed as she got to her feet. The room was filled with cats of every color, size, and mood. Some hissed. Some swished their tails; others licked their paws, like, *Boring visitor alert.*

The huge room had a total Palace of Versailles vibe. Ren had never been to Versailles, but she'd done a report on King Louis XIV for school (the guy did so much he could've passed for a mini god). She stared in awe at the vaulted ceilings painted with images of... cats wearing crowns? The chamber had gilded crown molding, a gigantic crystal chandelier, a marble floor, and ornate furnishings that felt too large for the place and made Ren feel small.

"Where the heck are we?" Ren asked.

"Seven Death?" A.P. shouted, his voice echoing across the chamber. "I really hate cats." The god sneered back at the felines.

Just then, a lithe woman with short, sleek purple hair, an impeccable neckline, and startling black eyes sauntered in. She was wearing white silk pajamas with an sd monogram and a matching smock splattered with gold paint.

S.D.... Was Seven Death a person and not a place? Ren wondered.

"Can we please reduce the noise levels?" The woman purred as she took in her visitors. Her dark eyes grew bigger. "Is that you, Ah-Puch? I heard about your trip through time, but I didn't expect... You are the god of death and you look like—" She broke off.

"Yeah, S.D., I know. It's rather dreadful, but what matters is my dark heart," A.P. said, hinting at a growl. "It's still beating away, waiting for all my powers to return."

So Seven Death *was* her name. Her gaze turned to Ren. "Who is this?"

"This is Ren. A godborn and shadow witch. Ren, this is Seven Death, retired demon lord of Xib'alb'a."

Seven Death studied her. "Godborn." Chuckle. "Shadow witch." Bigger chuckle. "Things have grown ever more complicated since our heyday, Ah-Puch."

The god rubbed his forehead and planted himself on a velvet settee, forcing two cats to recoil and leap onto the floor. "What's with all the cats?"

"They just keep showing up."

"In the middle of the freezing North Pole?" Ren said.

"This isn't the North Pole," Seven Death said. "This is a hidden realm of my own making, and the cold is a metaphor for the first layer of my soul, child. But, like all creatures, I am complicated. I have many more layers. Come, let's have some tea."

Ten minutes later, they were sitting on a veranda that overlooked spacious gardens filled with hedges, rows of flowers, and marble statues of Seven Death.

"This place is really beautiful," Ren said as a mousy demon servant appeared carrying a gold tray with a golden teapot and teacups etched with *SD*.

"It's warm-your-toes tea," Seven Death said as the servant poured some for everyone. Even A.P., who waved her away with a scowl.

It was hard to believe that this lady was ever a lord of the underworld. She seemed more like someone's eccentric great-aunt with too much money and not enough ways to spend it.

"I need a favor," A.P. said, getting to the point ASAP.

Seven Death leaned across the table, looking way too eager. "You want me to come out of retirement and raise some hell? Sever some heads? Disembowel your enemies?" Then she sat back, ladylike, genteel, raising her cup to her lips. "The answer is no. I'm happy now, at peace. Well, if I could just get my sleep under control, then I'd be at peace. Insomnia really is life's greatest tragedy."

"Have you tried meditating before bed?" Ren said, taking a sip of the bitter brew that was not even close to deserving its name. She tried to hide her grimace.

A.P. let out an exaggerated sigh. "I'm not here to ask for any of that. I need you to remember some things for me. My memory is . . . Well, it isn't all tuned up." He glanced at Ren and explained, "Seven Death was a spy during the time the Lords of Night were put to sleep. She investigated the entire ordeal."

Seven Death smiled, purred, and straightened the linen napkin on her lap. "Oh, the bad old days. Such violence, such treachery. I really did love it," she said, arching a single purple eyebrow. "But then I retired, discovered a world of art, of beauty, of painting. I'm working on a piece now that I call *Flesh Eaters*. It's quite stunning." Her dark eyes zeroed in on Ah-Puch. "And here I thought this was going to be something exciting, something worthy of a visit from the god of death himself."

"Just tell us everything you remember about that period."

"Well," Seven Death said, her black eyes sparkling with memory, "there was something called the Night Prophecy."

Ren's spine tingled. Her palms started to sweat. The edge of her vision blurred with menacing shadows threatening to pull her into one of her blackouts. *Hold it together,* she told herself. She'd come so far, gone so long without blacking out. Ren thought she had outgrown the absence seizures that always came at the worst times. Taking slow, deep breaths, she focused on the present moment, and when that didn't work, she began tapping her eyebrow.

"What are you doing, child?" Seven Death asked.

"Oh...just trying to chill. If I get too worked up, I sort of pass out, so I tap."

Seven Death made a sour face like she didn't understand weakness. "Well, if you're going to faint, I have a lovely fainting couch you could use. Just don't get it dirty. But if you want to know the truth, breathing and meditating and...Well, that doesn't work for anyone who has magic flowing in their veins." She clapped once. Lady Gaga's "Poker Face" boomed from... everywhere. The veranda trembled with the bass.

"Seven Death!" A.P. growled. "Turn off this blasted noise!"

"Feel better?" the lord said to Ren.

Strangely, Ren did. She nodded. "But why?"

"I shocked your system. Short-circuited it so it would stop focusing on the one thing you didn't want—fear, nerves, whatever. Got it?"

"Seven Death..." A.P. warned.

A black cat jumped onto Seven Death's lap and began to lick its paws. The lord turned off the music. "You know I hate talking about those days," she said. "But for you I will endure. Where was I?"

"The Night Prophecy," Ren said.

"Oh yes. Those prophecies are the worst, right? Always getting you into trouble. Talk about anxiety!"

"What did it say?" A.P. asked, his voice and manner too subdued for Ren's comfort.

Seven Death sipped her tea. "That one would be born many years in the future, one with the power to wake the Lords of Night."

Ezra.

Seven Death scratched the cat between its ears. "The last part is a little strange, though."

A.P. froze, like he was bracing himself. "Tell us."

"When the lords wake, they will wake to a queen, a queen who will change the course of their history."

Ren's heart stopped. She didn't dare look at A.P., terrified that his eyes would burn her.

"They called *me* queen," she said to Seven Death.

Seven Death dumped the cat on the floor, cleared her throat, and began to fan herself with the napkin. "Oh."

"Oh?" Ah-Puch pushed away from the table, rocking the golden teacups, and stood. He paced across the sunny veranda. "That's all you have to say?"

"What does it mean?" Ren asked, trying to ignore A.P.'s outburst.

The lord's eyes met hers. Even in the swirling darkness, Ren could see regret in them, like she didn't want to say whatever was already on her lips. "Well, when the lords went into their slumber, they knew it could change them. That when they awoke, they could find themselves just like . . ." She glanced at

Ah-Puch, nudging her chin toward him. "Time has a peculiar way of transforming things."

"I bet that's why the Smoking Mirror and the Prince Lord look so young," Ren said under her breath.

"So," Seven Death said, "they planted some of their most powerful magic in a few humans, sort of like a stockpile. These were people they trusted, who had served them well. I was quite struck with the brilliance of their plan. No one would look for magic hidden in a bunch of pathetic puny mortals."

Ren asked, "What... what kind of magic?"

Seven Death traced a long finger around the rim of her cup, thinking. "Shadow magic."

Everything went still, like nothing existed except Ren's heart, which was kicking its way out of her chest. "Like *my* shadow magic?"

Seven Death sighed. "I thought perhaps you knew?"

A.P. made a pained sound.

"Your magic," Seven Death confirmed, "comes from the Lords of Night themselves."

Ren shook her head, and yet she knew it was the truth. So many times she had asked her father where her power originated, and he had always refused to answer. *Why?*

A memory, way back in her mind, tugged itself free. It was about the first time she met Ixtab, goddess of the underworld.

Ixtab had scowled as she circled Ren. *Small for a child of a great Maya god. And yet so much...*

So much what? Ren had asked.

I will ask the questions, Ixtab had said. *Tell me, Renata...*

Where did you come from, and how is it that your skin buzzes with so much magic?

Had Ixtab known? *No way,* Ren thought. *She wouldn't have let me live.*

A.P. collapsed back into the chair. "Do you have anything stronger than this tea?"

Ren's mind was a machine of gears and cogs and cranks all trying to click together. "But why would the lords give away the shadow magic and not some other kind?"

Seven Death smiled for the first time, a small smile that carried the weight of whatever she was going to say next. "It is the only magic in existence that does not sleep."

Those words whirled around Ren.

The only magic in existence that does not sleep.

Ah-Puch looked like he might be sick. "And now they want Ren so they can take back the magic they gave away so long ago."

"Is that why they called me queen?" Ren asked.

Seven Death tossed her hair. "They can call you queen all they want, but until you agree to *be* their queen, they cannot reclaim their magic."

Oops.

Something collapsed inside Ren. Her mouth went dry. Her entire being grew cold, so cold she could feel her kidneys and liver and spine freezing over.

She waited for A.P. to blow into a storm of epic magnitude, but he only stared at her, shell-shocked. "She already did."

Seven Death took a long breath, shaking her head like, *Girl, you are so in deep.* "If you uttered those words, then I am afraid there is nowhere you can hide. And as each lord awakens, you will be drawn back to your source of magic, you will betray your own friends, and you will join the lords, because it is what you were always meant to do."

"NO!" Ren pushed her chair back and stood. "I'd...I'd never do something like that."

"Ren is the purest of heart and—" The god's voice broke.

But Ren had already felt the Night Lords' magnetic power; she had already felt her shadow magic rising up and away from her. "How did Serena know any of this? How did she know where to find the lords or how to wake them?"

A.P. rounded out the details for Seven Death. "It *is* strange that anyone would know such a well-guarded secret."

"And *why* do it?" Ren cried. "What's Serena's angle? What's she got to gain?"

When the lords wake, they will wake to a queen.

All the air rushed out of Ren as the answer came to her. She placed her palms on the table to steady herself. "Serena thinks *she's* going to be queen," she mumbled. Which meant she didn't know about Ren's destiny.

"Who else knew this 'well-guarded secret' about the hidden shadow magic?" A.P. asked Seven Death.

The death lord hesitated, fumbled with her napkin. "I only delivered the report to one person."

"Who?" he demanded.

"You, Ah-Puch."

The teen god's face drained of color. He stood and fell against the wall, muttering words Ren couldn't make out.

"But...how...?" He clutched his hair. "I never would have divulged this.... It's this memory of mine. It's so...But how could I have forgotten something so important?"

The time rope warmed against Ren's throat. She grasped it, fighting back the tears that wanted to fall. Had A.P. sold or traded the report hundreds of years ago?

But there was no time to worry about how Serena had found out the lords' secret. Ren had a bigger problem that no one had yet mentioned. "If I really do join the lords like you say," she said quietly, "they will have access to time itself."

"I'll kill them all first!" A.P. thundered.

"I am afraid that isn't a choice," Seven Death said to him. "Not while their magic still lives in her."

Blow after blow after blow. Ren didn't know how many more she could take. "Why not?"

Seven Death swung her gaze slowly back to the godborn witch. "Killing them would mean also killing pieces of you. Who knows what will and won't survive? You are tied to them now, don't you see? *You* are the prophesied queen."

Ren had never felt so alone, so trapped. So...

The walls were closing in, the roof was collapsing, the freeze was coming, and all she could do was sit on this retired death lord's veranda and reel.

Pull it together, Ren. Now! So what that the rules and circum-stances have changed! This is still your quest.

"Then why did the Prince Lord let me go?" she asked, claw-ing away at the questions, searching for any shred of an answer she could find.

Seven Death's gaze wandered to the garden. "They must awaken at least five lords for the circle to be complete."

"*Five?!*" Ren shouted. "What happened to nine?"

Waving her hand nonchalantly, Seven Death said, "Majority rules."

"That only gives us two days," A.P. snarled. He threw back his head and squeezed his eyes closed. "This changes everything."

Ren understood. A.P. would never bless a battle with Serena and the Lords of Night now, not if it might harm Ren in any way. Which meant there was only one course of action: They would have to go through the Maze of Nightmares to the Dark Mercado. To retrieve the one thing that mattered. The object that would return the Lords of Night to their slumber.

The Obsidian Blade.

32

Ren didn't want to do it. But she had to tell her friends *JK—plans have changed.*

Back at the safe house, A.P. left her to it, saying he didn't want to be there for the drama.

Marco paced, his eyes wandering along the floor. "Night Prophecy? Gods, I hate prophecies."

Ren could only nod.

"You're a . . . a . . ." Edison's eyes grew two sizes. He stammered, unable to get out the word that Ren knew was on the tip of his tongue.

"Queen?" Monty said. "Should we bow or something?"

"NO!" Ren cried. "It's just a prophecy, a title—it doesn't mean anything."

Marco harrumphed. "Only that you're going to side with the enemy. Man, this sucks."

"Not unless I can help it, Marco," Ren said with a heavy heart. *And I only have two days to stop that from happening.*

"This isn't just about you and your magic," Marco spat. "This is about that time rope, too! That thing is a . . . a . . . kick-butt weapon. We can't ever let them get their hands on it, Ren."

"Can't you talk to your mom about it?" Edison said, his voice miles away from the harshness of Marco's. "Give it to her for safekeeping?"

Ren said, "Like all magic, the rope has rules. Once she gave it to me, it became mine. No one can take it from me, and I can't give it back."

"But you could give it to someone else, right?" Monty said.

Ren had already thought about this option. But that would mean giving up her connection to Pacific, to time, to a power she had only begun to explore. During her SHIHOM training this past summer, she had practiced connecting to her Maya power over and over, but it was like she couldn't get past the shadow magic. As if the two magics couldn't coexist inside one body. She knew it was selfish of her, but she couldn't abandon the hope that she could control both someday.

"Listen," Ren said gently. "You guys don't have to go to the maze *or* the mercado with me. I know it's—"

"This quest seriously bites," Marco huffed. "And quit telling me what to do." Then he blew out of the room.

Yeah, it does bite, Ren thought. *Big-time. But I didn't choose this. I didn't know it was going to turn into this complicated web of deceit . . . and terrible truths.* Something about this thought left her feeling empty and vulnerable and scared. She was supposed to be the leader, but that was when she thought the quest was one thing and not *this. But doesn't a commander lead all the time?* she wondered. *No matter what the mission is?*

Edison clapped loudly, startling Ren out of her thoughts. "Okay, no más funk," he said. "Things could be worse."

"They could?" Monty asked like she didn't believe him.

"Things can always be worse," Edison said. "And look, it's not like we have zero options. We've got the Maze of Nightmares, and I don't know about you, but I'm super up for the challenge. I saw this movie once where the hero was in a no-win situation, ya know? Like the chips were way down. And he had to make a choice—walk away or die trying."

"What did he do?" Ren said.

"Oh, well, he, uh . . . He died," Edison said, rubbing the back of his neck. "That was a really terrible example. Let me think of another one with a better ending."

Ren couldn't help it—maybe it was the expression on the demon's face, or maybe it was the absurdity of it all, or maybe she just needed to let out all the tension that had coiled so tight in her spine she thought she might break in half. A small bubble of laughter escaped her mouth, then two or three more, until she was busting up, holding her belly, fighting for air. And before she knew it, Monty and Edison were laughing, too. It was a good moment there in the safe house with the not-bear watching. The kind Ren hoped to remember for a long time.

But, as with all good moments, reality dove in headfirst.

Monty stood taller and adjusted her bow. "I'm here for the quest no matter what it is." Ren could almost understand Monty's desire to finish this—it was the only way for her to claim her magic and the arrows. But Edison? What was he getting out of it?

"Thanks, Monty."

Edison thrust out his hand for Ren to shake. "Me too. No matter what kind of ending it is."

After Ren showered, she found some clothes Citla had laid out for her on an oversize bed a with deep purple velvet cover. There were three pairs of leggings: blue, green, and black, and four choices for the top: two black hoodies and two gray long-sleeved tees.

A dark and twisted thought ballooned in her mind: *What if this is the last outfit I ever wear?*

"Do you always keep clothes in every size?" Ren asked as Citla whisked her old ones away.

"Ah-Puch leaves nothing to chance. And yes, he keeps an entire selection for any guests he might have," Citla went on. "Of course, over the years we've scrambled to keep up with the latest fashion choices. Would you prefer something else? Maybe a cowboy hat and some chaps to go with your boots?" Then, with narrowed eyes, she added, "A crown?"

Ren stared at the mountain spirit, trying to decide if she was being playful or serious or something in between. "I'll never wear a crown."

"I hope not," Citla said. "I certainly hope not."

Ren had just put on the leggings and tee when her phone buzzed. It was a text from Marco.

I'm no good at good-byes. Had to take off. See ya.

Ren sank onto the bed, her heart and spirits sinking lower. She read the message again, not believing he would leave when she needed him most.

She felt a stab of anger. And the more she thought about Marco abandoning her without even a good-bye, the more her fury grew. Dark shapeless shadows surrounded Ren, their power surging through her.

"How could I ever have trusted someone called the son of war?" she hissed.

It turned out there were four entrances to the Maze of Nightmares, each located at the end of one of the cosmic roads: north, south, east, and west. But Ah-Puch had destroyed them all to prevent anyone from infiltrating the underground and finding out what he'd been up to. Yet, being the conniving god he was, he'd kept a private entrance just in case.

It was located in the Actun Tunichil Muknal cave in Belize.

"Also, known as ATM," Ah-Puch explained.

"Like dinero?" Monty said.

A.P. didn't answer.

Monty went on and on about Belize, but the god squashed her excitement. "You'll never see Belize."

An hour later, Ren understood why. They stepped through a gateway straight into the cave.

Ren felt the chill first, and then came the smell of death.

"This is an intricate cave system," Ah-Puch said, guiding them deeper into the cavern, past sprawled skeletons.

"Are these real?" Monty asked, sidestepping the long-dead.

"Sacrifices from hundreds of years ago," A.P. said casually. "And before you pin it on me, I didn't do it, okay? People always blame the god of death, but guess what? There are other dark forces, and other gods who required sacrifices."

"Gross," Monty mumbled.

They came to a chamber where another skeleton was laid out on the ground. "That's the famous Crystal Prince," A.P. said. "His bones have calcified, so he shimmers. Hence the name."

The bones did sparkle, and they were sort of beautiful.

"Was he another sacrifice?" Ren asked.

A.P. shook his head. "No, he was just a seventeen-year-old kid who owed me a favor, so now he guards the maze."

"Seems like more than a favor," Edison muttered.

At the same moment, the bones shifted and changed shape, forming a ... boy. He had smooth brown skin, a wide jaw, dangerous eyes, and the kind of hair that could make him TikTok famous. Well, if it weren't for the board shorts and muscle shirt, which made him look more like a lifeguard than the guardian of a killer maze.

With a snarl, he thundered, "Who are you?"

Wow, his voice is really deep.

"Why are you in my cave?"

"Stop with the theatrics!" The god's shoulders sagged. "It's me, Ah-Puch, just looking depressingly younger. Long story. Time travel, bad year, blah, blah, blah."

The Crystal Prince blinked, and his mouth widened in a big surprised O. "My lord," he said, bowing and scraping. "You look so ... so ..."

A.P. held up a hand. "Please do not say it."

The prince's gaze swung from Edison to Monty to Ren, studying them. He sniffed the air. "You brought a demon here?"

How did he know? Ren wondered. Maybe it was a dead thing. And then she wondered, if Edison was half demon, did that make him half-dead? Or only *of* the dead?

Edison scanned the cave, tilted his head back to get a better look at the craggy ceiling.

"We're here for the maze," Ren said.

"The maze," the Crystal Prince repeated like he had forgotten his role. "Oh ... yes! The Maze of Nightmares." He threw a hard glance at Ah-Puch. "You left me here for the last four hundred years. Do you have any idea how boring this place is?"

"I was otherwise occupied."

"Yeah, I heard. Locked away by the gods, huh?" The prince shook his head. "That's a raw deal right there. I would have testified on your behalf, but they never asked me."

Ren could never forget that A.P. had spent four hundred years imprisoned in a piece of paper before Zane released him. Apparently, Ah-Puch had been trying to take over the world and it hadn't gone so well.

"The gods don't do trials," A.P. growled. "You know that."

The Crystal Prince smirked. "Right. Of course. I just meant that if they did ... Well, I've got your back." He threw in a smile at the last second.

"Good," A.P. said, "because I need you to take them to the mouth of the maze." He gestured at Ren, Edison, and Monty.

"A Death Walk?" The prince smiled so big Ren worried he might split his face in two. "You betcha! I haven't done anything exciting since—"

"Death Walk?" Edison echoed.

"I named it," the prince said proudly. "Because the maze *is* a death trap. So yeah, you're basically walking to your demise. Pretty smart, yeah?"

"Just make sure they get there safely," A.P. commanded.

"Get to our deaths safely?" Monty whispered.

"Wait a second," Ren said as understanding dawned. "You mean *we*."

"I won't be coming with you." A.P. dropped the words like a live bomb.

"What?! Why not?" Ren said. "Don't go all Marco on me."

A.P.'s gaze was intense—not the eyes of a kid, or even a god. More like a forgotten monster, and it sent chills down

Ren's legs. "If I were to step foot on its soil," he said, "the maze would instantly collapse on us all, so no, Ren, I won't be reducing your chances by tagging along." He swept a hand over his black hair. "But I will tell you this—don't believe what you see, do the unexpected, take the route that seems the wrong one. Do the exact opposite of what your instincts tell you. The maze loves twisting reality, so to succeed you will have to beat it at its own game. Do you understand?"

Ren didn't know if she was built to throw her instincts out the window—they had always been her guiding light.

Monty ticked off the rules on her finger. "Do the unexpected, games, twisted reality. Got it. I'm totally down for this. I once did a simulation with a blindfold where I had to—"

Edison threw Monty a look that said *Not now.*

The god turned to Ren. "Listen, the maze walls shift, and fast. So be quick."

Ren felt like she was made entirely of water—the sea. With unpredictable currents.

Edison pressed his hand more firmly against the cave walls. Light radiated around his fingers. "Whoa! That's a ton of energy in there."

"Godly energy!" A.P. groaned, pushing him aside. "Listen up, children. You have never seen anything like what you are about to see. You will be tempted to ask stupid questions and ooh and aah and make useless comments. Don't. The stairs value silence above all else. If you speak, you will lose your voice, and if you touch anything you will lose a hand. Are we clear?"

"Except for me," the prince put in. "Since I'm your ghost guide, I can talk all I want."

Ren's nerves were ricocheting all over her body, thumping against her bones and organs, racing through her blood at a top-notch speed that screamed excitement or terror, she wasn't sure which.

"Swear," Monty said. "Not a peep from me."

After Edison and Ren agreed to the god's terms, he stepped back. The Crystal Prince said, "Follow me to the stairs and take them down into the darkness. At the bottom, you'll find a door that will lead you to the maze."

Edison was nodding.

"Stick together in the maze," Ah-Puch went on. "If you manage to get through in one piece and make it to the market, you will be tempted by all its magic. You will want to stop and linger. Don't. As a matter of fact, to have the best chance of finding the blade, you will have to separate. You will only have one hour."

"Oof." Monty grimaced. "Couldn't we have two?"

"Why only an hour?" Ren said.

"After that, the market will get inside you. It will sense your magic," Ah-Puch said begrudgingly, like he didn't want to admit that his brilliant security tactics were now coming back to bite him. "And when it does, it will use all of its power to keep you, to possess what you have."

"How will we find the blade?" Edison flexed his fingers. "What does it look like?"

The god said, "You don't *look* for a thing of magic—you *feel* it. Sense it."

"But it's a whole *market* full of magic!" Ren argued.

Ah-Puch huffed impatiently. "It's entirely impossible to

teach the ways of gods to . . ." He hesitated. "The Obsidian Blade will know you are seeking it. It will make itself known to you."

Monty frowned. "Why would it do that?"

Slowly, almost imperceptibly, Edison began to nod. His chest rose and fell with rapid (excited?) breaths. "Because it doesn't like being locked away. It wants out . . . to be used."

"Bingo!" A.P. said, pointing to the demon like he'd just won a car on a game show.

There were so many moving parts, so many directions and rules, and yet this one was simple. *The magic wants out.*

"And when we find the Obsidian Blade," Ren said, "how do we actually get it? Like, do we steal it or trade or . . . ?"

"You won't know until that exact moment," A.P. said. "That's the hard part. There's no way to plan ahead. Whichever one of you finds it, or whom *it* finds, you'll have to improvise."

Monty said, "I can totally improvise. I've been doing community theater since I was three. Last year, I even did a four-minute monologue. The audience went crazy."

"And one more thing," the god said, ignoring the hunter. "No using magic in the market. You'll give yourself away, create chaos, and very likely earn a nonrefundable one-way ticket to Xib'alb'a."

Every word from the god's mouth felt like a brick laid on Ren's chest. She hadn't realized she had started pacing. "Just to be clear," she said, "we're going into a maze of nightmares that will try to turn our brains to mush, and if . . . *when* we get through that, we're going to face some market that sounds like its own brand of monster, and we won't have any of our powers to protect ourselves while we're looking for a magical object that isn't supposed to exist."

"Don't forget the price we have to pay," Monty said.

There was a moment—a second, or maybe two—when Ren wanted to give up, throw in the towel, and let the Lords of Night win. To be their queen, let them have whatever they were after. Maybe they just wanted to live in peace? She might have clung to this hope if she hadn't felt the dark power of her/their shadows. If the Prince Lord's eyes hadn't glittered when she'd suggested that the lords just wanted to overthrow the gods. But then he had said, "That would be wholly unoriginal," like that wasn't their plan at all. Well, whatever it was, Ren was certain of one thing—it centered on power and who had it and who was going to wield it. Plus, knowing her magic came from the lords, feeling it pulse beneath her skin, she was certain they weren't here to play nice.

"Very well." Ah-Puch tugged a long black chain from beneath his shirt. Dangling from the end of it was a small gold orb, which he pressed into the wall. "Why can't anything ever be easy?" he muttered as the cave wall cracked, groaned, and split down the center. Blue light poured from an opening no wider than two feet.

"Shall we?" The Crystal Prince gestured for the trio to enter.

Monty and Edison went first, leaving Ren with the god. "We're going to make it," she said to him, drawing on her deeply held belief that positivity is half the solution to any problem.

A.P. didn't flinch. "You have the best team."

"I know." She went in for a hug, but the god inched back out of her reach. Did he really think pretending he didn't care was

going to make this any easier? "Seriously?" Ren said, not caring
if she looked foolish. "If I'm walking into a deathtrap, then the
least you can do is hug me."

She didn't wait for his response. Instead, she threw her arms
around the god's skinny waist. He didn't move, and just when
she thought he was going to peel her off him, he gently kissed
the top of her head and whispered something into her ear she
didn't catch before he pulled back and cleared his throat.

"Look for the golden arrows. They'll lead you to the market
exit," he said to the group. "But when you escape, there's no telling where you'll land."

With a half-hearted, hopeful smile, Ren said, "But you'll
find us."

"I'll find you."

Then she stepped through the wall.

33

The Crystal Prince guided the crew into a dim corridor lit only by flickering candles that hung from the low ceiling. Edison had to duck a few times to avoid singeing his hair.

Lengthy vines covered the walls, pulsing with life. They gently swayed from side to side like they were sniffing out the squad.

Monty was a broken record of enthusiasm. "Whoa. Cool. Whoa. Cool." Ren couldn't help but smile, remembering that not long ago she used to be the same way. *When you go on your first quest, you don't know what to expect, and everything is exciting and new,* she thought. *Then reality sets in and you see things you'd rather forget, and they get inside and change you.*

"This is the most excitement I've had in at least a hundred years," the Crystal Prince said. "Last time it was to deliver a piece of magic to the maze. The thing sucked it in like a black hole."

So the Crystal Prince was not only the guardian but the delivery guy, too.

"Like, what have you delivered?" Ren asked.

"You'll see when you get there. *If* you get there." He chuckled.

"Meaning you don't actually know," Edison said. His tone was curious and not at all accusing, but Ren winced anyway. She knew it would be misinterpreted.

"I wouldn't *want* to know, demon. That kind of darkness eats away at you." He snapped his fingers. "Oh yeah. You already know that, don't you?"

Edison was quiet. He lowered his gaze, and Ren wanted to nudge him, tell him not to let the ghost get away with being a rude jerk.

Just as she was about to come to Edison's defense, the demon said, "Must be hard being a ghost locked in a cave. I'm sorry, man."

That instantly defused the situation. The Crystal Prince hesitated, then nodded. "So hard. And not many people come in here, so I don't even have anyone to haunt."

"But your bones are so shimmery," Monty said brightly.

"And ghosts can walk through things," Edison put in. "You never have to worry about getting hurt, and you're some of the nicest people I know."

"Oh yeah? You know a lot of them?"

"They're really the only friends I've ever had."

"Hey!" Monty cried.

Edison laughed, flicked a glance at Ren. "Until now, that is."

Soon they hooked a right and then a left, and with each new turn, more candles vanished and more vines dissolved, until almost complete darkness overtook them.

If it hadn't been for a strange golden glow coming from the ground, Ren wouldn't have been able to see two inches in front of her.

They came to a dead end. The dark wall was slick with some kind of liquid that oozed down its surface and pooled into a tar-like black substance.

"The maze is through this door," the Crystal Prince said, "and down a steep hundred stairs that will feel like thousands. You can't speak until your feet have touched every stair."

Everyone nodded somberly.

"You will want to take shortcuts and skip some steps, but be warned—if the soles of your feet do not touch each and every stair, you will not be permitted to enter the maze."

More nodding. Ren could tell he'd given this speech many times. He sounded more like a tour guide than a guardian of a magical maze.

"Once you enter, there is no turning back."

"How many people have you taken on a Death Walk?" Ren was suddenly curious.

"Mmm . . . let's see . . . Maybe fifty? Ah-Puch used to use it as punishment." He smiled, then turned suddenly serious. "Just don't scream. The maze *loves* fear and screaming and all that."

"Have you ever heard of anyone making it out?" Edison asked.

The prince hesitated. "You really want to know?"

Everyone nodded, even though Ren was pretty sure she *didn't* want to know. Negative thinking always equaled bad energy, and bad energy always equaled unwanted consequences.

The ghost said, "Back in the old days, yeah. But now, with so much darkness consuming it all, uh . . . no. No one's made it out in over a century."

Edison clapped him on the back, smiling like he was about to hand him a good-citizenship certificate. "Until today."

"Attaboy," the ghost said, moving to the right to make room for the trio.

Ren took the lead, stepping over the threshold first. When she looked back, the ghost was already gone. Edison and Monty were right behind her, and she had the strangest sensation—a prickling of her skin that reached her scalp. Someone else was here.

She descended the stairs into utter darkness. And with each step, the sensation grew stronger. The prickling was now like cold fingers tap-tap-tapping her arms and legs and the back of her neck.

It was enough to make her want to jump out of her own skin.

Then came the low, menacing voice. She knew it immediately.

I go where you go, the Smoking Mirror said.

Ren paused. Edison bumped into her. He gave her arms a brief squeeze. She'd only known him a day, but the gesture told her *You can do this*. She *had* to do this.

Ren couldn't speak, couldn't tell the dumb Smoking Mirror to get lost. But maybe ... Since godborns could communicate telepathically through touch, maybe it would work now.

Go away!

She paused, wondered if the lord had heard. She'd tried to scream it as loudly as possible in her mind.

There was a dark laugh.

As long as you are afraid, I will be here.

What does that mean?

Your fear is a gateway, the lord said with way too much pleasure.

Why would you tell me that? But what Ren was really asking was, why would he show his hand?

Does it matter? You can never be rid of me because you will always be afraid.

A heavy dread filled Ren. She knew the lord was right. But how could she ever control her fear? There was just so much of it. Fear of the quest going bad. Fear of her friends getting hurt. Fear of failure. Fear, fear, fear.

As they continued their journey through the now-silent dark, the air was chilly one second, hot the next. And it smelled like a bag of putrefied potatoes.

Ren was woozy, her skin felt flushed.

Wishing there was a handrail, she counted each step, trying to focus on anything other than the Smoking Mirror.

Ninety-eight.

He's not here.

Ninety-nine.

It's just a fear echo.

One hundred.

But I am here, he said.

When she reached the last stair, Ren stepped onto what felt like a bouncy, foamy surface.

Soon Monty and Edison joined her in the glow of a faint light coming from beneath a door.

Monty pointed to her mouth and raised her brows as if to ask whether it was safe to talk.

Ren figured since they were down the stairs they were in the clear, but she thought she should be the one to make sure. Her voice came out a cautious whisper. "Testing, one, two, three." A.P. had said if anyone spoke too soon, they would lose

their voice; she was about to find out. She cleared her throat
and said louder, "Testing."

Nothing happened. *So much for the Crystal Prince's "Death
Walk,"* thought Ren.

"Phew!" Monty let out a long exhale and fanned her face
with her hand. "Did you smell that place? I thought I was going
to barfola all over."

Edison pressed his hands against the door. Light bloomed
from his fingertips. He closed his eyes, took a deep breath.
"There's a ton of magic behind this door. It's cold and dark
and . . ."

"And what?" Ren asked.

"Hungry."

"Oh," Monty said. "Well, that doesn't sound terrifying! *Psh.*
Keep the bad news to yourself, Edison."

With her hand on the knob, Ren asked, "You guys ready?"

"Wait!" Monty blurted just as Ren was about to open the door.

"What?"

"We should make a pact," Monty said. "It's what all good
warriors do. They swear to protect their friends with their lives.
They swear to have their backs. And they swear that if something happens and one of them doesn't make it, the rest will
go on without—"

"I'm not leaving anyone behind," Ren said, feeling like she
might barf all over Edison's shoes. "No matter what."

"You're not thinking about the mission," Monty said. "You
have to keep your eye on the prize. We have to complete the
quest."

Was she Marco's distant cousin or something? But Ren knew the hunter was right—she understood the cost if they chose one person over the many. And yet Ren couldn't bring herself to accept it.

"I swear to protect you," Edison said, his eyes focused on Ren before they swept to Monty. "To have your back. And if that means leaving you behind..."

He didn't finish the oath, and Ren was glad. She hated the words, hated the sound of them coming from the demon.

"I won't do it," Edison whispered.

Ren felt a surge of warmth flutter across her chest and up her throat. "Me neither."

Monty groaned. "You guys make terrible warriors."

With that, Ren opened the door to the Maze of Nightmares.

34

A great gust of frigid air blasted them.
Monty gasped.

Edison threw his arms over his face. Ren instinctively snapped her head down and squeezed her eyes closed. A moment later, when the air went still, she slowly looked up.

A massive formation stood before them. As tall as the sky and as wide as the horizon. A pyramid unlike any Ren had ever seen, made entirely of mirrors.

Light and shadow rippled across their reflections. The trio looked small, dwarfed by the maze and the sky of blue-and-black swirls. Purple lightning flashed. Winds screeched from a distant place.

Slowly, an entrance materialized. Ren could only see darkness beyond it.

Monty clutched her arrows. Edison stared in awe, as if he were taking mental measurements of the structure's monstrous scale.

Together they entered the Maze of Nightmares. Ren wasn't sure what she had expected—a maze of hedges? Cornstalks? At least that would have been something identifiable, something familiar.

Inside there was a dim light, like the sky just before dawn.

The ceiling was low, and the walls were shifting panels, changing direction as if they were on rotating platforms.

"Watch out!" Monty shouted as a panel came right at them. Everyone drop-rolled, slipping under the partition. They ended up in a small chamber at the edge of a waterway, like the first stage of a theme-park ride. An empty rowboat bobbed on the current.

Everywhere Ren looked, she saw her and her friends' reflections. "It's like a house of mirrors."

"Except these mirrors want to slice us in two," Monty added.

Ren scanned the area. The only way out was by boat. "Looks like we're taking a cruise," she said, stepping into the dinghy. Monty and Edison did likewise.

Ren took one oar, Edison the other, and together they paddled along the dark surface. The air was still and heavy with the smell of vanilla.

Black Flower. The darkness is where all the flavor comes from.

Dip, row. Dip, row.

"Hey, Eddie," Monty said. "How about a vanquisher bubble to protect us from the killer walls?"

"Don't think that'll work."

"Why not?" Ren asked.

"Remember when I told you I draw on energy?" Edison said, rowing at a nice, smooth pace, unlike Ren, whose movements were more like jerks and twitches. "Well, this place is loaded with the dark kind. Like bad. I've only ever used dark energy once, and it was sort of a disaster."

"Disaster how?" Ren thought the details were important.

"I blew up a couple things, and . . ." He shook his head.

"And what?" Ren said.

"It's nothing."

"Seems like something," Monty sang, perched in the back of the boat, looking from side to side like they were on an It's a Small World tour.

The demon twisted his mouth. "It's just that . . . I think the darkness made me sick. Maybe there was too much or . . . I don't know, but it wasn't nearly a tenth the size of this place, so . . ."

"If you use your magic here, you could get sick again." Ren finished his thought.

Edison exhaled sharply. "I don't mind that as much as . . . It's hard to explain, but it took a while for the darkness to get out of me."

Oh. OH.

A few moments of silence passed. Edison said, "These aren't really mirrors. They're made from a rare substance found in Xib'alb'a. Sort of like crystal, but not."

"Is it poisonous?" Ren said. "Lethal? Toxic, or any other thing that could kill us?"

Edison hesitated. "No, but supposedly it shows you a future."

"What do you mean *a*?"

"In this maze, we'll take different turns, right?" Edison said. "Like in life—the turns determine where you end up. And the reflections show you the most likely result based on your current path."

"Sounds kind of woo-woo," Monty said.

Ren was taking tiny, short breaths, waiting for the nightmare part of the maze to kick in as they came to a crossroads. Right or left? Left or right? Which path to choose? Which future?

The massive walls began to grind into gear again, slowly, like a Ferris wheel just getting started.

"Which way, Ren?" Edison asked.

Ren was studying the area when her gaze locked on her refection. But instead of seeing her usual self, she saw another version. She was wearing a crown made of jade and shadow, and her eyes were nearly black, her smile glittering. And she was driving a green dagger through Edison.

Ren shrieked.

Edison snatched her oar before she dropped it in the water. "Are you okay?"

She couldn't get out the words. Couldn't erase the image from her brain. She dared another glance, but the evil-queen picture was gone. "Did you . . . ? Did you see that?"

"See what?" Monty asked.

"The maze is trying to get into your head," Edison said. "Remember?"

Don't believe what you see. That's what A.P. had said. But Edison had been clear. *The reflections show you the most likely result based on your current path.*

Mostly likely. Most likely.

As if he knew what she was thinking, Edison said, "Despite what you just saw, you can still make decisions, Ren. There are multiple possible outcomes."

"But the Night Prophecy . . ." Ren barely got the words out. She swallowed the lump in her throat, wishing away that image. *I'll never be that queen. Never,* she resolved.

"We're going to stop it," Monty insisted. "Swear."

"Thanks, Monty." Ren believed the hunter, trusted in her loyalty and good nature. If she could handpick a little sister, it would be Monty. Always Monty.

"You decide," Edison said, barely above a whisper.

Ren hesitated, caught her breath, looked left, then right. She considered the god's words.

Do the exact opposite of what your instincts tell you.

Her instincts told her to go left. She was about to turn right when she noticed Edison's eyes on a mirror. All color drained from his face.

"Edison!" Ren shook his arm. "Don't look. It's wrong, remember? It's not real!"

The demon's body went rigid.

"Edison?" Ren's voice was small.

"Can demons go into shock?" Monty asked. "'Cause he definitely looks like he's in shock."

Slowly, Edison turned, his gaze fastened on Ren's. "You . . . You were a queen . . . and you killed me."

"The maze is playing us against each other!" Ren cried. When she'd first heard the name Maze of *Nightmares*, she thought it would be like a house of horrors, with a spooky mist, crazy clowns, and shrieking winds. But this was so much worse, because this maze really did get into your head. It filled you with doubt and brought out your innermost fears. And worse, it showed you a possible future—one you didn't know you were galloping toward because there were too many paths to choose along the way.

Edison's mouth turned up in a forced smile. "I know" was all he whispered.

"Go right," Ren finally commanded, dragging the oar through the water with a fresh anger that fed her godborn strength. The new passage was even narrower than the first, and shorter, too. A few seconds later, they came to an eddy where the river branched off in three directions.

The water swirled, forcing the little boat to dip and rock. Ren had been white-water rafting a few times, where the river's strong current carried you and all you could do was go along for the ride. But here she didn't want to give in to it.

A sudden vortex spun the boat.

"Row!" Edison shouted.

Ren paddled hard, digging her oar into the river, trying to control the direction of the boat, but it was useless. She threw a shadow platform under the boat to buy them some time, but for what? They couldn't sit here forever. But the thought of getting sucked into a nightmare vortex was *not* on the agenda.

The time rope pulsed and warmed against Ren's throat. In the mirrors' reflections, the chain glowed and glimmered, then flashed like lightning, blinding Ren for a few seconds.

When she looked back, Ren saw her mom, the goddess of time. And she didn't look happy at all.

35

"Pacific!" Ren shouted. Her mother floated above
the water—she was wearing a black fur cape, its hood draped
over her unearthly beautiful face.

"That's the goddess of time," Monty said, pointing.

"Oh, child," Pacific said, dropping the hood. Her white gold-
streaked locks spilled over her shoulders. "You are always in
trouble." She raised a single finger, and the current slowed; the
boat stopped rocking.

Ren didn't know what to say. *Great timing—no pun intended?
Hey, Mamita? How's the goddess life?*

"Are you here to save us?" Monty asked excitedly, like being
rescued by a Maya goddess was one of her life goals.

Edison stared at the goddess, ran a hand over his messy
hair, and straightened his shirt.

"No, I am not here to save you," Pacific sneered. "I'm here
for the rope. It is calling to me."

Yeah, thanks for the support, Ren thought. And then the
weight of her mother's words came down on her with the force
of a tidal wave. "Wait. You can't be here for the rope. You . . . You
said I can never give it back."

"That doesn't it mean it doesn't call to me. And here you are
in this dreadful place, about to meet your demise, and I will not
have my rope destroyed because you are irresponsible."

Ren couldn't believe what she was hearing. "Irresponsible? Seriously? I'm the only one trying to save everyone." Her mom clearly didn't know what was at stake. "The Lords of Night..."

Pacific raised a single lithe hand. "I care not. Do you know how many takeover attempts there are each and every day? It's exhausting. We cannot get involved with them all."

"But the Aztec Lords—we think they're connected to the Unknowns," Edison said, enunciating every word like he was trying to make an impact.

Ren waited, watched for any signal that the word *Unknowns* had unnerved her mom, but there was nothing except for a smooth, striking face and sparkling eyes the color of the deep blue sea.

"Also," Pacific went on, "I've been absorbed in a more important matter. I'm still puzzling over why the time travel affected the gods. For creation's sake—I am the goddess of time. You would think *I* could determine the truth!"

She extended her hand and the time rope slipped off Ren's neck and floated toward Pacific. Ren's heart sank. The goddess stroked the rope as it split into individual strands, wiggling through the air like worms, dancing around the goddess in brilliant flashes of gold.

Thanks a lot, Ren wanted to say. The time rope had never shown *her* that kind of respect.

"What's it doing?" Edison asked.

"It's communicating with me." The goddess caressed the rope with her cheek. "Yes, my darling. I missed you, too. Oh, did she?"

Great. So now the rope was a tattletale?

"Well, if you're here just to visit your...*pet*," Ren said, "then can you at least get us through this maze, or blow it up or something? We have to get to the Dark Mercado."

Pacific gave her daughter a tenuous smile. "I am afraid that is impossible. This maze was created by Ah-Puch. One god cannot destroy what another has created. Perhaps I could go to the council, but that would take time, and, well..." She glanced around. "It looks like you are running out of that very quickly."

If Ren didn't know any better, she would have thought that Pacific was completely and totally entertained by her predicament.

"Then make that...that chain work," Ren said, her frustration mounting. "Show me how to stop time."

"Even if I could," said the goddess, "time is unbound here. The rope has no power in this bleak, horrible place. But be cheered, daughter. I am working on another timepiece for you. It's not easy. It took me eons to create the rope from the universe's power. I can't just snap my fingers. Now, you must think your way out of this."

The frustration exploded. "I can't!"

"You are the daughter of time," Pacific growled. "I am of the greatest intellect and imagination. None of the other gods even considered that we needed a marker of time for the human world to function. It was I!"

Unexpectedly, her gaze fell on Monty. She studied the hunter like a shiny new thing she wanted to devour. "A Jaguar Warrior..." she whispered.

How did the goddess know? Then Ren remembered that her

mother had fallen for Ren's dad, an Aztec brujo, so she knew more than she let on.

"The blood of King..." The goddess's sea-colored eyes flashed gold. She turned to Ren. "I will leave you with one bit of information."

Everyone stared at the goddess, waiting as the time rope floated back to Ren and once again encircled her throat.

Pacific pulled her hood over her head and said, "The maze abhors indecision. The longer you linger, the more indecisive you are, the angrier and hungrier it becomes. So, the answer is obvious." She flashed a knowing smile. "Give the maze what it wants."

And then she vanished.

"Seriously?!" Ren shouted. Her voice echoed in the chamber. "That's it?! Give the maze what it wants? What kind of advice is that?" Having a godly parent wasn't at *all* as cool as it sounded.

Go against your instincts.

"Maybe she means to *make* decisions," Monty guessed.

"That still doesn't get us out of here safely," Edison said. "We could make the wrong choice too easily."

The realization was slow at first—nearly unbelievable until it bloomed so big Ren couldn't contain it. Her belly fluttered with excitement as she said, "Edison, I need you to throw as much of the vanquisher as you can at these walls."

"I already told you, the darkness—"

"Use its energy against itself and don't take it in," Ren said. Edison caught on. "Got it."

The walls began to close in. The three paths that had once floated before them were now just one. The water churned.

"Looks like it took away our choices," Monty said, her bow poised, arrow nocked.

"Monty, when I tell you, let the arrows fly," Ren commanded. "Do you understand? Let them all fly!"

Edison looked concerned. "Ren..."

"Just trust me."

Edison set down his oar, raised his hands, and with a deep breath, he released his magic. Two hollow silvery spheres flew from his palms, swelling into a wave of energy that sped toward the walls.

The walls didn't break; they didn't collapse. They sucked in his magic like it was nothing. At the same moment, Ren hurled every ounce of her shadow magic at the maze.

"Now?" Monty shouted.

"Wait!" Ren said, cuing Edison to go again. Together they launched demon and bruja magic in a display of force and strength that felt more powerful than a rocket liftoff.

The walls quivered and swelled, sucking in the magic hungrily.

"Now!" Ren shouted to the hunter as she kept feeding her shadows to the maze.

Monty's arrows flew through the air, one after the other, with such speed that Ren wouldn't have been able to see them if it hadn't been for the blue whizzing past.

Onetwothreefourfive.

They shattered the bloated glass now overfed on magic.

The crack was louder than thunder. The world shook, and the maze came down wall by wall. Shards flew, slicing Ren's skin as the water rose higher and higher.

The maze collapsed into the black water, which swelled and crested in a massive wave.

Instantly, Ren threw up a shadow of protection, but Edison had beat her to it. His demon magic was all around them, a barrier of light. How had he made light when the only energy for him to draw on was darkness? It must have been the arrows, Ren thought, which were now safely back in Monty's quiver.

The trio stared in horror while the water churned violently, tossing them about like they were nothing more than a beach toy. They clung to the sides of the boat.

"What if the boat doesn't hold?" Ren shouted.

She thought she heard Edison say, "It won't."

The wave reached its peak, curled.

And here it came.

Down, down, down.

Ren braced herself, holding tight to Monty. "If it breaks—" she hollered, but there were no more words because the wave crashed with the boat, obliterating their magic.

Ren was sucked under, tossed up and down, thrashed from side to side.

In the struggle, she reached for her time rope. She didn't know why. Maybe it was instinctive; maybe it was desperate. Her lungs were going to explode. She needed air. She launched the glowing rope across the dark, praying to anyone who would listen, *Please get us out of this alive. Please get us out of this alive.*

A pulse of magic. There. Pushing at the water, breaking it apart like glass.

Edison.

Ren would recognize his brand of magic anywhere. There

was a hum to it, a barely there fluttering like a summer breeze sweeping across your skin. And it carried Ren to a moonlit shore. She rolled across sand as green as jade, then spit up dark water while on her hands and knees. As soon as her vision cleared, she scanned the beach for her friends. On the opposite end of the shore, she could make out a shimmering, ragged-edged black door floating in space.

Just then, Monty staggered out of the water like the weight of the entire maze was on her shoulders. Ren got to her feet, her legs nearly buckling. She pulled the hunter into a hug. "Are you okay?"

"I'm...a...Jaguar...Warrior," Monty said through chattering teeth. "Did you see my arrows fly? Did you see them?"

Ren nodded, but her eyes were on the water, searching among the chunks of the maze that bobbed on the surface.

"Where's Edison?"

Monty swiveled. "I...I thought he was with you. Hey, what's that door?"

Ren wasn't listening. Her heart pounded in her ears. *He's going to come out right now. Right now. Right now.*

"Ren...um...the door kinda looks like it's fading."

"We aren't leaving Edison." *What if he's too sick from the darkness to get out?*

Monty shuddered. "We said we wouldn't sacrifice the mission for anyone."

"I never made that promise, and I'm not made like that, Monty." Ren fought back tears. "I'm illogical and have a stupid big heart and—"

At the same moment, the ground began to tremble. Mirror

shards started rising out of the water. A cold terror washed over Ren's skin. "The maze..." she cried. "It's rebuilding itself!" Everything tilted, blurred, darkened.

"It's going to swallow us!" Monty shouted.

The hunter was right. They had to get to the door...now.

She grabbed Monty's arm, and they began to run. Ren pushed her legs faster, farther, and longer than she ever had. And with each footfall she thought of one thing—Edison.

When they reached the door, she spun. The dark maze was expanding toward them. A sharp and violent wind whipped across the shore.

All the air rushed from Ren's lungs with the words "We can't leave him."

"We have no other choice," said Monty, her voice trembling.

The doorknob was warm beneath Ren's touch. She knew that once she opened it, she'd never see Edison again. He'd be locked in the dark maze forever. How could she do that to him? She couldn't. Wouldn't.

"You have to open it," Monty said more firmly now.

Ren wasn't strong enough. She had never abandoned anyone. And yet here she was. She'd either save herself and the hunter, or—

"Hurry!" Monty cried. "The door's fading."

Ren's hand turned the knob, tears streaking her cheeks. Dim shadows floated around her. Her heart withered.

Then she sensed it. A flicker of magic. A familiar hum.

She whirled to see the demon stumbling out of the water. The maze was close behind, its darkness tugging at him. He pitched face-first into the green sand.

Ren bolted across the beach, grabbed him under his arms, and began to drag him toward the door, but he was deadweight, heavier than she could have ever imagined.

Monty was there in an instant. Her small hands pushed Ren's away as she lifted Edison into her arms like he was nothing more than a pillow.

Ren blinked in astonishment. "Monty?"

"No time to explain," the hunter said. "The door's vanishing. Run!"

The ragged wind screamed. It reached for them like it wanted nothing more than to drag them back into the Maze of Nightmares.

This time Ren didn't hesitate. Panting, she threw open the door to see a darker sky gleaming beyond. She ushered Monty in first since the hunter was cradling Edison. Once Monty was beyond the threshold, Ren moved to follow, but in her haste, she stumbled and lost her footing. She quickly righted herself and had begun to step over the threshold when the door shimmered and pulsed.

"Ren!" Monty screamed.

And before Ren could cross, the door evaporated.

36

Centeotl

There was no thunder.

No storm. No quaking earth. There was only a single breath. One. Then came the blinding light, layered with flecks of gold that clung to the lord's hair, his skin. He breathed in the light, drank it hungrily until it spilled from his mouth and onto the earth, spreading. The Maize Lord stood, staring at the golden seed in his hand. He smiled, blew a single breath on the kernel that was pulsing with life... until it shriveled and turned black as night.

He smiled, set the kernel on his tongue, and said, "I am ready."

37

Chilled and dazed, Ren stood alone in a barren landscape of ocher sand and blinding-white skies. The air was hot and dry. Gilded kernels of corn were scattered across the earth, glittering in the sun.

She heard the whistling first and then, "So you're the queen."

Ren whirled to find a guy with golden eyes and skin. His short dark hair was a bed of waves, their tips glittering. He looked about eighteen, older than the other lords had appeared to be.

"And you're Centeotl, the Maize Lord." Ren's heart thrashed against her ribs. That meant only one more of these gods had to awaken before she'd have to make good on the deal that she'd struck with the Prince Lord.

He frowned. "You have a small head."

Of all the things she'd been expecting him to say, it wasn't *that*. "What?"

"I am designing your royal wardrobe and your crown, so I thought I should introduce myself, take measurements, see what I'm working with." His expression went flat.

Ren's hands flew to her head. "I don't want your crown." *And I already know what it's going to look like.* No, that had only been a nightmare, she told herself. It wasn't real.

But what if it was?

The lord drew closer, keeping his golden gaze fixed on her head. "The Night Prophecy described you as taller, but I suppose I can work with what I have. And it doesn't matter what you want," he said, deepening his voice. "You have a destiny, and you have agreed to accept it. No exchanges. No returns. All sales are final."

Ren didn't have time to sit around talking about crowns and destinies, not when she needed to get back to her friends. "Okay, fine," she groaned. "Take your measurements. Then can I go?"

The lord sighed. "I have already taken them. Weren't you paying attention? A royal who doesn't pay attention spells trouble."

"Listen," Ren said, leaning into the situation with optimism. "What if I wasn't your queen? I mean, you guys don't want someone telling you what to do, right? You're gods! Gods don't need rules or rulers."

Centeotl laughed. He clutched his waist and shook his head like Ren had said the most hilarious thing he had heard in the last millennium. Catching his breath, he managed, "You think you are going to rule us?"

But don't queens rule? A prickling heat made Ren's palms itch. She could feel the shadows building, wanting to lunge at this guy. "Exactly," she pivoted. "So, no need for me to be queen."

"Oh, but"—the lord blinked—"didn't anyone tell you?" Then, with glittering mischievous eyes, he smiled. "Of course they didn't, because where would be the fun in that? You *will* be queen. You *will* fulfill the Night Prophecy."

Ren threw a hand on her hip, confused but doing her best to

look like she was in control. "Oh yeah?" *Oof... such a pathetic comeback.*

"A queen never says *yeah*, but we'll work on your training soon enough."

Ren knew her time with Mr. Corn Flakes was short, so she figured she might as well put it to good use. "Hey, when you send me back, make sure I land on the right side of the door."

The lord's expression screamed boredom. "You *were* on a threshold, so I suppose I can choose which side you land on."

"Well, if you want me to be queen, I think you should make sure I land on the correct side, the side I was heading to, because I was just about to get swallowed by—" Ren stopped herself. She didn't want to give too much away, encourage questions, reveal her plan.

The lord's gaze was cold and cutting even though he was smiling like they were besties. How much did he know? Had he seen where she was?

"Details, details," he sang. "I am all about the details. Why do you think I've been charged with your wardrobe and crown? But that isn't the point, is it, Renata Santiago? The point is sharp and precise like a needle, and thresholds can be quite menacing. This side or that, one step or two."

Ren was barely following this guy. What was he even saying?

"Before you go," he said, "do you prefer blue or green? With your dark hair and those blue eyes..."

"I, uh...Whatever."

"Whatever?!" he growled.

It did her no good to infuriate the guy, not when she needed him for the few inches that would make a difference to her quest.

"I mean, green is good," she said. "It's practically my favorite color."

"Yes, that is good," he said. "I'll go with blue. And one more thing. Perhaps the most *important* thing." His eyes glittered. "How do you feel about a jade-and-shadow crown?"

38

No. No. NOOOOO!

The lord's last words thrashed between Ren's ribs with an immediacy that made her feel sick. And all she could see was her nightmare vision, the one where she was wearing a jade-and-shadow crown as she drove a dagger into Edison.

Ren opened her eyes to a glittering starry sky. Silver bursts of light raced across the black canvas. A dozen moons floated above her. No, not moons. Planets, or at least they looked like planets—large and small and blue and gold, and fantastically beautiful.

The ground beneath her was made of cold wet sand.

"Ren?" Edison's voice found her. And her first thought was *I made it! I'm on the right side of the threshold. Or maybe the corn lord got confused.*

Ren blinked, brought the demon's face into focus.

"You should have gone through the door before us," he said, kneeling next to her. "That was really dumb."

Ren rolled onto her side and sat up slowly. "I wasn't going to leave you behind." Then she remembered the shape he'd been in when he was in the hunter's arms. "And you . . . You're okay?"

The demon nodded. His jaw was clenched, his eyes fixed. She glanced at his face and neck. He didn't have a single wound.

"How?"

"Demons can heal pretty fast," he said as his gaze fell to her chin. He unpocketed a handkerchief and handed it to her. "You're bleeding."

Ren touched the cloth to the gash on her chin, wincing at the pain. "You seriously carry a handkerchief?"

"I saw it in a few different movies and thought it was a smart and logical move." He gave a small shrug. "Think of all the ways a handkerchief could be useful ... I mean, aside from blood and tears and stuff."

Ren felt an overwhelming wave of gratitude or relief—she wasn't sure which, but it felt like a warm ball of energy that drew her to Edison. She had doubted A.P. when he brought the demon on board. But now? She saw that Edison was the perfect teammate and an even better friend. She could sense that he cared about her, too, that maybe together they could "imagine" a better world. That had to mean that the horrible image of her knifing him in the mirror was a false future. It couldn't be true. She wouldn't allow it, no matter what. He had to know that, right?

"That's going to be a killer scar," the hunter said to Ren, pulling her from her reverie.

The memories of their escape felt so far away and yet so close. "Monty," Ren said. "How did you ...? When did you get so strong?"

Monty chewed her bottom lip. "When a hunter faces grim— Is that the word? Or ominous? I can't remember, but when things are super bad, a hunter's strength grows. It's kinda like a switch that gets triggered, ya know? And once it's triggered, it's a part of you." She gave an uncertain smile. "I'd always wanted it to happen, thinking it would be so cool, like all Hercules, but now I think maybe it's not. I mean, I'm really glad I saved Edison, but..." She took a deep breath. "At least I know I'm not broken, right?"

"It's amazing," Edison put in. "And I owe you."

"But I didn't get a handkerchief," Monty teased.

Edison reached into his other pocket, pulling another free. "You want one?"

"What are you," Ren said with a laugh, "a hankie factory?"

Edison gave her a blank stare. "Hankie?"

"Maybe you should hang out with fewer ghosts and watch less TV," Monty said.

Ren got to her feet and was brushing herself off when the demon said, "I guess we can assume another lord is awake, right?"

"Yeah, the corn guy. What do you know about him?" she asked Monty.

The hunter twisted her mouth, pressing her lips together. "He's super private, but supposedly really detail-oriented, and gold is his favorite color. Was he creepy? Cute? Tall? Goth?"

"None of the above." It was then that Ren turned. Her eyes settled on a crumbling stone archway in the distance with a flashing pink neon sign: ENTER AT YOUR OWN RISK.

Beyond was a small mountain that seemed to be floating a few feet above the ground. Its black edges were ragged like torn paper. Dim lights flickered across its belly.

"That must be the Dark Market," Ren said with a trace of wonder in her voice.

A lightning bolt flashed across the sky, illuminating the

looming planets. Black clouds formed around the market. It
was almost like it knew intruders were coming.

"Listen," Edison said. "It might look impressive or magical or whatever, but I grew up around dead things. I know the
way darkness thinks and acts. It keeps things hidden, puts up
a false facade, waits until you're right up in its face, and then—
boom!—everything changes. So, don't make any quick moves
or do anything that screams *tourist*."

Ren pocketed the hankie. "Well, we only have an hour, so
we can't move like snails, either."

"And don't use any magic," Monty reminded them.

"How do we find each other?" Edison asked. "I mean, once
one of us finds the Obsidian Blade."

"Ah-Puch said there was an exit in the back of the market
and to follow the golden arrows," said Ren.

"Exit, golden arrows, got it," Monty said eagerly, counting
her own blue-feathered ones, which had obediently returned to
her quiver. "All accounted for. Can we go now?"

Together they stepped through the archway. A cool wind
carried them toward the floating mountain. They hauled themselves up onto its bottom edge, which was actually a stone path-
way that looked like it encircled the entire formation.

Ren lifted her gaze to the dozens of walled stairways that
zigzagged up the landscape.

"I'm going right," Monty said, clutching her quiver and bow.
"It's my lucky direction."

Edison said, "I guess I'll take center?"

Ren nodded, turning to the left. The stairs were steep,
way too steep to climb. So she grabbed a long, thick chain that

was fixed to the wall and hauled herself up until she reached a curved passage that ran in two directions. She took a right, inching slowly along the walkway's edge, following the glow of the dim lights. She could feel the hum of magic all around. Forbidden magic.

You don't look for magic. You feel it. Sense it.

Ren could definitely feel her shadows stirring, as if they were responding to the power that was hidden in this place. Heat boiled in her veins, racing toward her heart, her throat. She felt a flicker of longing. She *wanted* the forbidden magic. All of it.

The time rope blazed hot, then cold against her skin. The sudden pain jerked Ren out of her trance. She gripped the chain tightly as she shoved away that horrible thought. That strange longing she had felt.

Ren reached a wide landing where she spied rows and rows of booths tented in fabric as gray and drab as a winter storm. Figures in dark clothing milled about, picking up wares and setting them back down. *Ghosts*, Ren thought. The ones who never made it out of here, she guessed. One brushed past her—a woman. Her touch was ice-cold and sent shivers through Ren.

Stopping at the first table, Ren eyed a small jar of cacao beans.

"Would you like to buy a dream?" a shopkeeper asked. She was no older than Ren, with a twisted smile, dark-circled eyes, and tangled hair that looked like it hadn't been brushed in a thousand years. How had the girl ended up here? And what was so forbidden about a chocolate bean?

"A dream?"

The girl's lips pulled back in a sneer. She took a bean and set it on her tongue. The air around her shimmered, there was a flash of light, and in an instant, she was transformed into the most beautiful girl Ren had ever seen. Glossy hair, polished skin, full lips, soft angled brows, and the kind of eyes that could compel you to do her bidding. "You can be whoever you want to be," the girl said, her voice like honey.

Ren had never aspired to being the most beautiful. She appreciated her brain above all else, and now her magic. "I'm not looking for that kind of dream," she said, moving on as the girl returned to her deathly condition.

Ghosts milled about, floating too close for comfort, staring with vacant eyes. Leaving everything cold and gray in their wake.

Feel the magic, Ren told herself. *Let the blade call to you.*

But there was so much energy in this place, so many bits of forbidden magic, and it felt like they *all* were calling to her. While clutching her necklace like an anchor, Ren waded through the corridor.

As she passed, the merchants stirred as if waking from a long daze.

"Make them desire you," a rickety old woman called. "Try my honey love potion."

Soon the voices rose fast and feverish.

"Live forever. Look! The beetle of immortality."

Despite her keen curiosity, Ren hurried past. She had less than forty minutes now. If she didn't hustle, she'd end up a clueless ghost wandering around aimlessly.

"Know the secrets of the universe!" a vendor called. "Come see the Flower of Knowledge."

Ren was tempted. She wanted to see and touch and know all the forbidden magic, but she couldn't get distracted by it, not when she needed her senses to be in top form to recognize the Obsidian Blade's call to her.

"Create your own prophecy," a short toothy man said. "Don't you want to see the godly bone?"

Ren understood why these bits of magic were off-limits, why the gods didn't want them to exist. Secrets of the universe. Immortality. Prophecies. Each was enough to thwart the gods' power or at least challenge it.

"Or you can break a prophecy," he added, as if he knew Ren's troubles.

She froze. A prophecy breaker? Again, she was enticed, but she wasn't here to procure a bone. Sure, it might be an answer to her queen problem, but it wouldn't stop the Lords of Night and whatever they were up to, which had to be no good. No good for the gods, for sobrenaturales, for humans.

A voice—her voice—came to her from deep within. *Do it. Save yourself first.*

Ren felt the longing again. She found herself gravitating toward the table. A cold jolt of terror coursed through her veins as Seven Death's words wrapped themselves around her.

You will be drawn back to your source of magic, you will betray your own friends, and you will join the lords, because it is what you were always meant to do.

Ren was shaking her head, willing the words not to be true.

But she couldn't ignore the moments when her shadows had felt more powerful, more menacing than ever, when their darkness had called to her. Like now.

She turned on her heel and ran, hard and fast and with so much desperation she thought her legs would buckle. Her shadows whispered, *Give in to us....*

Ren collided with a ghost. His freezing touch burned her skin like dry ice. She gasped.

"You're hiding your magic," he growled under his breath.

With a hard twist, Ren tried to jerk free, but he had a death grip on her. "Let me go!" she demanded.

His gaunt face and black eyes drew closer. "Never," he whispered. "I want all your magic."

Ren could feel her shadows waking, growing, pulsing with anger turning into rage. This time, she didn't fight it. She let the shadows grow, let their fury build.

"You'll never have my magic!" she snarled. Her shadows flew from her eyes, hands, and mouth. They rose in a cloudlike formation, consuming the ghost. He screamed into the night as he fell to his knees, batting the air.

Another sombra encircled Ren, breathed her air, watched the ghost through her eyes, matched her movements until it looked as if she were the shadow itself.

The realization came fast and furious.

Do not use your magic in the market.

39

Chaos erupted. Ren heard shouts, scrapes, and growls. The other ghosts whirled toward her, their vacant eyes black as midnight. With a flick of her wrist, Ren threw a wave of shadow at them, then darted away, dodging her pursuers. Voices hollered, "Come back! We just want your power. Give us your magic. Give us your life."

Ren catapulted herself over a half wall at the end of the aisle and barreled full steam ahead past a stone garden with a giant statue that might have been of Ah-Puch. She sped around a corner and planted herself against the wall, panting, trying to figure out her next move. What sounded like a thousand swishing pieces of fabric swept past her. The sound of ghostly footsteps, she guessed.

The moment they passed, a strange quiet settled over the place. Ren peered in both directions, then set off at a clipped pace up the steep walkway until she reached a narrow alley with high stone buildings on either side. There were no tents here. No ghosts. No merchants.

A faint light coming from the planets or moons illuminated the walls, which were riddled with holes the size of grapefruits. A sign read YOU TOUCH, YOU BUY.

Then there came a light, feathery sound—the flapping of wings—and a high whistle like birdsong. Ren froze to listen.

She caught a flicker of movement in her peripheral vision. Turning, she saw her own shadow growing on the wall. It was strange for two reasons: First, it was three sizes bigger than it should have been. And second, there was a shadow bird perched on its shoulder.

Her hand flew to her own shoulder. Empty.

Ren's gaze focused again on the dark formation on the wall. The bird peeled itself off the stone and took flight. Ren followed it, watching in wonder as the shadow bird dipped and soared, skimming the wall with the tips of its wings.

And then...

The bird flew into one of the holes.

Ren halted, peered into the opening. Something glimmered inside. She reached in and wrapped her trembling fingers around a cool hard object.

The Obsidian Blade will call to you.

Just as she was about to remove the object, the hole closed around her wrist, clamping her in place. "Hey!" Ren wrestled and wriggled and twisted and groaned, trying to break free. But the more she struggled, the tighter the stone's grip became.

Her panic was near its peak when a woman draped in black appeared. "You think you can steal my goods?"

"No—I've come to trade."

"Looks like you've got your hand stuck in the cookie jar. You're a thief, not a trader," she snapped as she stepped into a wedge of light. The woman, who had a sunken face, hollowed cheeks, and shriveled lips, said, "And besides, what do you have that I would ever want?" Her eyes fell on Ren's chain as she clutched her own red-coral necklace.

Ren's nerves were in rapid-fire mode. No way would she ever give this ghost her time rope. "I can give you a thread from my necklace—a thread of time."

"I care not for time," the woman scoffed. "What does it matter to me? I have been here so long, I no longer remember who I am. But I know I came for a great purpose, a purpose that is lost to me forever." Her cold gaze terrified Ren. "I could take something else from you, but what, oh, what should it be?"

Sweat trickled down the back of Ren's neck, and she was finding it hard to breathe. "I can give you a shadow." She had never given away a shadow and was pretty sure it wouldn't last, but it might buy her enough time to escape.

"What kind of shadow?"

"Any kind you want."

The woman seemed to think on this with narrowed eyes. "A dragon shadow?"

Before Ren could answer, the woman said, "Too cliché. And anyway, you have your filthy little hand on my blade. It is so powerful, it can even put a god to sleep."

The Obsidian Blade. The magic *had* called to Ren! But it hadn't told her how to get out of this predicament. . . .

The woman was still talking. "What good would one of your little shadows do me when I can have all of you *and* your shadows?" Her sinister smile seemed to split her ghostly face in half.

The hole squeezed tighter around Ren's wrist. "Please," she said. "I would make a terrible ghost and—"

An arrow sliced the air.

The woman pivoted. Just in time for the arrow to stab her chest. There was an explosion of dust. Monty came running.

So fast, it was like she was flying, like her feet weren't even touching the ground. Ren blinked.

Even in the twirling specks of dust, she was sure.

Blink.

Monty's feet *weren't* touching the ground.

Blink.

And as fast as Monty was moving, it felt as if time slowed, as if the moment was stretched wider than the sky so Ren wouldn't miss a single detail.

Blink.

The hunter's arrows glowed. Not blue, but silver.

"Why are you just standing there?" Monty scolded as she lifted one of her arrows from the pile of ghost dust.

"Monty...you...Your feet. How...?"

"How about you ask me the questions later so we can get out of this zombie nightmare?"

"My hand!" Ren cried. "It's stuck, but I found the blade!"

Well, the shadow bird showed me the blade.

Monty spared a quick glance over her shoulder. "We have to go now!"

"Over here!" someone shouted.

"I realize that," Ren said through gritted teeth.

Without another breath, Monty nocked an arrow, pointing it at Ren's hand. "Hey!" Ren shouted.

"It's just a hand," Monty said. "Stay very still."

"You can't be serious!"

The hunter shot two arrows with such speed Ren didn't see them coming, and didn't see their magic break the wall's hold on her hand.

"Good thing I'm a perfect shot," Monty said with a triumphant smile as the arrows flew back to her quiver.

As Ren threw a deep scowl at the hunter, she removed the Obsidian Blade. She'd been expecting a shiny carved dagger or ritual knife, but this "blade" was just a black shard about the size of a guitar pick, and there was no handle on it.

"Come on!" Monty shouted, taking off.

The hunter and the godborn ran up the passageway. Not in the direction Ren thought an exit should be. But who was she to question her rescuer?

"They're getting away!" a voice hollered.

"We need . . . to find . . . the golden arrows," Ren said between breaths.

"I'm way ahead of you," Monty yelled.

They reached the apex of the narrow stone corridor, coming to a terrace. A dozen ghosts raced toward them from the right—a mass of darkness. They chanted as one: "Give us your magic. Give us your magic. Give us your magic."

Monty and Ren tumbled down the ashy hillside. The dark world became a blur, a fuzzy dark dream. Until *splash*.

They had landed in a small fountain. The ash from their bodies turned the water black.

Ren looked over her shoulder. A swarm of ghosts were coming at her and Monty from above. *Flying* at them with hands extended, mouths open, eyes bulging.

"They're too close!" Ren shouted. "We have to fight."

"Heck yeah!" Monty launched herself to her feet, an arrow already poised.

Ren stood, black water dripping from her hair as she faced

the zombielike ghosts that A.P. had *not* warned them about. "Let 'em fly!" she shouted.

Arrows and shadows, shadows and arrows zoomed toward the specters. With every hit, there was a burst of gray, like a storm cloud. Ash rained down on them until they couldn't see clearly.

Just when Ren thought the battle was over, a ghost bolted from a cloud of dust. It swung itself around Monty's ankles, bringing down the hunter.

Ren ripped the time rope from her throat and lashed it through the air, connecting with the enemy in a brilliant flash of light. The specter disintegrated.

Monty jumped up and stomped the ground where her attacker was now nothing but ash.

"Are you okay?" Ren said, securing the rope.

With a short nod, Monty said, "This way!" They bolted down a dirt lane.

"Are you sure this is right?" Ren shouted. "I don't see any golden arrows."

"Trust me."

A minute later, they came to the top of a winding stone staircase. A golden arrow flashed a short distance below another, which was a good one hundred steps away. And on the last step was a figure—Edison.

He threw his hands in front of him, creating an enormous bubble of magic that encircled the hunter and the godborn. It lifted them off their feet and carried them to the bottom of the stairs in three seconds flat.

Edison gave them a once-over. They were soaked, filthy, and exhausted. "I don't think I'm even going to ask."

"Good," Ren said. "Where's the exit?"

Edison pointed to a silvery gate that was shrinking by the second.

The trio raced through it, out of the Dark Mercado with its ghosts, clawing hands, and forbidden magic, and into a bright space. The hot sun hovered above them.

Ren blinked, letting her eyes adjust to the light. For miles and miles there were hills of blindingly white sand and nothing else.

She unpocketed the object that had created so much trouble. Edison and Monty gathered closer to inspect it.

"Looks like an arrowhead," Monty said.

"It's amazing," Edison said. "I can feel its power without even touching it."

Ren fingered the shard and turned it over. On the back she found an engraved symbol.

"The shadow bird," she whispered.

"Shadow huh?" Monty said.

The symbol began to glimmer silver, and the bird's wings shifted, expanded.

"What the . . . ?" Edison breathed.

And then the bird took flight.

40

The shadow bird flittered and fluttered, dipped and swirled.

It wasn't that Ren had never seen a living shadow before. She just had never seen one she herself hadn't created. And she was mesmerized.

The bird expanded to the size of a lion, only to circle back and shrink to the size of a mouse. Ren thought she heard a distant "WOO-HOO!" She shook her head. Shadows don't talk, she reminded herself.

"That thing is awesome!" Monty's smile was wider than the sky.

"That thing is powerful." Edison shook his head and raised his hand toward the bird like he was going to take its temperature. "OH!"

"*Oh* what?" Ren was afraid of the answer.

The shadow swept over the demon as he said, "The power isn't in the blade—it's the bird that has all the magic." And then he collapsed onto the sand.

"Eddie!" Monty cried, falling to her knees. She shook him, but he just moaned a little and turned over. Then he started to snore.

"So that's how it works." Ren spoke quietly. "It puts things to sleep."

"Hey! Earth to Ren," Monty said. "Man down . . . or, uh, demon down. No time to go all heart eyes on the bird. Wake up, Eddie!"

Except that Ren didn't know how to awaken him. It was a stretch, but she told the bird, "Wake Edison." The bird just flitted about like it had nowhere to settle down.

That CREATURE, the bird replied in a female voice, *is rude and deserves to sleep forever. How dare he sense my magic!*

Ren startled. "Did you . . . ? Did you hear that?" she asked Monty.

They can't hear me, the bird said. *Only the one who possesses the blade can.*

"Hear what?" Monty squinted against the sun.

See?

"The bird, it . . . She talked to me."

As a godborn she was used to telepathic communication with other godborns, but this? An ancient shadow bird?

She lifted her gaze to the bird. "Please wake Edison. He wasn't being rude, I promise. He's just—"

This is so humiliating, the bird said. *To be bossed around like this, to be used for my magic. I'm only going along with it because you rescued me from that wretched place.* Then, after a sigh: *Just set the blade on each of his eyes. Left to right, and make sure not to slice his lids open as you're doing it.*

Ren did as instructed. The blade glowed an iridescent silver.

HIS left.

Half a second later, Edison woke with a gasp, bolting upright and patting his chest like a madman or someone who was looking for a pen but couldn't find one. "Where am I?"

Ren checked their exact location on her watch. "White Sands, New Mexico."

Edison glanced around at the rising hills of glittering sand. "This place was formed out of gypsum crystals over thousands of years."

"Is there anything you don't know?" Monty said.

"A lot. But I don't know I don't know it, ya know?"

"No idea what that means," Monty said. "All I *know* is that this place looks like the Sahara desert. Well, except the sand is white."

Edison blinked at Ren. "Did that... bird thing put me to sleep?"

Tell him if he calls me thing *one more time*... the bird warned.

Ren relayed the message, followed by "And the blade woke you up."

The bird swooped down closer and closer until it landed on her shoulder.

"How come *you're* not asleep?" Edison asked.

Because she saved me, the bird said. *Jeez... You guys aren't very intuitive.*

Edison and Monty stared at the shape. "It's... weird," the hunter said. "It doesn't have any eyes."

I don't need eyes to see! the bird said. *Tell them. Tell them what I said.*

"Shadows are featureless," Ren said, reaching up to touch the bird. Anyone else would have just felt air, but she could sense the shadow beneath her fingertips, its cool, rhythmic, powerful pulse.

Edison looked intrigued and peered too close for comfort.

Ren stepped back as the bird said, *Can we please get on with whatever task you have?*

Monty said, "Well, if it doesn't want to be called *thing*, then we should name it."

"It's not exactly a pet," Edison said, frowning at the bird like he had a bone to pick with her for knocking him out.

I HAVE a name! the bird shouted, flapping its wings wildly. *I am Zyanya. Do not call me Z, or Anya, or anything else. We are not friends. Do we understand one another?*

Ren nodded. "Her name is Zyanya," she said to her friends.

"Zyanya," Monty repeated under her breath. "I like it."

"It means *forever*," Edison said.

"You're like a walking Google," Monty told the demon.

Well, he's smarter than he looks, Zyanya muttered. *So, here are the rules. One: Don't lose the blade. If you lose it, you lose me. Two: I can put anyone with a pulse to sleep, but I can't kill them. Three: You'd better be sure when you use my magic, because once I put someone to sleep, it's lights-out forever unless you use the blade to awaken them in less than five minutes. Six minutes and beyond is when it gets ugly. I once had a possessor who told me to put her husband into seventh-dream status and then, two days later, she changed her mind and tried to bring him back. Can you say* zombie? *Which is all to say that my sleep magic is the most powerful in the universe, so be sure before you use it. Got it?*

"What's she saying?" Monty asked, stepping closer.

Ren relayed the information, and Monty's face brightened. "She's like a genie bird, but instead of a lamp she lives in . . . a knife."

I don't like this child, Zyanya groaned. *Get rid of her.*

Ren changed the subject. "So, you can put gods to sleep, right?" She had to be one hundred percent sure.

As in plural? asked the bird.

Oof. Ren didn't like the tone of that question. "You said you're the most powerful."

Edison raised his hand and let it hover over the shadow bird. *What's he doing? Why is he measuring my magic? This is insulting! Tell him to get away.*

"She doesn't like what you're doing," Ren told the demon.

Edison rubbed his chin, gazing at the bird. "She is...Her magic is old and *super* powerful."

See? Like I told you, Zyanya said. *He can stay.* The bird spread her wings and bounced onto Ren's head. *Now, where were we? Oh yes, I am the most powerful, but every power has limits. How many gods are we talking?*

Ren said, "Like maybe four or five," and then shared Zyanya's words with her friends.

I don't do maybes.

"Five," Ren said, thinking it was better to overshoot than undersell.

I can't knock out five gods in one fell swoop. Has to be one at a time with at least ten minutes between each knockout. So I should go get some rest. Call me when you're ready. And with that, the shadow bird flew into the blade with a brilliant flash of light.

Ren pocketed the blade as she told her friends about the ten-minute rule.

"A lot can happen in ten minutes," Edison groaned as he toed the sand.

"A lot can happen in ten seconds!" Monty said.

After a quick check of her watch, Ren said, "There isn't a gateway to get us back to the safe house." She quickly texted A.P.

We made it. I have the blade. Need ride.

The god of death sent her a smiley face, then wrote:

How do I use location share again?

"Is he coming?" Monty said, dancing on the balls of her feet.

"What's your deal?" Ren asked.

"I really have to pee."

"Can you hold it?" Edison said.

Monty scowled. "Do I look like I'm five? Of course I can. I just need to dance, okay?"

"Listen," Ren said. "We wait for Ah-Puch, get back to the safe house, and then, Monty, is there any way you can find Serena again? I mean since you don't have anything to track her with?"

"Oh, I took a few of her things from SHIHOM," the hunter said. "Figured we'd need to track her more than once."

"You're such a genius," Ren said to a beaming Monty. "We'll go to wherever she is and stop her from waking the fifth lord." That was the one Ren was the most terrified to meet— Mictlantecuhtli, the Underworld Lord. "Then we'll have Zyanya knock out the other four."

It sounded like such an easy plan when Ren put it like that, but there were so many what-ifs between each of its steps. What if they couldn't find Serena? What if they couldn't stop her? What if they got attacked by more killer bees? What if Zyanya wasn't as powerful as she claimed?

In real life, Ren wasn't such a catastrophic thinker. But this wasn't just a quest to put the lords to sleep and stop Serena. This was about Ren staying Ren. About her never, ever, *ever* wearing a crown of shadow and jade.

Night would fall in a few hours. And once the fifth lord woke up, the Night Prophecy would come to pass. Ren would return to the origins of her magic. She would become the lords' queen and betray her friends. She couldn't fathom it, or stomach it.

Monty twirled an arrow between her fingers. "Hey, check it out. If we can knock out any lord before tonight, won't that stop the prophecy? You said they need five, right?"

Ren said, "Good thinking, but that would only delay things until tomorrow."

"Tomorrow is better than today," Edison said, but his face told another story. He was worried or unsure or scared, or maybe all the above.

It felt like a bomb was ticking in the middle of Ren's chest. And it wouldn't stop ticking until *all* the lords were asleep. She hadn't wanted to admit it—not to herself or to her friends—but there was a strange darkness stirring inside her, calling to her. And there were moments when she wanted to answer, wanted to see what the dark had to offer. *No*, she thought. *I can't trust myself until this is over for good. I'll never side with the Lords of Night*. Never.

Edison had begun pacing. "How will we find the Night Lords to put them to sleep?"

Ren had known the answer before he had asked the question. "I'll get them to come to me."

Within ten minutes, Ah-Puch stepped through his Lake Tahoe gateway. He looked like he'd been put through a sieve. His eyes were sunken, his skin ashen, his spine hunched over like he might collapse any second. But then he saw Ren and there was a spark, a flicker of something—life? Relief? It seemed he might smile, or hug her, or do the Chicken Dance, but instead he hardened his stance, threw on a scowl, and said, "I've been waiting forever. It was agony! Do you have any idea what it's like to be a parent?" He cleared his throat. "I mean..."

Ren's heart swelled with love for the god of death. He had always protected her, sacrificed his own safety for hers. He had always been there for her no matter the consequences. And now she had to be there for him. She had to finish this thing and find a way to restore him to his godly status. But Ren couldn't say any of that without breaking down into a blubbery, snot-nosed mess. So instead, she said, "I'm sorry. We went as fast as we could." Then she unpocketed the blade, and the god's eyes glimmered.

"Hey, Ah-Puch," Monty said, pointing to the still-shimmering rainbow gateway. "Uh, is it supposed to be shrinking like that?"

"Hurry!" the god shouted as everyone dove into the portal.

Back at the safe house, while Edison and Monty got cleaned up in other rooms, Ren told A.P. about the maze and the market and the blade.

"I'm...sorry...I couldn't...go with you." Ah-Puch dragged out the sentence like it hurt him to say it.

Ren nodded in acknowledgment of the apology. "I can feel it deep inside me," she whispered, tears pricking her eyeballs.

"Feel what?"

She looked up at him with moist eyes.

"You're not going to do that crying thing, are you?"

Ren wiped a tear away. "It's allergies. And you know what I'm talking about."

With a clamped jaw, A.P. said, "I know a thing or two about the dark, Ren. It's all-consuming, and it tricks you into making you think you want it, that you'd rather dwell in its depths than seek the light."

Ren stood by the window with her back to the god. "If—"

"No!" he growled.

"Just hear me out. If it happens...If the Night Prophecy comes true and I side with the lords, if I become their queen and betray you and my friends, I need you to do something for me."

"I said no."

"A.P." Ren turned to face him. His pallor was deeper than it had been at White Sands. "Please. Tell Monty to shoot me and take me to Xib'alb'a. I'd rather die than live and be evil."

"You could never be evil!"

Ren took three deep breaths. "I saw myself. In the maze. I was queen, and I...killed Edison."

The god collapsed onto the sofa. His face fell. "The vision could be wrong."

But Ren knew otherwise. She knew deep in that place where instincts grow and the truth is spelled out. "It's not wrong." She went to the god and sat next to him. "Wouldn't you rather I be a ghost in the underworld than their queen?"

A.P. stood abruptly. "What I'd rather have is you . . . the way you are now. You're like . . . Well, don't ever tell a soul, but you're sort of like a daughter to me. No father could watch his child die, so what you're asking is impossible."

Ren grew a shadow, shapeless and black. It hovered over the god.

"Ren, I'm not afraid of your shadows."

"You're still the god of death, darkness, and destruction. Tell me—what do my shadows feel like to you?"

Ah-Puch sighed. He swept his hand through the blackness, recoiling just as quickly. Throwing his hands on his hips, he looked down at the floor, refusing to meet Ren's eyes.

"That's what I thought," she said quietly.

"Okay," he finally said with a heavy note of defeat in his voice. "You win. I won't let you . . . live as their queen."

41

It didn't take Monty long to locate Serena, and within the hour, Ren and crew stood on the shores of Lake Zirahuén in Mexico. "I can see why they call it the Mirror of the Gods," Edison said as they took in the sparkling water surrounded by hills forested with pine, ash, and oak trees.

It was so beautiful that Ren felt her heart stir.

"There's a legend," Edison said, "that after the Spaniards came, a captain fell in love with the Aztec princess Eréndira. Well, the king wasn't going to marry off his daughter to some Spanish dude, so the captain kidnapped her and hid her in a valley. She was devastated, cried night and day, and the gods took pity on her and turned her into a mermaid." Edison gestured toward the water. "Supposedly all her tears made this lake and she's still living under there."

"Mermaids?" a surly A.P. growled. "You're talking mermaids when . . ." He blew his hair off his forehead. "Can we get on with this?"

Monty dipped her hand into the water. "That's terrible. I hope that captain got hung up by his toes."

Ren was captivated by the tale, but this wasn't the time to get distracted. She checked her watch for the coordinates Monty had given her. "We're about a mile out."

Edison tossed a twig into the lake. "The sun will be going down in about an hour."

"Then get your feet moving!" A.P. ordered.

With each step, Ren could feel the Night Lords' magic hanging like a thick fog in the air. She carried the blade in her hand, worrying its handle as she stared into the glittering lago and wondered if the mermaid had realized she had merely gone from one prison to another.

Zyanya huffed, *Can you quit rubbing the thing? I'm trying to rest!*

"Sorry."

And by the way, the bird said, *you didn't tell me you have shadow magic.*

"How did you know?"

A.P. and the others were a few paces behind Ren, talking in low whispers that she couldn't make out.

Zyanya flew out of Ren's pocket as a tiny shadow, flitting back and forth in front of her face. *We shadows recognize each other. And yours are powerful. A little dark, but who am I to judge?*

"Yeah, but..." Ren paused, too exhausted to explain. "I'm working through some stuff."

Nothing wrong with darkness as long as you control it, Zyanya said before perching on Ren's head.

That's the problem, Ren thought. *I can't control it.*

Zyanya let out a ginormous yawn. *Wake me when I'm needed. For now, I shall rest.*

At the same moment, Ren's watch vibrated. She glanced at the message: YOU HAVE ARRIVED.

She looked up at the wooded hill far above the lake. "That's it," Ren said, pointing to a large stone house.

"We'll circle around the back," Edison suggested as he lifted his hands, drew them back, and made a protective blue sphere of magic around the group. "Hey, guys?" he said.

"Nice vanquishing." Monty was nodding her approval.

"That lake has some real magic going on. You think that mermaid tale is true?"

A.P. snorted. "As if mermaids are special."

Ren so badly wanted to ask, but she knew it wasn't the right time. But as she turned up the incline, she thought she saw movement in the water.

A few moments later, they reached a small hill. They hunched down behind it to get a good look at what lay beyond. In the valley below was a sprawling hacienda with iron gates and a long dirt road leading up to it. Strangely, there were no guards, no demons circling the place. Music drifted from the house. The last of the day's light was vanishing into the horizon.

"Kenji will have bee scouts," Ren said, scoping out the scene.

"Don't worry—they won't get past my shield," Edison said.

"When we get to the house," Ren said, "we'll need to separate."

"No way," Edison said, shaking his head. "I can't protect us unless we're together."

A.P. pinched the bridge of his nose and sighed loudly. Ren was sure he was going to start a bickering fest with her. Instead, he said, "Ren's right."

Ren felt her whole being swell with pride, but she didn't have time for that now. She needed to be the team captain, and that meant assigning roles. "Edison and Monty, you find Serena. Stop her from waking the fifth lord."

"What are you going to do?" Monty asked.

"I'm going to find the other four lords."

"How?" Edison asked, his eyes filled with concern.

A.P. studied her with an intense knowing gaze. "I'll go with you," he insisted.

Ren shook her head. "I need you to be the lookout."

A.P. scoffed, threw his hands onto his hips, scowled, and scoffed again. "Renata Santiago, I am the god of death. I do not play *lookout*."

Ren nodded sympathetically as she took the god's hand in her own. "I know it's a lot to ask. But if—"

Just then, a familiar voice said, "Could you guys be any more obvious?"

Ren spun to find Marco walking down the path toward them. And at his side was Nakon, the Maya god of war. Nakon hadn't traveled back in time with the other gods, so he was in his usual adult form—dark hair, stone-cold gaze, chiseled jaw, and humongous muscles that were pretty intimidating. And yeah, he was wearing his signature cliché leathers.

"Marco!" Ren's eyes filled with tears of happiness—or maybe relief. She wanted to throw her arms around the friend she thought had abandoned her. "What are you doing here? I figured you—"

"I went to find this guy," Marco said, jabbing a thumb at his dad, who merely deepened his glare.

A.P. grunted.

"Why didn't you tell me?" Ren cried.

Marco twisted his mouth in that smirk Ren usually hated, but not today. Today she loved every inch of his face. "Didn't want to get your hopes up," he said. "What if I couldn't deliver?"

"I'm not here to help," Nakon managed. "Not in the way you think. I'm a god worthy of great, spectacular wars, not itty-bitty battles unlikely to win me any glory."

Ren stared at him openmouthed. She would never get used to the selfish and totally self-centered ways of the gods.

"What do you got, then?" Edison asked with a confidence that practically screamed *I am totally used to dealing with wicked gods.*

Nakon surveyed the valley, the hacienda. "You've got a few demons keeping watch on the other side of the gate. An army of security bees buzzing around." He rubbed his chin with his knuckles. "A few godborns on the east side of the house. And"— his black eyes continued to scan—"some baby Aztec gods on the west side."

"Baby gods?" Ren asked.

Nakon didn't even pay her the courtesy of looking at her when he spoke. "They are weak, just woke up after a long sleep. But something else is containing some of their power." His tone was ominous.

"Like what?" Ren asked.

The god didn't answer. Instead, he said, "These worthless beings are nothing you *kids* can't handle." His eyes fell on A.P. and Ren could feel the dig there. Nakon looked like he might start laughing.

"Whoa," Monty said, all breathy and impressed. "You can see all that from here?"

Nakon's dark eyes were now merely slits. He turned to Marco. "I have fulfilled my . . . duty." He said the word *duty* like he might choke on it.

What the heck? What duty? Ren wondered what Marco had given up for such worthless intel.

Marco patted his dad on the back. "Hang tight."

The words made the god visibly stiffen.

Marco turned back to the crew. "Do you need anything else from my old man before he goes?"

"Can't he help us knock everyone with a pulse into orbit?" Monty asked innocently.

"Not part of the deal," Nakon growled.

"How . . . ?" Ren was having trouble forming the words that would help her make sense of Nakon's presence. "Why is he doing this for us, Marco?"

"I'm not," Nakon said at the exact moment as A.P. said, "He's not."

Marco barked out a laugh. "He lost a little wrestling match with yours truly."

Nakon looked like he was going to implode. His eyes were nearly bulging, and so was a big vein in his neck. "I'm an insomniac, okay? I was tired."

"Sure," Marco said. "That's what they all say."

"Well, thanks," Edison put in. "No matter the reason, it's really a stand-up thing to come all this way and help us."

Monty nodded vigorously while Nakon inhaled slowly, growled once, and vanished into thin air.

A.P. screwed up his face. "*He* should have played lookout!"

With the sky nearly dark, Ren didn't have time for A.P.'s

godly ego. "Marco, can you take out the demons on the other side of the gate?"

"I can blast them," Edison said.

"Too much commotion," Ren replied.

Marco popped his knuckles and smiled lazily. "Heck to the yes, I can take out those blue-skinned, gnarly-smelling losers." Then he winced. "No offense, Edison. But what about the bees?"

Pressing her lips together, Ren ran through her options, always landing on the one that made the most sense and would cause the least attention. With a deep breath and a single thought, a massive formless shadow rose from her hands, looking like a dark storm cloud floating above them. In the next breath, the form shattered into a few dozen shadow butterflies. Ren sent them on their way before turning to her friends. "That should keep the bees busy. Marco, you ready?"

With a smirk, he merely said, "I'll send the signal when I'm done." Then, way too cheerfully, he made his way into the valley, racing ahead as if there was a prize to be had at the end of all this and not heads on platters.

Everyone watched him go and waited in silence for his signal. Ren's heart thumped fiercely. Not because she was nervous for Marco, or anxious about being near the end of this quest, but because beneath her heart thumping she felt something else. Shadow and power and hunger swelling inch by inch by inch. She could feel herself being drawn to something inside that house, a missing piece she needed to find.

In what seemed like a very short time, Marco opened the gate and bowed to them. Then he flexed his arms and kissed a bicep.

"He's so cool," Monty said.

"You guys ready?" Ren asked the crew.

A.P. said, "I'll be your lookout, but only until the sky darkens and the moon rises high."

Ren nodded before they descended into the valley. And with each step she took, she could feel the Night Lords' presence, thick and heavy like a midnight shadow.

42

Ren wanted to turn back. She wanted to run to the god of death, but she knew that wasn't an option. She had to see this through.

And even though she couldn't read her friends' minds, in that moment, she knew they were as apprehensive as she was, heading toward something bigger than any of them had imagined, bigger than the now-awakened gods, bigger than the rogue godborns. And the bigness of it all felt like an avalanche just before it picks up speed and power, before it becomes unstoppable, before it destroys everything in its path.

Marco rushed them all inside a courtyard marked by an uneven stone floor, high border walls, and dried-up vines and bushes that looked like creepy skeletal formations in the waning light. They stood in the shadows for a mere five seconds— long enough to share glances that said *Good luck*.

And then there was another look—one shared only by Marco and Ren. His eyes were almost narrowed, but not quite, and in them Ren saw something she'd never seen in the son of war before—deep concern. It made her want to hug him, to tell him she would be careful, that they'd been through so much worse. She wanted to laugh and remind him she still had all his essays to write, so she wasn't going anywhere.

Without a word, she split off from the group in search of

the four awakened lords. She knew they were close—she could feel their magic. Clutching the Obsidian Blade, she created a shadow ladder and climbed up to the roof. As she touched each dark rung, she found herself wishing, *Please let my friends be okay, please let my friends be okay.*

When she stepped onto the roof, she felt her shadows stirring, reaching. The sensation carried with it a strange want, as if Ren *was* her shadows, as if *she* were doing the reaching. Ren crouched low and tiptoed across the flat surface. She heard music echoing from below—a slow and steady beat from inside the walls—and then she heard muffled voices. But they didn't belong to the person she was looking for, so she continued on, keeping a single idea in her mind: *All I have to do is find the four lords, release the bird, and watch her knock them all back into a forever sleep.*

Ren came to the edge of the roof. Below, a dark landscape stretched out before her. She could almost imagine the green grass that once grew down the slopes, the white flowers that once crawled up the trellises, and the leaves that once clung to the thick tall trees, but now all she saw was death, a winter-like garden that didn't belong here.

Gingerly, she gripped a fat vine and lowered herself to the ground.

It was eerily quiet here. So quiet Ren could hear her own breathing.

Dried leaves crunched beneath her feet as she picked her way across the land, down a dark knoll, and into a dense forest. With each step, she could feel her shadows growing, almost whispering to her, *Yes, this is the way.*

A warm wind swept through the trees, shaking the spindly limbs, rustling the scattered leaves. And then a glow appeared a few feet ahead, as if a candle had just been lit.

Instantly, the wind ceased, the trees grew still, and a girl stepped out from behind a blackened trunk. She was carrying a glass lantern that cast shadows beneath her eyes, giving them a sickly hollowed-out look.

Ren didn't move. She only stared at the godborn, the daughter of spells and magic. "Ezra?"

"I knew you'd find it," Ezra said. A smile played on her lips.

Ren blinked. Her mind was working overtime to put all the pieces together. "It?"

Stepping closer, Ezra said in a soft yet menacing voice, "You could have died getting the Obsidian Blade, and that made me feel bad. Sort of. But you know these things are always risky, right? And someone has to do them, so . . ."

"I . . . I don't understand." Ren felt hot and shivery all over. Her shadows pulsed at the edges of her fingertips. "And how are you stopping time?"

"Not time, exactly," Ezra said, quirking her mouth to the side. "More like a moment that's asleep."

Ren's first thought was *So that's* her power. *Or one of them. She can put moments to sleep and wake sleeping gods. Cool.* Her second thought was *How long does the frozen moment last?* And her third was an echo of Ezra's words that were only now sinking in: *You could have died getting the Obsidian Blade.*

As if she could see the questions forming in Ren's mind, Ezra said, "I knew you were the only one who could get the blade. I knew Ah-Puch would share the location with you and only you." She smiled, overly pleased with herself.

"How did you know the blade even existed?"

"My mom told me about it. I knew it was the golden ticket I was looking for, because let me tell you . . ." Her voice trailed off as she realized she'd said too much.

"So . . . this was a setup?" Ren asked, knowing the answer before Ezra answered.

"A setup? No. I'd call it a plan."

"But why? Just to get your hands on the blade?"

"It's powerful," Ezra said. "Like your time rope. My mom created the blade and then Ah-Puch took it from her like the thief he is, so I'm only making things right."

Ren thought Ezra had a point. It didn't seem fair for Ah-Puch or *any* god to take what someone else had created, even if the magic wasn't supposed to exist, but Ren didn't make the rules. And at this moment, those rules didn't matter. "So, you tricked me into thinking you needed my help," she ground out both haughtily and gloomily. "You fed me some bogus clues to get me to do your dirty work so you could have the blade, and then what? Give it to Serena? Control the Aztec lords?"

As the words passed Ren's lips, she couldn't help but wonder if that was it—the blade was the final step in Serena's plan to control the lords.

Ezra sneered. "You think I'd give this power to Serena? *Psh.* Seriously? Would you give your time rope to someone?"

Ren shook her head. *Not unless it was absolutely necessary.*

"Serena wouldn't even know what to do with it," Ezra spit

out. "Even if she is going to be some queen or whatever she thinks."

Ren decided it was time to play dumb. "Queen?"

"Some prophecy about waking the Night Lords and becoming queen. To be honest, I barely paid attention because I don't really care. All I care about is the blade, so hand it over."

So, Serena really *did* believe she would be a powerful queen if she awakened the lords. She had done all this over some terrible misinterpretation that now made Ren feel like she was going to be sick.

Ren stepped back. "I can't give it to you."

"Because you're going to put the Night Lords back to sleep with it?" Ezra's eyes grew darker, as if her pupils had enlarged and all that was left was a pool of blackness. She hesitated, studied Ren. "I'm an astral traveler, and right now I can see that your friends are fighting a battle they can't win."

She was bluffing. Ren stood her ground, readying her shadows.

Ezra closed her eyes and took a breath. "Your hunter—her arrows are impressive, but they're useless against Kenji's bees, which have stung her a few times. And that tall boy . . . He's trying to throw up some kind of barrier, but it keeps crashing to the ground like a wave of water."

Ren watched Ezra in horror, imagining the scene the daughter of spells and magic was describing and wondering if any of it was true. *No, it has to be another trick.* "I don't believe you."

Ezra shrugged. "Give me the blade or things are going to get a lot worse for you and your friends."

"Ezra," Ren said as calmly as she could manage, "we're both

godborns. We should be on the same side, helping each other. We don't have to fight."

Ezra hesitated just long enough that Ren thought/hoped her words had penetrated somehow. At least until Ezra said, "You call yourself a godborn? You're not even pure. You're tainted with Mexica blood, a shadow witch, a descendant of dead gods."

Those last five words landed with force. *A descendant of dead gods.*

Instantly, Ren's anger rose to the surface. She was sick of being discounted, of being called names, of being bullied and pushed around. She was sick of giving people the benefit of the doubt only to be disappointed by their power grabs and selfish ways. Her shadows called to her in dark voices that whispered, *Hurt her like she's hurt you. Demolish her. Ruin her.* Ren's heart raced as she consumed the words and wanted to make them happen, wanted to show Ezra just how powerful she was. The darkness spread beneath her skin and bones, into her blood, and she did nothing to stop it. She welcomed it, let it roil within as she growled, "I'm the most powerful godborn alive."

And then she raised her hands to unleash her anger, her shadows. But they were locked in place.

Ezra laughed. "Hmm . . . Hate to tell you this, but your shadows won't work in a sleeping moment." And then she lunged.

Ren sidestepped, leaping out of Ezra's reach as she ripped the time rope from her throat. She snapped it out in front of her, and its golden light glowed across the black forest. "Don't come any closer," Ren warned, fighting the longing, the terrible desire to wrap Ezra in the rope and watch it hurt her the way she had hurt Ren.

Ezra looked unafraid as she lifted one hand in Ren's direction. "I think it's time for you to take a nap."

Ren's eyes suddenly burned, her eyelids felt heavy, her head throbbed. She could feel herself being pulled under... deeper and deeper. And she would have slept if it hadn't been for her shadows, thrashing inside her, forcing her awake. With her last ounce of awareness, she whipped the rope toward Ezra and coiled it around the godborn's ankles. Ezra screamed as her skin burned, and she collapsed to her knees.

The wind awakened, rushing through the trees with a ferocity that nearly knocked Ren off her feet.

Ezra didn't struggle against the rope's power. Instead, she closed her eyes and said, "Looks like the fifth lord..."

Underworld Lord, Ren thought shakily as the earth quaked hard beneath her. Heat and strength coursed through her with such swiftness, she had to fight to catch her breath.

Ezra opened her eyes and grinned. "She's waking."

Ren stumbled over the words, or one in particular. "She?"

"Jade Is Her Skirt, the great water goddess," Ezra said with a desperation in her voice that unsettled Ren.

Wait! No, it was supposed to be the lord of the underworld. Not that Ren was complaining—a water goddess sounded much more appealing.

"Give me the blade," Ezra commanded. "I'm the only one strong enough to put all five to sleep now."

Ren realized that that might be true, but Ezra didn't want to put the lords to sleep. Ren understood that now. She wanted to control them with the blade. Ren released a shadow that wrapped around Ezra, instantly taking the form of a cage.

"You won't win without me," Ezra growled. "They're too powerful."

Ren knew her shadow cage would only hold Ezra for so long, but it was enough to give herself a head start. She spun toward the deeper part of the woods and followed the darkness that was calling to her.

43

Whispers sailed through the trees.

Yes, yes. This way.

Dazed, Ren followed them. Until she found herself on a hill staring at a small lake below.

Thunder pounded the sky. Lightning shredded the night.

And there, on the water, by the light of the full moon, tiny ripples began to appear. They grew into rings, and the rings formed a tight spiral made up of dozens of little circles. At the center was a glowing seven-pointed star.

It was the symbol.

Ren was so mesmerized she didn't hear the woman calling to her. Not at first. Slowly the voice brought her back to the present moment.

"Lovely, isn't it?"

Ren turned to find a petite woman standing behind her. She had short dark hair that hugged her refined-looking jaw, and she wore a silvery top and a long, flowing jade skirt that glittered in the moonlight like diamonds. She was so beautiful Ren couldn't tear her eyes away from her.

The woman introduced herself. "I am Chalchiuhtlicue, the Aztec goddess of rivers, streams, lakes, and storms. Some call me Jade Is Her Skirt. You may call me Jade."

Oh. Ren wanted to say something like *Why are you here?*

Or *How do you get your skin to glow like that?* but her mind was a jumble of total bewilderment.

The goddess came closer. "I am the sixth lord of the night. And you..." She hesitated before she smiled. "You are the shadow queen."

Queen. There was that word again. The better part of Ren shook her head, but the other part, the one lost in her own shadows, wanted to say yes. Just like she had done with the Prince Lord when she'd made that terrible promise.

"I have waited eons to meet you." The goddess spoke so softly her voice was on the edge of kindness. A kindness Ren sorely needed right now.

"Um... How come number five... I mean the Underworld Lord... didn't wake up?"

"Because he matters not."

Well, to be fair, he does run Mictlan, Ren thought. *And underworlds are pretty big places with huge responsibilities.* Ren clutched the Obsidian Blade, fingering its edges like someone ready to pull the trigger. She knew she had to put Jade back to sleep, and this was her chance. All she had to do was release the bird...

And yet she couldn't do it. She felt some strange connection to the goddess, as if she'd known her forever, as if they'd been friends in some other life.

But that didn't mean Ren couldn't get intel. "Five of you are awake," she managed as the implications exploded in her head. Now they'd have enough power to do whatever it was they were planning. "What are you going to do?"

The goddess turned her head to the right, studying Ren.

"Your magic runs deep." Then she sighed, but barely. "So much power, and soon we will grow that power together. You have bound yourself—you have accepted your destiny, and now we can begin."

Ren stood frozen, afraid to move. Seven Death's words rang in her memory. *Until you agree to be their queen, they cannot reclaim their magic.*

Ren knew that the lords wanted their magic back, and a part of her couldn't blame them, but it was the unknown of what they wanted to *do* with that magic, the same kind that was coursing through her veins, that worried her.

It is the only magic in existence that does not sleep.

The time rope warmed against Ren's throat, sending a jolt of sadness and regret through her. Jade's gaze fell on the golden necklace. "She is not your only mother," she said, barely above a whisper.

Ren's insides coiled tightly. She wasn't sure she had heard the goddess right. "What's that supposed to mean?"

Jade stood taller, looked more regal. She pressed her graceful hands against her shimmering skirt and its greenish-blue color seemed to deepen. "*I* am the mother of your shadow magic."

Ren felt cold all over. She remembered what Seven Death had said: *Your magic comes from the Lords of Night themselves.*

"You mean all the lords," Ren said, fumbling with her thoughts and words. "It was all of you who made it and ..."

The goddess's gaze intensified. "They assisted in hiding the magic, but it is I and I alone who gave it to some humans. To your ancestors. To you."

A newfound anger gripped Ren. She hadn't asked for any

of this. She hadn't agreed to accept the shadow magic that was just passed down to her without her having any choice in the matter. But she had a choice now. She clutched the Obsidian Blade tucked carefully in her pocket.

Yet if she put Jade to sleep, every question Ren had about her history, her family, her shadow magic might go unanswered forever. . . .

"The shadows have been speaking to you," the goddess said. "And they speak to me now."

Ren felt the weight of her sombras twisting inside her. Yes, they had spoken to her, and she had found it both terrifying and exhilarating. What else didn't she know about her own magic?

The goddess's dark eyes glittered in the moonlight. "They tell me you are afraid, that you want to save your friends, that you do not want to be queen, and yet . . ." She stretched the moment with a long meaningful gaze. "You have felt it, Renata Santiago. The desire to assume your throne, to wield your powers. To accept your destiny . . . as queen."

Hot tears stung Ren's eyes, threatening to fall. And it wasn't the goddess's words that split her in two and shattered her heart—it was Seven Death's promise.

You will be drawn back to your source of magic. You will betray your own friends and you will join the lords, because it is what you were always meant to do.

NO! Ren wouldn't, couldn't, let that happen. Scorching anger bubbled in her chest. "I never got to decide, to choose for myself!" *But I'm going to choose now. Loyalty, love, friendship. I'm going to send you back to dreamland!*

"Oh, but you did," the goddess said gently. "You tell yourself that because it makes you feel better about what you chose. You chose your destiny. You chose to be queen. You chose the truth."

Ren's eyes took in the glowing symbol floating on the lake. And all she could think was *No, I chose to save a life. And I'd do it again.*

A shiver grabbed hold of her and shimmied up and down her spine, making her tremble violently. She knew what she had to do even if it meant killing the truth forever. She reached for the Obsidian Blade, nearly ripping it from her pocket, when the goddess fanned out her skirt like a parachute and wrapped it around both of them.

In an instant, Ren was floating in a tunnel of glittering green and shimmering gold. Its walls were made of water running down in rivulets of silver and white.

Ren had a single thought of *Where am I?* when the goddess said, "Not where, but why?"

The sting of betrayal ran deep inside Ren. Her own shadows had given her up. At the same moment, a new image materialized in the water. Marco was leaping through the air like a panther, his teeth bared, his face distorted. Ren's heart raced double time as she peered closer. He was wounded—he had a gash on his forehead. Blood seeped down his face and neck. And in that moment, Ren could feel his hate, his anger. His regret.

He'd never wanted to come on this quest, yet he had, and now look!

"Stop!" Ren shouted. Her voice reverberated painfully in her ears.

Her shadow magic pulsed hard and fast in her fingertips, ripped through her heart.

"This is their fate," the goddess said just as Marco's image was replaced by Edison's. He stood in a dark garden, his jaw clenched, his eyes narrowed, his chest heaving like he couldn't get enough air into his lungs. Slowly, he lifted his face to whoever it was he was fighting. Serena? Kenji? Another godborn? One of the Lords of Night?

Edison's sharp features wore a look of rage. And in that moment, Ren saw the blue of his demon skin shining through. She watched his fangs curl over his lip. His hands thrust outward with a force that made the entire image shake then vanish. And as it did, she felt his fury, his inner darkness. She sensed the monster living inside him.

"Do you understand?" Jade purred. "Your friends, too, are consumed by the dark, by their anger and hatred. It lives in all beings, Renata. It is nothing to fear or run from."

"Please," Ren said shakily. Tears rolled down her cheeks. "I don't want them to get hurt."

"But they have already been hurt," the goddess said matter-of-factly. "They wear the invisible scars of your friendship and love."

A deep ache throbbed inside Ren. She knew the goddess was right. Her friends were at risk because of her. She suddenly thought of Monty. Where was she in all of this? Why hadn't Ren seen her image? And A.P.? Was he still keeping watch?

She glanced down at the now-faded letters inked across her wrist: *WWMD*.

"Let me guess," Ren growled through her tears. "You want me to make some deal with you to save them." It was the oldest tactic in the world. And she wasn't going to fall for it this time.

Jade gave a small laugh. "Not at all, Renata. I merely wanted you to *feel* what they were feeling."

"Why?"

"It will make your surrender easier for you."

At the same moment, the water tunnel was swept away, and Ren once again stood on the shores of the moonlit lake, trembling with a cold she had never felt before. A strange sensation curled around her feet, ankles, and legs, coursed through her blood toward her heart.

The goddess placed a hand on Ren's shoulder. This simple touch sparked the godborn's magic like an electrical current. Instantly, shadows flew from Ren's eyes and nose and mouth, wrapping themselves around her so tightly the cold vanished, the trembling ceased.

"Give yourself over to the magic," the goddess purred.

Ren struggled against the power consuming her, a power she both rejected and craved. She fell to her knees, trying to catch her breath, willing herself to hold on. Just a second longer. Just until she could pull the Obsidian Blade from her pocket and awaken the bird within.

Just until she could watch the bird finally take flight . . .

44

Ren watched as, in a single breath, Zyanya's
wings expanded. The bird orbited the goddess, flapping its
wings with the magic of sleep.

The goddess looked up like she'd been expecting Zyanya.
She smiled at Ren. "Such a clever girl." And then she vanished
in a trail of smoke.

Ren gripped her sides and gasped for air as she waited for
Zyanya to zoom back to the Obsidian Blade. But the wait would
be a long one—maybe forever. The bird had disappeared along
with the goddess and what was left of Ren's faculties, because
she could feel herself slipping into the darkness. She could sense
her shadows reaching, longing for a place that finally felt like
home.

At the same moment, the Smoking Mirror materialized.
"You look rather uncomfortable," he said in that ridiculous velvety voice of his.

"Where are my friends?"

The Smoking Mirror said, "They are alive and well. All but
one, that is. He was a real fighter."

He. Marco? Edison?

Ren shook her head vigorously. This was her fault. All of
it, just because she'd wanted to prove something to the world,
that she was smart and capable and not a loser. In the end, it

hadn't even needed proving. Because it no longer mattered. It no longer felt important. And now it was too late.

Ren lingered, closed her eyes, took deep even breaths, transported her mind to another place. A quiet place, a still place. She imagined herself at the edge of a tranquil bright blue sea. The sand was cool between her bare toes. The waves rolled gently in and out. A salty breeze caressed her face in the warm morning sun.

Pacific. Help me.

But her mother didn't answer. Instead, Ren's shadow magic called her back. Or was it the voice echoing through the trees?

"Ren!"

Marco!

She glanced up. The Smoking Mirror was gone. Footsteps pounded the earth.

"Ren!"

She spun, redoubled her focus, but the insatiable power of her magic spread across her memory, throwing shadows across her mind, blocking out the memories of who she was, who she had been. The time rope pulsed around her throat as Marco reached for her.

In that moment, everything shifted. The world contracted; the forest closed in. A sensation spread through Ren like warm water, coursing through every inch of her until all she could feel was the power of her ancient magic, from the "dead gods."

She pushed Marco away with such force he flew through the air, landing on his back with a *thud*. Quickly, he jumped to his feet. Confusion swept across his still-bleeding face. "What the hell is wrong with you?"

Ren felt nothing. Only the desire to get away from this godborn and all his rage. She turned and made her way toward the lake, on the surface of which the symbol still shimmered. The ground shook with such ferocity Ren nearly stumbled. She spun to see Marco on his knees, his fist jammed into the earth.

"Stop!" he shouted. "Don't let them win! Fight!"

Ren continued to walk away.

Marco launched himself toward her. With a flick of her wrist, she commanded a shadow to pin him to the ground. He thrashed beneath her magic.

She stepped toward the lake, toward the symbol now calling to her. Just as the water touched her ankles, she felt a warm sensation around her throat—a spark of a memory, of light, of something she couldn't name.

The god of death's whisper. *Not like this.*

And then she walked deeper into the water.

45

Hours later, before the sun rose, before the light rolled back the dark, a plan was made.

There was nothing sophisticated about it, no extra steps or layers to complicate things. Only a promise made between the god of death and the most powerful godborn to ever live. Now the god felt hollow, his ache and loss so profound he didn't think he would ever come back from it. And truthfully? He didn't want to.

As he sat hunched in the dark forest, keeping watch, sensing Ren's movements and the darkness inside her, he snapped twigs in half over and over and over, wishing he still had the power of a god, wishing he wasn't a useless kid with no strength or ability to save the only being he had ever loved. Maybe even wishing he had never loved her at all.

The symbol on the lake's surface glowed brighter and brighter.

The god's secrets, deals, and incessant need for power had finally caught up with him, because for the first time he had something he couldn't stand to lose.

Aside from all that had happened, the god knew that Ren would hate their epic defeat. She'd hate that Marco had been captured along with the rogue godborns and that Edison had been swarmed by bees before he collapsed on the ground and evaporated like a trail of mist. She'd even hate that Serena had shrieked with fury and agony when she learned she wouldn't be queen. When she realized she had been led astray by a prophecy that was never about her. But Ren would love that the hunter got away. That Monty had escaped with her magical arrows and would soon be a true Jaguar Warrior.

Still, even that minuscule victory felt empty. It was a victory that now forced A.P.'s hand.

The god breathed slowly, deeply. He remembered the words he had spoken to the godborn just days ago: *I know a thing or two about the dark, Ren. It's all-consuming, and it tricks you into making you think you want it, that you'd rather dwell in its depths than seek the light.*

"Hey," Monty said, sitting next to the god. Her face wore a few gashes—some would heal, others would scar.

A.P. didn't want to acknowledge the hunter's presence. It only reminded him of his promise, of what Ren had asked of him.

If the Night Prophecy comes true and I side with the lords, if I become their queen and betray you and my friends, I need you to do something for me.

Clenching his jaw and fists, A.P. shook his head, remembering a truth he wished had never existed.

Please. Tell Monty to shoot me, take me to Xib'alb'a. I'd rather die than live and be evil.

It was an unfair request, one the god was sure Ren hadn't thought through—or at least not what the act would do to the hunter. And still, Montero had insisted. She had told the god, *I'm a warrior first and I will do this. For Ren.*

A.P. got to his feet, sensing Ren's presence drawing closer. "You should take your position now, Montero," he commanded limply.

"I never thought this would be the way I'd finally earn my title," Monty said shakily as she squeezed the tears from her eyes before shouldering her bow and quiver and climbing into the tree that would give her the best shot. She had already suggested that Ah-Puch just knock out Ren, but he had refused, saying it was a temporary solution that would only make her darkness grow.

Just then, Ren emerged from the forest. She wore a long silver dress, and its hem dragged along the earth. Her hands were clasped in front of her, her head bowed.

A whisper floated from the god's lips: "I won't let you live as their queen."

At the center of the lake, on a misty platform that hovered near the glowing symbol, three Lords of Night appeared: the Fire Lord, the Smoking Mirror, and the Prince Lord. As Ren approached, the symbol pulsed and its spiral unfolded, creating a path of light that she stepped onto as she made her way toward them.

A.P. watched in horror as the Maize Lord appeared next to Ren, gripping a crown made of dark jade and writhing shadows.

The black night began to give way to the gray morning light. Even from here, A.P. could sense the darkness twisting inside Ren, the shadow magic's unfathomable power, and it nearly broke him.

But he wouldn't look away. He wouldn't make her do this alone. He'd stay here until the end.

A.P. stole a quick glance at Montero. She was in position. Tears flowed down her cheeks, but her grip was steady, focused.

"On my signal," he muttered.

If there had been time, he would have begged the Maya gods for their assistance. He would have given anything, become anything, promised anything to save Ren.

The Smoking Mirror was speaking—Ah-Puch wouldn't be able to remember any words later except for: "Her blood is ageless. Worthy of being joined to the gods. To the Prince Lord."

A.P.'s knees nearly buckled. He swallowed the bile rising in his throat as the realization daggered his heart. Ren would be *wed to the prince and that would make him king.*

Look at me, Ren, he willed with a desperation he had never known before. *Give me a sign. Any sign, and I'll burn down the world for you.*

Ren bowed to the Maize Lord, who held the crown over her head, chanting indecipherable words. The symbol in the water burned brighter.

Trembling, Ah-Puch raised his hand, giving Montero the signal.

The warrior was true to her word. The arrow flew.

Just as the crown of jade and shadow was placed on Ren's head, she looked up. Her steady gaze found A.P.'s. There was a distant flicker in her cold blue eyes, a light that told a story he would now never hear.

Because the arrow had already pierced her heart.

El Fin (sort of)

GLOSSARY

Dear Reader,

This glossary serves to provide some context to Ren's story. It is merely a bird's-eye view of a vast and complex mythology that has been passed down for generations and in no way represents the enormousness of this lore and culture. I was captivated by these myths growing up, by the way humans sought to understand their place in the universe and their relationship to something greater than what they could see, touch, and hear. I grew up listening to various narratives of the same tales, featuring the same Aztec and Maya gods, and with each iteration my fascination grew. My grandmother used to speak of spirits, brujos, gods, and the ancient civilizations that further ignited my curiosity for and love of myth and magic. I hope you, too, are inspired and fascinated by these tales, that they lead you to open your heart to the possibilities of what-if.

Actun Tunichil Muknal (*ak-TOON too-nee-CHEEL mook-NAL*) a cave in Belize whose name means Cave of the Stone Sepulcher. Many Maya artifacts have been found there, including skeletons thought to be sacrifice victims. Creepy!

Ah-Muzen-Cab (*ah-moo SEN KAHB*) Maya god of bees.

Ah-Puch (*ah-POOCH*) Maya god of death, darkness, and destruction. Sometimes he's called the Stinking One or

Flatulent One (oy!). He is often depicted as a skeleton wearing a collar of dangling eyeballs that came from those he's killed. No wonder he doesn't have any friends.

Akan (*ah-KAHN*) Maya god of wine.

Centeotl (*sen-THE-oat*) one of the nine Aztec Lords of Night; also called the Flower Prince or Maize God.

Chalchiuhtlicue (*chal-chee-wit-LEEK-weh*) one of the nine Aztec Lords of Night; also called Jade Is Her Skirt; goddess of water.

Eréndira (*eh-REN-dee-rah*) according to legend, she was a princess captured by Spanish conquerors. They imprisoned her in the forest, where she cried night and day, begging the gods to save her. The gods sent her a flood of tears that transformed into a beautiful lake. She dove into it and became a mermaid.

Ixchel (*eesh-CHEL*) Maya goddess of the moon.

Ixkik' (*sh-KEEK*) mother of the hero twins, Jun'ajpu' and Xb'alamkej; also known as the Blood Moon goddess or Blood Maiden. She is the daughter of one of the lords of the underworld.

Ixtab (*eesh-TAHB*) Maya goddess (and often caretaker) of people who were sacrificed or died a violent death.

Nakon (*nah-CONE*) god of war.

Piltzintecuhtli (*peel-tseen-TEK-wit-lee*) one of the nine Aztec Lords of Night; also called the Prince Lord; god of the rising sun.

Tezcatlipoca (*tes-kah-tlee-POH-kah*) one of the nine Aztec Lords of Night; also called the Smoking Mirror; god of the night sky.

Xib'alb'a (*shee-bahl-BAH*) the Maya underworld, a land of darkness and fear where the soul has to travel before reaching paradise. If the soul fails, it must stay in the underworld and hang out with demons. Yikes!

Xiuhtecuhtli (*shee-wit-EK-wit-lee*) one of the nine Aztec Lords of Night; also called the Fire Lord; god of fire, day, and heat.

Yohualli (*yoh-WAL-lee*) the Nahuatl word for *night*.

Zirahuén (*see-rah-WEN*) a lake in the central highlands of Mexico, also known as Mirror of the Gods.